Praise for the Novels of
MARY HIGGINS CLARK,
Editor of
THE NIGHT AWAKENS

"Mary Higgins Clark is truly a mistress of high tension."
—*The New Yorker*

"Clark's mastery of suspense will keep 'em guessing, and the bad guys are truly creepy."
—*New York Post*

"What's amazing is how expertly Clark manages to keep us hooked time after time, and even better, create new plots, each fresh as a mountain stream."
—Ruth Coughlin, *Detroit News*

"She's one of the biggest storytellers ever."
—Larry King, *USA Today*

"Mary Higgins Clark does not traffic in mundane murders. Her victims tend to be dispatched with imagination and dramatic flair."
—Joyce Slater, *Minneapolis Star Tribune*

Mystery Writers of America Anthologies

Guilty as Charged (Edited by Scott Turow)
Diagnosis Dead (Edited by Jonathan Kellerman)
The Night Awakens (Edited by Mary Higgins Clark)

Published by POCKET BOOKS

A MYSTERY WRITERS OF AMERICA ANTHOLOGY
EDITED BY MARY HIGGINS CLARK

THE
NIGHT
AWAKENS

POCKET **STAR** BOOKS

New York   London   Toronto   Sydney

For further information about membership in The Mystery Writers of America, please contact The Mystery Writers of America, 17 East 47th Street, 6th Floor, New York, NY 10017.

An *Original* Publication of POCKET BOOKS

A Pocket Star Book published by
POCKET BOOKS, a division of Simon & Schuster, Inc.
1230 Avenue of the Americas, New York, NY 10020

ISBN 13: 978-0-671-51918-6
ISBN 10:   0-671-51918-2

First Pocket Books printing February 2000

20 19 18 17 16 15 14

POCKET STAR BOOKS and colophon are registered trademarks of Simon & Schuster, Inc.

Cover art by Ben Perini

Printed in the U.S.A.

Contents

CONTENTS

Introduction

Mary Higgins Clark

I have been frequently asked why I chose to write suspense novels and why there is always a hint or a dash of romance in almost all of them.

A simple answer: suspense mystery—crime stories have been part of the human experience since Adam and Eve. Think about it. Only two people on earth, and she persuades him to commit a felony. They have two kids, and one murders the other. The die was cast for the rest of us.

As to the romance, I think a touch of it is emotionally satisfying for the reader as well as the fictional characters who have endured a very hard time indeed in achieving their goals: identifying and trapping the guilty party—the one who often has a smiling face and bloody hands.

The touch of romance works in other ways. It inspires betrayal, jealousy, hatred and need for revenge. Sometimes the assailant gets away with the deed, and we wryly or wholeheartedly applaud. Sometimes, because we understand the motivation, we put ourselves in that character's shoes and decide that what was done for love, or lack of it, is understandable.

Years ago I read that a prominent writer, Catherine Drinker Bowen, had a simple note posted in her study. It read: "Will the reader turn the page?" I think that question asks and says it all. We want you, the reader, to keep turning every page of this book, and I'm happy to say that I think you will.

Sally Gunning's story of a jealous lover will make you think twice before accepting an invitation to a remote cabin.

Joseph Hansen's part-time private investigator, who takes time from tending horses to learn why a gentle elderly widower bit the dust, will keep you guessing.

You'll sympathize to a point with Sarah Shankman's main character, a beautiful young woman who was left at the altar.

You'll share the young reporter's fear of the dark if you get trapped in a tunnel with a dead man, the predicament Nancy Pickard presents to us.

A missing Vietnamese child and the search to find her by the woman who loves her father comes from the pen of Eleanor Taylor Bland.

Brendan Dubois examines the sibling rivalry of an estranged brother and sister who have markedly different versions of what's lawful.

Sometimes a literary society isn't the thoughtful meeting of the minds it's cracked up to be. Edward D. Hoch finds other uses for The Haggard Society.

It's not a bad idea for a new bride to know more about her husband than what he's chosen to tell her, especially if his activities put her life in danger. Writer Leon D. Estelman explores that premise.

Angela Zeman zeros in on a harassed employee who makes an unfortunate choice to finance himself into a new life.

And finally, Noreen Ayres invites us to the Delta Region with a tenderhearted investigator who wants justice for the murdered younger brother of his lady-love.

In all, a collection of short stories I feel you will thoroughly enjoy as I did. I can safely promise you, the reader, will happily turn the page.

All best,

Mary Higgins Clark

The Perils of
Pond Scum

Sally Gunning

Two minutes after it happened, I wasn't sure it had. I could see the glass on the floor from the broken picture, I could feel the throb in the back of my head where it had snapped into the wall, but I could also see and feel Jeffrey, his face contorted with shock, his hand trembling as it touched my face.

"My God, Hannah, look at us. Do you see what you've done? Is this how you want it?"

I pushed his hand away, trying to focus. What *had* I done? I had walked into the dark apartment. My apartment. Jeffrey's voice had come at me. *Where have you been?* I'd reached for the light, but something had kept me from it. Hands. Strong. Angry. *Had* they grabbed me? Thrown me? I'd crashed backward into the wall. I knew that much. I'd crashed into the wall, and the light had come on, and there was Jeffrey.

Jeffrey. In my apartment. A week after I'd told him I needed some time alone.

"Forgive me," said Jeffrey now. I could see the rise and fall of his chest under the shirt as he struggled to calm himself. "I frightened you, didn't I? I wanted to talk. I let myself in. But you upset me, Hannah. I had no intention of—" He broke off and dashed a hand across his face. "Are you all right?"

I felt my head and winced.

"You're not. Here. Sit down." He led me to the couch and sat beside me. Skillful, gentle fingers probed my scalp. That was one of the first things I'd loved about Jeffrey. First the wide, easy smile, but second had been those competent, reassuring hands. No, it couldn't have been his hands.

Jeffrey stopped probing and smoothed back my hair. "Not even a goose egg. But you see what can happen. I'm sorry I barged in and frightened you. This isn't me tonight. But this isn't you, either. This isn't like you, sneaking around."

"I wasn't sneaking around. I went with Ellen and Paul to—"

"You can leave Ellen out of it, Hannah. We know Ellen wasn't there, don't we? It was you and Paul. But Ellen's part of the problem, too, isn't she? Your sister doesn't like us spending all our time together, does she? I don't know why you listen to her. That's where the problem lies. *You* don't need time alone. *We* need time alone. Just the two of us, without all this interference. I know what we'll do, we'll go the cabin."

"Jeffrey—"

"Hush." Jeffrey leaned back, bringing me with him until my cheek rested on the hard plane of his chest. "You know I'm right, Hannah. You don't solve problems by hiding from them. We'll get out of the city, go to the cabin for the long weekend on Saturday. We'll be alone. We'll talk. We'll sort this out." While he talked, his hands, those hands, stroked my hair, my neck, my face.

I knew I should move, get up, ask him to leave. Why did it suddenly seem so hard, so pointless, so . . . so silly? And what if Jeffrey was right? Maybe if we were alone, if there was no third party to make him angry, if *I* didn't make him angry . . . And what had he done, after all? He'd gotten jealous. It was flattering, really.

Jeffrey's hands gripped my shoulders and eased me sideways. "Look, you're right. You need time of your own. I can see that. I'll go now. I'll pick you up Saturday."

When he picked me up on Saturday, and I saw the fresh haircut, the face shaved to the bone, the jacket I particularly loved that made him look so broad in the back, I thought of Harry's. That's where we'd met, Harry's Tap. Jeffrey had worn that jacket at Harry's. Everything had been fresh and new at Harry's. Jeffrey had met me, wanted me, wooed me.

"We're getting a good early start," said Jeffrey now. He smiled at me from the driver's seat, that smile I'd first met at Harry's. "Or should I say a good fresh start?"

A fresh start. To go back to the way it was at Harry's. Suddenly, the weekend ahead of me glimmered brightly.

My daydreams dissolved as Jeffrey started talking, filling me in on the history of the cabin. It belonged to Jeffrey's father, divvied his way in a nasty divorce settlement. It was a treasure beyond compare, said Jeffrey, sitting virtually alone in the middle of two thousand acres of conservation land. Most of the year, it sat there empty, waiting for Jeffrey's father to remember he owned it and blow down the expressway for a getaway summer weekend with most of the people you'd expect him to want to get away from. He brought business associates, politicians, friends, acquaintances, anyone he could find, said Jeffrey.

Except Jeffrey.

But Jeffrey didn't seem to resent this parental neglect as much as I thought he might. He talked calmly of arranging with his father, once he came of age, for his own time at the cabin. July and August were his father's. The off-season months were Jeffrey's own. Usually, because of the risk of frost, Jeffrey drained the pipes and closed up the cabin the last weekend in September. It was only the unseasonably warm October, a true Indian summer, that had prompted the late visit this year.

At first, as Jeffrey talked about the cabin, I listened attentively—how there were plenty of deer, fox, trout. How there were no phones, electricity, neighbors. But as the sun beat through the windshield and the tires hummed over the highway and Jeffrey's voice rose and fell, I began to feel drowsy. I closed my eyes.

I woke when we hit the first rut in the dirt road.

"You just missed Fairnham," said Jeffrey.

"Fairnham?"

"Our last sight of civilization. If you could call it that. A post office, a laundromat, and a town hall."

I looked around. On either side of me was nothing but wilderness—deep, black, wild. Huge pines blocked the light from overhead, and thick seedlings and bull briars and dead stumps obliterated the ground.

We rattled in and out of the ruts for what seemed

like another ten miles, until Jeffrey suddenly yanked the wheel hard right and we plunged into the trees.

I gasped.

Jeffrey laughed. "Almost there now."

When I'd collected myself, I could see that we weren't forging a new trail through virgin forest, as I'd first supposed, but were actually following a faint track through the pine needles and dead leaves. It seemed to go on forever, the forest crowding closer and closer on each side, until finally, just when I was sure if I didn't see sky or light or air I would suffocate, I saw the glimmer of the water through the trees.

The car rolled to a stop fifty feet on.

"Like it?" asked Jeffrey.

I didn't answer right away. I wasn't sure. If I looked straight ahead, the gloom of the woods seemed to have disappeared as if someone had waved a magic wand, and the sun stretched a welcome pool of light across the surface of the pond. A narrow dock of rough planking bridged the gap between sun and cabin, but when I turned to look at the cabin itself, I saw that neither sun nor water had penetrated that far. The cabin was nestled in shade so dark it seemed like night, and the deeply stained clapboards of the porch wrapped what I could see of the doors and windows in even blacker shadows.

I felt Jeffrey's eyes swivel in my direction. "Well, Hannah?"

"I . . . yes. It's . . . the pond . . . it's beautiful."

He grinned. "Wait till you see the inside." He pulled me after him up three stone steps to the cabin. When I stepped onto the porch, the floor gave slightly under me. Jeffrey pulled a rusty key from his jacket pocket, scraped it into the lock, and the door opened with a moan. He stood back, and I stepped inside.

It smelled of must. A pale green light oozed through a crack in the shutters and wobbled across the floor, illuminating what the previous tenants had left us—chewed mattress batting, empty seed casings, mice droppings. My eyes traveled to the farther wall.

A pair of beady black eyes stared back at me.

I shrieked.

Two paces took Jeffrey across the room. He snatched something off the wall, pulling it into the light. The glass eyes of a stuffed fox gleamed at me. Jeffrey laughed. He put the fox down and showed me around.

The room we stood in seemed to be most of it—living area to the left of the wood stove, with an iron cot for a couch and a wooden crate for a table. The kitchen was to the right of the stove—a wood table, two chairs with missing rungs, a small ice box, a sink complete with rusty pump, a metal cupboard. A collection of fishing rods hung suspended from the rafters.

Jeffrey led me into the bedroom. The bed seemed to fill it, with no more than a foot to spare all around. I looked for the bathroom and found it through a crack in the shutters, a box like a wooden phone booth twenty yards off in the pines. I must have peered through that cracked shutter a long time.

Jeffrey spoke from behind me. "Who's out there?"

"No one. Aren't there any neighbors at all?"

"Not anymore. I told you, we're smack dab in the middle of conservation land. Our cabin and the Blakes' down the beach were the only ones here before the park came in. By law, we both have lifetime use, but Blake abandoned his a couple of years ago. Come on. You clean up while I open up. The broom's behind the ice box."

Jeffrey went out, and almost at once I heard the sound of creaking boards as he removed the shutters. The light that filtered in through the trees did little to lighten the dark rooms. I found the broom and swept up the mouse residue. I unpacked our sheets and made the bed. By the time I'd filled the kitchen cupboard with our provisions, Jeffrey was no longer there.

I stepped out onto the porch. No Jeffrey. The sun was high above the towering trees, but I could see the spot where it would later disappear behind them, off to the west, and I felt a moment of panic. I didn't want to see this place without the sun. I crept onto the dock and looked along the beach. I saw a second dilapidated dock a hundred yards to the left but no signs of life. Jeffrey had been right. Our lone neighbor was gone.

I turned around and called, hoping I'd defeated any sounds of panic. "Jeffrey!"

"Down here." The voice came from underneath the cabin somewhere. "Pipes are all right. Try the pump, will you?"

I went inside and pumped the handle. Rusty brown filth sputtered out into the sink.

"Keep going," said Jeffrey behind me. "It'll clear."

He disappeared again, but by the time I'd pumped the water clear, he was back with an armload of wood. "I'll have to cut more. We'll need the stove nights."

Nights.

Suddenly, I felt the need of air. Sunlight. "Could we take a walk?"

Jeffrey followed me out. I stood on the dock and looked left and right. The choice was clear. To the east, the white sand beach disappeared into choking reeds and undergrowth twenty yards beyond our dock, but to the west, the sand stretched in a welcoming crescent all the way to the absent neighbor's dock and beyond. We stepped off the dock and walked west.

Sun or no sun, I found myself reaching for Jeffrey's hand. As we neared the Blake cottage, his fingers tensed in mine.

"What's the matter?"

"There's a chair on the porch."

"Oh? You think he's here?"

"No. He hasn't come in years. And there's no car. I just never noticed that chair before."

Jeffrey stared at the cabin, and I stared with him, curious. It seemed much like ours, only smaller, if that were possible, with the same dark clapboards and tiny windows, but the sticks and leaves on the roof, the rip in the screen door, made it seem somehow lonely and forlorn.

Jeffrey seemed to find it the same. He turned us around. "Come on, let's go back. We've got work to do."

Jeffrey assigned me my usual chores—washing the dishes, making the stew. After I'd figured out the ways and means of the primitive kitchen and the stew was bubbling on the stove, I stepped outside and was surprised to see most of the day was gone.

The sun brushed the tops of the trees. I could hear the sound of Jeffrey's ax behind me in the woods somewhere. I walked out on the dock and sat down, feet dangling just above the water, watching the sun disappear.

Suddenly, one of the tall, dark posts on the distant dock moved. Something splashed out of the water, danced into the air, flopped back into the water. After I saw the fish, I noticed the black rod, arching between the long shadow of the man on the dock and the fish. I watched, fascinated, as the rod dipped and reared, the man rocking with it, until the fish blasted out of the water again. It gave one last sharp, silver twist in midair and seemed to grow wings. The rod snapped backward, the fish soared in a graceful arc and splashed into the pond, free.

I hadn't meant to clap. The sound seemed to echo over the water like a small burst of cannon fire. The shadow on the dock turned in my direction. I felt the dock tremble under my feet, and Jeffrey spoke from behind me.

"So he *is* here."

I turned, surprised at his tone, the words more hissed than spoken.

I touched Jeffrey's arm. "So he's here. It doesn't matter."

"Doesn't matter? Of course it matters. That was the point. I wanted us to be alone."

I laughed, waving a shaky hand at the miles and miles of blackening woods. "I think we've got enough room."

Jeffrey looked down at me. The lumpiness in his jaw eased as he smiled. The odd sunless panic I'd felt moved off. He put his arm around me, and we walked together up the dock.

Just before we stepped onto the porch, I looked again for the fisherman, but he was gone.

The lantern helped. So did the wood stove. So did the bubbling stew. So did Jeffrey, the old Jeffrey, the Jeffrey of Harry's Tap, talking and laughing and reaching across the rickety table to touch my hand.

Once the stew was gone, the plates washed, the wine glasses refilled, he stood up and led me to the cot. He propped the pillows behind him, pulled me down against his shoulder. "Now," he said. "Let's hear it. What's wrong? What's happened to us, Hannah? Or should I ask what's happened to you? I still feel the same. And you know, deep down inside where it counts, I think you do, too."

"Jeffrey," I said, and stalled. It must have been the wine. My mind seemed to have slipped into neutral.

"That's it, then. I was right, wasn't I? It's not us. When it's just the two of us, away, alone, there's nothing wrong. You belong with me, Hannah, can't you see that?"

"I . . . yes . . . sometimes . . ."

The arm around me tightened. Was he angry? I didn't want Jeffrey angry. And now, right now, it did seem that I belonged there with him. The wood crackled comfortably in the stove, the lantern warmed the dark wood walls, Jeffrey's hands warmed my skin, and any misgivings I might have had about him seemed to recede with the black woods.

But I slept badly that night, just the same, too alert to woods noises and cabin smells and phantom visions. When daylight came, I did better and was still in a muddled half-doze when Jeffrey's lips brushed my cheek at nine.

"I have to run into town for ice. Stay put. The coffee's on the stove."

The words hardly registered. I only snapped wide awake when the car engine roared. "Jeffrey!" I grabbed my robe and raced onto the porch, but I was seconds too late. The car's brake lights winked once through the trees and were gone.

But the sun was there, a glorious lemon balloon floating over the treetops, already dispelling the shadows and warming the air. I went inside for coffee and brought it out onto the dock. I stretched my toes to the water. It was surprisingly warm. When I finished the coffee, I went back inside, put on my bathing suit, took a running start off the dock, and plunged.

It was colder down below. I broke the surface gasping and struck out along the shore in a stiff crawl. It had been some time since I'd done any serious swimming, and I tired way too soon. I was twenty yards from our neighbor's cabin when I stopped, exhausted. I decided to cut straight to shore and walk home. I angled toward the beach and climbed out onto the sand, shivering. I was leaning over wringing out my hair when a voice spoke from behind.

"Stabbed in the back?"

My heart bucked. I turned. A man stood there, not smiling, hands on hips, bare feet planted. The fisherman. It had to be the fisherman. But the long black shadow from the night before now seemed all gold. The sun glinted off the fine hairs on his head, chest, legs, arms. Even the khaki shorts looked gold.

"Stabbed?"

He pointed at my back. "That cut."

I stumbled backward, babbling. "No. No. I wasn't stabbed. It was glass. A picture. A piece of glass. I fell into the wall, and the picture broke, and I was cut with the glass. It was an accident. A silly accident. I—"

By the time I realized he was smiling, he stopped. He seemed to be looking at me oddly. "It was a joke. Stabbed in the back. No need to explain. But I brought it up because it looks like it could use some attention. I guess you can't see it, but it seems to be infected."

"I . . . oh." I stood there, breathing.

The man continued to watch me, still with the odd expression. Finally, he stretched out a hand. "Peter. Peter Blake."

I took the hand. "Hannah Templeton. I'm staying over there." I pointed to Jeffrey's cabin.

"I assumed so. You're the clapper. So you enjoy seeing men starve?"

"I . . . starve?"

"That fish last night was my dinner. I'm not torturing them for fun." He half smiled. "But it *is* fun. Especially when they put up a good fight." He stopped. He seemed to be waiting. For what, an apology?

"I'm sorry," I said. "I didn't mean to clap. It was just so beautiful, and it fought so hard. It—"

That half-smile again. "I know. He deserved to win. Will you be here long?"

"A week." I paused, at a loss. "We were surprised to see you here."

"Surprised?"

"I suppose I should say Jeffrey was surprised. He said you didn't come here anymore. Do you know Jeffrey? Jeffrey Holtz? It's his father's cabin."

14

What smile there was disappeared. "I know Jeff. It's true I haven't been here in a couple of years. Last time I came, it wasn't too . . . pleasant."

"Well, it's certainly pleasant now."

Peter Blake didn't seem to agree. At least, he didn't answer. Maybe it had seemed more pleasant before I'd blundered onto what he must consider his front lawn.

"I'm sorry," I said again lamely. "I suppose I'm trespassing. But if I hadn't walked ashore here, I'd have washed up drowned. I don't suppose you'd have found that too pleasant, either."

Something happened to his face. What was it? He made no attempt to answer my inane babblings, not that they deserved it, but something about the way he continued to look at me convinced me it was best to shut up and move on. "I'd better go," I said. "Good luck with tonight's dinner. I promise to clap if you win."

I left him standing there, tall, gold, silent in the sun.

Jeffrey was on our dock, waiting for me. "What was all that about?"

"That's Peter Blake. He—"

"I know who he is. I asked you what you were doing."

I had one foot on the dock when he spoke. I took it back and left it in the sand. Not Jeffrey angry. Please, not Jeffrey angry. "I swam too far and decided to walk home. He came up and introduced himself. That's all."

"You jumped into the water without knowing the first thing about it, is that it?"

"No, I—"

"I don't know why your idiocies still amaze me, Hannah. I should be used to it by now. Just the same, you might be interested to know there's a huge drop-off out there. Don't you know if you tire yourself, you leave yourself susceptible to cramp? Don't you know how easy it is to drown? And don't think Peter Blake will save you. He didn't lift a finger when his fiancée drowned." Jeffrey turned and went inside.

I followed him. "Drowned?"

Jeffrey bent down, fidgeted with the stove, and spoke without turning around. "Two years ago. Right out there."

"Oh, no."

"Served her right. It was damned foolish. She had a few drinks, took the boat out, went over the side, and drowned."

"And he couldn't save her?"

"Couldn't or wouldn't. He *said* he wasn't even here. But if he had been, I doubt he'd have bothered. She'd been fooling around."

"Jeffrey!"

He straightened. The look he gave me was almost amused. "According to his version, they'd planned to meet here that weekend to talk things over, but when he got here, she was already dead. He was the one who found her body washed up on the beach over there."

"Oh, *no.*"

Jeffrey turned around. "For God's sake, Hannah, calm down. I was only trying to warn you, that's all. You'll be all right if you're careful."

"It's not that. I . . . I said something awful. To Peter Blake. I told him I almost washed up on his beach

16

drowned. He gave me the oddest look. I couldn't figure out—"

I stopped mid-sentence as Jeffrey tipped back his head and laughed.

We hardly spoke at lunch. My mind was on my conversation with Peter Blake. I could feel myself blushing with mortification, and I could feel Jeffrey watching me, but I didn't meet his eyes. If he laughed again . . .

I was reprieved after lunch when Jeffrey went off into the woods to dig worms. When he returned, he pulled a fishing rod from the rafters and an old battered aluminum canoe from under the cabin where it had been stored. "Want to come?"

I shook my head.

Jeffrey shoved the canoe into the water and paddled out until he'd disappeared around a bend in the pond. I watched him from the window over the sink as I scrubbed the lunch dishes. When I finished cleaning up, I pulled a blanket off the shelf in the bedroom, went down to the beach, and spread it on the warm sand. But I didn't sit down. I couldn't, not with Peter Blake on my mind. What must he think of me? He must have assumed I knew his whole story and had been goading him cruelly. I summoned most of what little courage I'd ever possessed and walked down the beach, to his cabin.

He was on the porch, fixing the torn screen in the door, still without a shirt, the long, smooth muscles in his back ebbing and flowing under the gold skin until he heard me and turned around. I didn't give him a chance to speak. "I've come to apologize for what must have seemed like some very pointed and unnecessarily cruel remarks. I promise you I had no idea what happened until Jeffrey told me an hour ago. I never would have said . . . I wouldn't make light . . . I certainly didn't . . . I only hope you can bring yourself to understand—"

There was no question of a smile this time, but his voice, when he spoke, sounded warmer than I deserved. "I understood two minutes after you'd gone. It was obvious you weren't the type to go in for cruel jokes. There's no apology necessary. I'm only sorry I wasn't able to recover enough to ease your mind at the time."

"Oh, please, don't *you* apologize. It was all my fault. Jeffrey says I always babble like an idiot whenever I'm nervous. Thank you for being so nice about it and for bearing with my babbling a second time. Good-bye."

I turned around and beat it out of there, already down all three steps and onto the beach when I heard him say, "Good-bye."

I returned to my blanket and collapsed on my back, exhausted but with conscience eased. I think I fell asleep, but I couldn't have slept long. When I woke, I sat up and looked around. Jeffrey was still nowhere in sight, but for once I was glad. I realized somewhat belatedly there were other things worth looking at. Driving through the acres of woods, I'd noticed nothing but pine and oak, but across the pond there must have been a decent smattering of swamp maples and beeches, identifiable by the bright swatches of red and yellow among the green and bronze. The pond glistened silver in the sun, the sky was that turquoise blue that only seemed to happen in October, and the air was just crisp enough for the sun to seem worth its weight in gold.

Gold. Was it the word that made me think of Peter Blake and look his way, or was it some unearthly intuition? Whichever it was, the minute I glanced down the beach, he emerged from his cabin and walked in my direction. He came up to the edge of the blanket and extended a hand. The hand held a white tube of some kind. "For that cut."

I reached up and accepted the tube. I read the label, an antibiotic cream. "Thank you, but it's not that bad. Honestly."

I tried to hand back the tube, but he gazed down at me solemnly. His eyes were the pale green of water over sand. "I wish you'd use it. I've seen things like that get nasty."

"All right." I laid the tube beside me on the blanket.

"I'd soak it first. In warm water."

I laughed. "Warm water's a little hard to come by around here."

His mouth jerked in that almost-smile. Now, of course, I could understand why that smile never made it any farther. And as I studied him closer, I realized the reason he looked so gold was because of the tan. I looked toward the water to rest my eyes and saw that Jeffrey's canoe had finally reappeared.

"Just how do you fall into a wall?"

I started, flustered. "Excuse me?"

"You said you fell into a wall. How do you do that, exactly?"

I could see Jeffrey facing our way, spine stiff and alert. I stood up. "Do you know, it seems colder out here now than it did this morning. I think I'd better go in."

"It'll be colder inside. Look, I know it's none of my business—" He broke off.

I kept my eyes glued to the pond. Jeffrey was paddling hard in our direction. I scooped up my blanket and the tube of cream. "I have to go. Thank you for this. I'll be sure to return it before I leave."

"I don't need it. Look—" He began again.

I turned to face him. There was no suggestion of a smile anywhere this time. His eyes seemed locked onto me.

And I stood there caught in the beam until the canoe scraped on the sand and Jeffrey bounded up the beach toward us.

I'd been foolish to be so afraid. Jeffrey's hand was out, his teeth gleaming, as he approached the other man. "Blake. Good to see you back. It's been some time."

But we weren't out of the woods yet. It was Peter Blake, not Jeffrey, whose face had turned to stone, and for a minute it looked as if he would ignore Jeffrey's hand. I think I closed my eyes. *Take it. Dear God, take his hand.* When I looked again, the two hands, one large and brown, the other large and white, were clenched.

I breathed.

The green eyes flicked toward mine, then back to Jeffrey, and Peter Blake withdrew his hand. "You're up late this year."

"Yes," said Jeffrey. "Decided to take a chance on the frost. Worth it, don't you think?" He smiled at me, and I smiled back. He held out an arm, and I moved close enough so he could drape it around me. I knew the routine.

Peter Blake watched. "I brought your friend some-

20

thing for that cut on her back. I noticed it this morning. I'm afraid it might need medical attention."

"I've been keeping an eye on it," said Jeffrey. "Thank you. Hannah, you look cold. Let's get you back inside. How long do you plan to stay, Blake?"

"A few days. I've got some work to do on the cabin."

"Then I'm sure we'll see you," said Jeffrey.

"Yes, I'm sure you will."

I said good-bye. Peter Blake nodded in return. Jeffrey led me inside, arm still gripping my shoulder.

To this day, I don't know just what it was, if it was Peter Blake's question or the way he'd watched Jeffrey and me, but it was there on the beach that I think I saw Jeffrey, the real Jeffrey, the man behind the smile, the man behind those hands, for the first time. Whatever it was, by the time I'd stepped out of the sun and into the darkness of the cabin, I knew.

I hadn't fallen into that wall.

And I didn't belong with Jeffrey.

My first thought as we walked inside was that I would tell him right away. I would tell him I didn't want to see him anymore, and we'd pack up and go home, and my life would return to normal. *Normal.* It had taken a silly conversation on a beach in the middle of the wilderness for me to realize how abnormal my life had become. I saw no friends, I saw no family, I saw no one but Jeffrey. And what had happened the minute I tried to reestablish contact with a few of those people I'd left so ruthlessly in the dust? Jeffrey had whisked me out of their reach.

I think that was when I finally realized how afraid I

really was. Suddenly, I knew it would be very foolish to tell Jeffrey of my decision to leave him while we were trapped here alone. Better to let him think everything was fine until we'd returned to civilization. That, then, was my goal: to return as fast as possible to civilization. With a great effort of will, I slipped my hand around his waist and smiled up at him.

"How was the fishing?"

"Nothing doing. Not that I expected it. They usually don't surface till around dusk. How about it? Want to learn how to fish? You seemed fascinated enough by Blake's poor effort yesterday."

"I'd love to," I said. What else could I say? To say anything else would convince him I was interested only in Peter Blake's fishing, not Jeffrey's. Oh, I knew him so well in so many ways. Better to agree to this one thing that didn't matter while I figured out how to get him to agree to the one thing that did. "Speaking of Peter Blake, he's got me nervous about this cut. It's been throbbing like anything, and I've felt feverish all morning. I really do think I should go home and get it looked at."

Jeffrey pressed a palm against my forehead. "You don't feel hot. Here, let me look." He turned me around and pulled up my shirt. "The man's got you worked up for nothing. I grant you it's blown up a bit."

"He said I should soak it in warm water. We don't have any warm water. Really, Jeffrey, maybe we should leave and—"

"Nonsense. Look, I've kept the coals going. We'll have water hot enough to scald you in no time."

Jeffrey opened the stove, stirred up the banked coals, and tossed in fresh wood. He filled an aluminum kettle at the pump, lifted off the stove lid, and fit the kettle neatly over the fire.

I didn't dare press it. In a matter of minutes, he had me stretched out flat on my stomach on the iron cot with a hot compress under my sweatshirt. "There. When it cools down, resoak it. Keep it up for thirty minutes. I'll be back in an hour."

I raised my head. "Where are you going?"

"Town. That junk Blake gave you is useless. I'll get something that works." He landed a kiss halfway between my left ear and my eyebrow and left me there.

So the gambit had failed. But at least Jeffrey had no idea how my feelings had changed. Certainly, I could keep this up for one more night, one more day, and then we'd be home. The only danger, as I saw it, was to stay clear of Peter Blake, to give Jeffrey no cause, however false, for alarm. It shouldn't be hard to avoid a man who had obviously come up here to be alone, to lay his own ghosts to rest. Our contact so far had been accidental. Medical. If I stuck to my end of the beach, there was no reason we should cross paths again.

And why, I wondered, did the remaining night and day suddenly loom twice as grim?

Knuckles rattled against the door. I bolted upright, and the compress slid off my back onto the floor. "Who is it?"

"Peter Blake."

There was no reason on earth for my heart to start kicking. I got up and opened the door. In the shadow of the porch, with his shirt on, he looked completely ordinary.

"I saw Jeff go out. Is everything all right?"

"Of course it is. Why wouldn't it be?" I waved the

compress. "See, I'm doing as you instructed. Jeffrey's run into town for some better medication, but he'll be back soon."

Did he catch the warning? No. The sun creases in his forehead deepened into a frown, but instead of leaving, he stepped through the doorway.

"Look, I came over here to . . . God knows why I came over here. All right, no. I know why I came over here. You have every right to think I'm crazy. But I don't think I am. Something's wrong, isn't it?"

I tried to laugh. "Wrong? What gave you that idea?"

"The way you acted when I asked about that cut, for one thing. And the way you looked at him. You might say I've seen it before. You were afraid of him."

"Oh, really?" I looked at my watch, trying to think, but the only thing I could think of was that I had to get him out of there.

"And you're afraid now," said Peter Blake. "Why? He isn't here. I saw him go out in the car."

"And if he comes back and finds you here—" I didn't have to finish my thought. I could see the light dawning across the strong planes of his face.

"Of course," he said. "That was the trouble on the beach, too. He'd have noticed it."

I didn't ask, "Noticed what?" If I had, I don't think he would have heard me. He appeared to be thinking about something else.

"But what happened to your back didn't happen because of me."

No, I thought, it didn't happen because of Peter Blake. It happened because of my brother-in-law, Paul. Poor, innocent Paul and his wife, my sister, with us the whole time. And a week ago, only a week ago, instead of seeing that blind, unreasoning jealousy for what it was, I'd taken it as flattery. But the important thing now, the crucial thing, was not to trip Jeffrey's jealousy switch again. And that meant I had to get Peter Blake out of there.

I braced myself to meet his eyes. "I told you what happened to my back. If I sounded odd, it was because I felt like a fool."

"You sounded damned odd. You'd have sounded better if you'd told me to mind my own business. That's what a normal person would have done."

"Thank you," I said coldly.

"Look. I'm sorry. Christ, I've got some nerve, talking to you about what's normal. I don't think I've said two normal words to you since I met you. The truth of the matter is, I don't much like this Jeff Holtz of yours. I have my reasons. Or maybe I don't. I don't know."

The painful honesty in his voice shot through me. How could I have called this man ordinary? There was only one possible way to answer him.

"So that makes two of us."

For a minute, it was hard to read his face. Then it flooded with something that would have looked like relief if it hadn't been too absurd. "You shouldn't stay here. Let me drive you home."

"And run into Jeffrey on the road? That would be the worst thing I could do, believe me. Honestly, the best thing you can do is to get out of here."

It seemed he looked at me forever.

He held out his hand. "Fair enough. I won't bother you again. If you need anything, you know where to find me."

"Thank you." I shook his hand.

After he left, I expected to breathe easier, but I found I could barely breathe at all.

When Jeffrey returned, I was lying under another hot compress. He checked my wound, slathered it with something, and set to work collecting our fishing gear, all without speaking. He handed me heavy rubber boots, two pairs of socks, a thick wool sweater.

"I need all this? If it's going to be that cold, maybe I won't bother."

"It won't be that cold."

I said nothing more.

Just as we were going out the door, Jeffrey cupped my chin in his hand and smiled at me. "We didn't need the whole weekend, did we? There was nothing wrong between us, was there?"

"No, nothing."

"I pity those poor sods like Blake. Come on."

The sun was just behind the trees when we walked to the boat. Out of my peripheral vision, I could see a lamp come on in Peter Blake's cabin. We paddled in the direction Jeffrey had gone before, and I wondered, foolishly, if Peter were watching. No. Why should he? And even if he were, it seemed in no time at all we were around the bend and gone.

Jeffrey found the spot he was looking for. He threaded a worm onto my hook and cast it for me. We sat there in silence in the growing cold and dark until finally the depth of the shadows gave me courage.

"Jeffrey? You're right. We don't need the whole weekend. There's nothing wrong between us. Why don't we go home tonight?"

Silence.

I didn't move or breathe.

"You're not still worrying about that ridiculous cut."

"No. Of course not. It's just that I'd like to go home." I tried a laugh. It rang false in the gloom. "Let's face it, I can only live so long without my hair dryer. And admit it, doesn't a nice, hot bath sound good right now?"

"Delightful. But it can wait till tomorrow."

I gave up.

The silence grew longer.

"Shouldn't we go in?" I said after a while. "The wind seems to be coming up."

"Good. It'll stir up the fish."

"Well, it's awfully cold."

"We'll move around the point and get out of the wind."

I heard the hiss of his line as he reeled it in. I reeled in my own. Jeffrey took the rod from me and stashed it in the floor of the canoe. He handed me my paddle. It must have been half a mile across the pond, and it was so dark now I could barely distinguish the trees on shore. The newly formed chop slapped loudly against the aluminum canoe, drowning out any sounds of our paddles. As we rounded the point, the first thing I noticed was that Peter Blake's light was gone. The second thing I noticed was that the wind was worse there. It cut through my heavy sweater and rocked the canoe dangerously.

I twisted around. "Jeffrey, let's go in. I've had enough, haven't you?"

"Yes, I think I've had quite enough."

Was something wrong with his voice? I wasn't sure. But suddenly, I wanted more than anything to get out of there. I faced front and dug in with my paddle, willing us closer and closer to the cabin and the car and home. At first, Jeffrey's paddling seemed as determined as my own, but as soon as we pulled within five hundred yards of the beach, I could feel our momentum slow.

When Jeffrey spoke again, it wasn't in his own voice at all but in a neat imitation of my own. " 'Nothing's wrong between us.' Oh, Hannah, do you really think I'm such a fool?"

No. Not here. Not now. I thrust my paddle into the water and pulled for shore.

"I saw you. I saw him. I knew he'd come the minute my car was gone. So I parked down the road and walked back. I must admit, it didn't take him long. What's the plan? We go home, you ditch me, the two of you come back alone?"

Don't panic, I said to myself. *You've been here before. The thing to do is . . .* But what was the thing to do? Nothing I said had ever cut through this insane jealousy of Jeffrey's. No explanation ever served. But maybe that was the whole problem, my attempting to explain. I thought of Peter Blake. *You'd have sounded better if you'd told me to mind my own business. That's what a normal person would have done.* And in this case? What would a normal person say here? I slipped my paddle across my knees and swung around as far as I could without upsetting the canoe. "If that's what you think, Jeffrey, you *are* a fool. Now, it's late, and I'm cold, and I'd like to go in."

I must admit, it seemed to give him pause. A brief one. "Well, well, well, listen to you. Getting perky, is that it? Let me warn you, the last person who tried it didn't fare so well."

"I don't know what you're talking about, and I don't care. I'm going in. Now." I resumed paddling.

"Not *what,* Hannah, *who.* Rosemary Stevens. Don't you want to hear what really happened to her?"

And now it was my turn to pause. "Rosemary Stevens?"

"Peter Blake's fiancée. I suppose I should say Peter Blake's deceased fiancée. And she'd be my wife right now if she hadn't been such a fool. We'd gotten along quite swimmingly for a month or two, much better than they ever did with each other. He never knew it was me, of course. At least, he was never quite *sure.* But something happened. Mr. God's Gift must have gotten to her somehow. She was supposed to meet him here. She came up early to see me and tell me we were through."

"No."

I hadn't realized I'd said it out loud until Jeffrey answered. "Oh, yes, Hannah, yes. But you would have approved of our meeting, I'm sure. I could see there was no hope of changing her mind, so I accepted her decision like a gentleman. I offered her a drink, and she was so relieved at my reaction she drank it straight down. It wasn't too hard to talk her into another. I walked her home. Didn't I tell you it's easy to drown? It only takes about a foot of water. I simply shoved her in and held her down. She was in no condition to save herself. All I had to do was to launch Blake's rowboat with her sweater in it, erase any evidence of my presence here, and go back to the city."

The wind—no, his voice—raked through me. I couldn't stop shaking. The *no* that had escaped me before had been a token denial. In actual fact, almost before he'd spoken them, I'd believed every word. "And Peter Blake—"

"Peter Blake *wasn't* here, Hannah. They weren't supposed to meet till the next day. He wasn't here that night, and he isn't here now. An interesting thing happened while I was in town a while ago, didn't I tell you? A call came into the police station that his mother was seriously ill. There are no phones up here. They had to drive up to get word to him. They really should check those things before they send the cruiser around, shouldn't they? But they didn't. I saw the police pull up to his cabin when we were rounding the bend. He's probably halfway to Hempstead by now. That's where his mother lives. He told me that a few years ago. So let's see, it's three hours there, it should take a couple of hours to sort out the confusion, then three hours back. Always assuming he'd try to come back here at all."

So Peter Blake was out of the way for eight hours or more. But why would Jeffrey want Peter Blake out of the way now?

Suddenly, it was as if someone had turned a key in my brain, stepped on the gas, and told it to go. Jeffrey had just told me he'd murdered Rosemary Stevens. No matter what I said or did now, he'd have to murder me, too.

We were in the middle of the pond. No, not the middle, but five hundred yards, or six hundred now, from the beach, the cabin, the car, the quickest route home. I heard the slap of the waves against the left side of the canoe, which meant the wind was blowing us toward the opposite shore. And what was on the opposite shore? Mile after mile of empty black woods. And what was in the canoe? Jeffrey.

I'd just made up my mind where my better chances lay when he lifted the canoe paddle, hands locked as if he were holding a baseball bat, and swung.

But for the first time in my life, I was a step ahead of him. Before he'd completed his swing, I'd begun my dive over the gunnel, and although the edge of the blade connected, it only grazed the thickest part of me—my skull. Then two things happened that should have sealed my fate but actually saved me. The first was that as I went over the side, I swamped the canoe, which meant that Jeffrey was too busy trying to stay afloat to have time to look for me. The second was that at Jeffrey's insistence, I was laden down with heavy rubber boots and layers of clothing topped with a thick wool sweater.

The minute I hit the cold, black water, I went down.

And down.

It seemed I stayed down there forever. By the time I'd managed to fight my way back up into the air, there were enough waves and darkness between us to conceal me from his view.

And at the moment, that was all I wanted, to be concealed from Jeffrey's view. I gulped every mouthful of air I could and went under again, kicking in a fury away from the canoe, and when I surfaced for a second time, Jeffrey was paddling again, but he and the canoe seemed smaller than they had before. I dove once more, and the next time I came up, I knew I was right. I'd swum away from the canoe, with the wind, toward the opposite shore. Jeffrey had assumed, as anyone might assume, that I'd head for the nearest land. He was paddling parallel to the beach, combing the water between where I went over and the cabin's shore. It was a big pond. He'd had to make a choice. And he'd chosen wrong.

I concentrated on regulating my breathing. I wouldn't, I couldn't panic. I moved my limbs just enough to keep afloat and stay warm, conserving every last ounce of energy, letting the wind and waves do the work. I'd lost all track of time and place and sense by the time my feet scraped mud, and I half stumbled, half crawled into the pitch-black wilderness of the far shore.

I learned something that night about wool. Even if it's wet, it will keep you warm. I don't know how long I lay where I landed on a sodden patch of reeds and grass before I could breathe again, before the cold drove me to move.

Finally, I struggled to my feet and looked around.

Behind me was nothing but a black tangle. I didn't have to peer into it long to realize that if I struck out into the middle of it, I would disappear forever. Jeffrey had said there were two thousand acres of untouched wilderness out there. I could give up hoping to stumble across a house or a car. I had no sense of direction even in broad daylight on familiar terrain. At night, in unfamiliar woods, I would certainly circle aimlessly until I froze or dropped from exhaustion. There was only one thing to do: work my way around the edge of the pond as best I could in the direction of the road that ran somewhere to the east of Jeffrey's cabin. But what if I overshot the road and stumbled into the vicinity of the cabin, the vicinity of Jeffrey? And even if I did successfully find the road without running into Jeffrey, what then? Which way had we turned off that rutted road? Which way was town? I almost laughed out loud. As if I'd ever have the strength to make it all the way to town, on foot, alone.

I don't know how long I sat there shaking with cold before I saw the light come on.

It wasn't my brain this time that threw me to my feet and sent me thrashing through the reeds along the edge of the pond, but I hadn't gone far before the old cells fired themselves up. Peter Blake was there. Of course he was there. He didn't have to drive all the way to Hempstead to find out if his mother was ill. All Peter Blake had to do was drive the ten miles or so to Fairnham and make a call. And when he found out about the ruse, he'd know what was going on. He'd come back. He'd come back because he'd seen my back and he'd seen my fear and he knew Jeffrey. And now Peter Blake was there, in his cabin, and as soon as I reached him, I was as good as home.

I don't know how long it took me to fight and claw my way around that pond. The wool sweater caught on every branch, the bull briars raked my face, and I tore my hands pulling myself through the swamp grass. My thick jeans protected my legs against the jungle, but they were wet and cold and dragged me down. Jeffrey's big boots were somewhere at the bottom of the pond, and I hadn't covered half the distance before my socks were in shreds, but I kept on. When I hit the smooth sand, I almost cried in relief, and when I hit Peter's first step, I know I did begin to cry, but I didn't care. There was no need for false pride.

Or fear.

Tears stung my lacerated cheeks as I flung open the cabin door and walked into the glow of the lantern.

And Jeffrey's eyes.

He was wet. Dripping. But he'd kindled Peter Blake's stove, lit Peter Blake's lantern, settled in Peter Blake's chair with his stocking feet stretched toward the fire as comfortable as any spider waiting for his fly.

"Hello, Hannah," he said. "You look surprised. Why? I'm not surprised. Although I must say, it took you so long I thought maybe you were really dead after all. But I knew if you weren't, you'd come running to him—it only took one look at you ogling each other on the beach today. Or perhaps, in all fairness, I should say trying *not* to ogle each other. It was, all in all, a most pathetic display." Jeffrey pushed back his chair and stood. "Now, now, Hannah, don't cry. You can't say I didn't play fair. I told you he wasn't here, didn't I? Come here, into the light. You're quite the mess. What happened to you?"

He grasped me by the arm and pulled me toward him. I couldn't have moved if I'd tried. I was drained dry. I should have known. Had I learned nothing? Running to Peter Blake to save me. There was no one to save me. There was only Jeffrey and me. As Jeffrey swung me around toward the lantern, he must have felt what there was, or wasn't, left in me. He laughed softly, tipping me backward. I dropped a hand to steady myself and brushed up against the lantern. It wobbled, casting wild shadows, making Jeffrey's face dance before my eyes.

Jeffrey.

And me.

My fingers closed around the lantern. When he pulled me upward, I brought the lantern with me and smashed it into his eyes.

Jeffrey screamed and let me go, clutching at his eyes. I fell to the ground. A lick of flame streaked across the cabin floor in the wake of the trail of lamp oil, and I rolled away from it, colliding with a metal box on the floor. It fell over and burst open. Fishing tackle. Jeffrey dashed his shirt across his face, saw me, came at me. I ripped a fishing knife out of the tackle box, and Jeffrey laughed.

"Really, Hannah, what exactly do you plan to do with that?"

I don't honestly know what I would have done if Peter Blake hadn't chosen that minute to come crashing through the cabin door. The door smashed back like a thunderclap, and Jeffrey leaped around, but not before I saw the look on his face as he went for Peter. Peter was taller and stronger, I was sure. But Jeffrey was insane. I stepped as close as I could to the two grappling men and drove the knife home.

Jeffrey's body stiffened, sagged. I saw the look of surprise on Peter's face.

"Stabbed in the back," I said calmly, and sat down on the floor, hard.

We left Jeffrey where he fell. I think I looked worse than I was, and Peter's primary concern seemed to be to load me into his Jeep and get me to a hospital. It turned out Fairnham didn't have one, but the next town over, Pittsville, did. Somewhere between the nurse and the doctor, Peter slipped away. He must have made a few phone calls. The police met me at the hospital. It was almost daylight before I saw Peter again.

He appeared at the door of my hospital room, looking tired and surprisingly filthy until I remembered he'd half carried me to his Jeep and I'd been covered in mud and slime.

"All right?" he asked.

"Right enough. They said I can leave."

"Then let me drive you home."

"It's a long ride. I can call someone. You should—"

He smiled, almost three-quarters. "Get out of here? I don't think so. Not this time."

Widower's Walk

Joseph Hansen

The new kid has overslept and, being not much more than a teenager, could sleep till noon. Bohannon drags on Levis and boots, flaps into a shirt, steps over the windowsill onto the long porch of the ranch house, and heads for the stable building, clean, low lines against the gray background of the drowsing mountains. Horses move restlessly, rumble, and blow air through their big sinuses behind the closed doors of their box stalls. "Buck?" he says. "Seashell? Geranium?" And names the rest as he passes. His own horses and horses he boards for folk in the little town of Madrone, at the foot of this canyon, beside the ocean.

He raps knuckles on the tackroom door, whitewashed planks. "Kelly? Time to get up." No reaction. He knocks again. Silence. He lifts the black metal tongue that serves as latch, swings the door inward, pokes his head inside. "Kelly? Wake up." But the steel cot looks empty. He steps inside. It's empty, all right. But slept in hard, sheets tangled, blankets half on the floor. He glances around in the weak morning light from the single window. Two of George Stubbs's horse drawings on the walls. (Shouldn't there be three?) No boots under the cot. He opens the drawers of the unpainted chest. Nothing. No clothes in the closet. He shuts his eyes and swears. Another one gone.

He walks back along the sheltered length of the stable building, opening the top doors as he goes. He doesn't turn to see, but he knows heads are poking out to watch him. Hooves move fidgety, hopefully. At the end stall, he opens the whole door and takes Buck's bridle and leads him out. He loops the reins around a post and goes inside the building and gets his saddle. "Come on," he says, throwing blanket and saddle over Buck's broad back. "Start you and me off with a ride today." He grunts, bending to cinch up the girth. Buck grunts, too. Bohannon puts boot into stirrup and swings heavily aboard. "Nice long ride." He nudges Buck's ample sides with his heels, and they move out onto the gravel under the rustling trees. "Hell, maybe we'll just keep riding." Buck heads for the gate, which has a wooden arch over it, which holds the single name "BOHANNON" in cutout wooden letters. "Maybe we'll never come back." He leans from the saddle to unfasten the left leaf of the gate and, when they're past it, leans and drags it closed again. Habit. This morning, he wouldn't mind if somebody came and stole the place, horses and all. They'd be doing him a favor. Out on the pitted blacktop road, he reins Buck to the left up the canyon.

He can't remember how many stable hands he's lost since losing first Rivera—he'd expected that; Rivera had been training all along to be a priest—and then

George Stubbs, the veteran rodeo rider who'd come to Bohannon already old, and whom arthritis at last had put into a nursing home. There'd followed drunks and itchy-footed men, green and lazy boys, even one girl, who worked hard but quit to get married. Bohannon promised himself when he hired young Kelly that he'd be the last. If Kelly walked out on him, it would be a signal to give up and sell the ranch to a land developer, the way everybody else in the canyons seemed to be doing. It was all work and no fun anymore. Why prolong the misery?

He's a couple of miles up the canyon now and no longer on the main track. Buck is paying more attention than he is to his surroundings, and Buck shies. Now, this is not the kind of shy that would unsettle any rider but the newest. Buck is, after all, no colt. He's got fifteen years on him, if not more. And he's heavy. So his shy only *almost* unseats Bohannon. For a second, the man has to fight to keep upright. At a hard-bitten fifty-two or -three, his reflexes aren't what they used to be.

"Whoa, what's the matter?"

But before the words are quite out of his mouth, he sees what's the matter. A man is lying facedown in the road, half in the road, half on the shoulder. "Easy." Bohannon turns Buck's head, and they cross the road, where Bohannon swings down and ties the reins to a tree. He gives Buck's trembling flank a couple of soothing strokes, then crosses the road to the man. He kneels and touches the man, lays fingers lightly on the man's neck below the ear. But there's no need to feel for a pulse: the man is cold. He's been dead for hours.

Bohannon was for a long time a deputy sherriff. He knows how to act in situations like this. From his crouch, he looks around him, first at the whole wide scene—canyon, trees, rocks, dry streambed below—then up the slope that climbs to his right. Next, he studies the immediate site. Close to the body. Spatters of blood. Then what's near his boot soles—dried leaves, sickle-shaped eucalyptus, curled oak, pine needles, pebbles, no bullet, no shell casing. Nothing is stuck to the soles of the man's shoes.

The man is well dressed and not for a rustic place like this but for city life. The suit is dark. There's a necktie. The shirt is white. Where it isn't blood-stained. Somebody shot this man. From the front. Bohannon knows an exit wound when he sees one, and he sees one. Right between the shoulderblades. Not much blood. The man died fast.

He doesn't touch the body again, or the clothes. It was his job once but no more. He stands, brushes grit off his hands, and looks to the right again. Some way up the slope, among trees, rocks, ferns, and brush, he thought earlier he'd glimpsed metal. He had. He climbs toward it, and his heart sinks when his guess about what it is turns out to be a fact. It is Steve Belcher's battered camper truck. Belcher is a bearded, longhaired Vietnam veteran who lives in the camper and leaves everybody else alone and wishes they would leave him alone. The best luck he has had in his four or five years here is since he took to the canyons. First he'd parked the camper different places in Madrone, and the citizens had moved him on. "On" proved to be a leaky old fishing boat he'd anchored in Short's Inlet, a body of water nobody cared about except some migrating ducks now and then but that everybody got protective about once Belcher had started to live there. Belcher was polluting, wasn't he? A beautiful natural wildfowl habitat.

So Belcher gave up after making some ugly scenes at town council meetings—he had a rough mouth on him, did Belcher—and he'd taken to the canyons with this rusty camper. He never went into town except to pick up his disability check every month and buy supplies. The rest of the time, he kept out of the way. Except for establishing his campsite once in the Mozart Bowl. Dr. Dolores Combs and the rest of the town's wealthy music lovers damn near had him hanged for that.

Bohannon's boots crunch across strewn paper and crushed cans and plastic packaging. Coyotes or raccoons have broken open a trash bag, looking for a meal. He hears a noise and looks up, and Belcher is standing, buck naked, in the camper's dented doorway, holding a Browning 9mm.

"It's me," Bohannon says. "Don't shoot."

"You woke me up," Belcher grunts. His dirty-blond hair and beard are tousled from sleep. "What do you want? You never give me no trouble. Not you." He narrows mistrustful eyes. "Not yet."

"There's something down on the trail," Bohannon says, "that shouldn't be there. Put on some clothes. I want you to take a look at it."

Belcher tilts his head. "What do you mean, 'something'?"

"A body," Bohannon says.

Belcher stares. "A dead body?"

"Shot through the chest. Middle of the night. You hear anything?"

"Nope." Belcher scratches his beard. "No."

"You want to answer me?" Bohannon says. "You want to hand me your gun to sniff at?"

Belcher jerks with surprise. He's forgotten the gun. "It ain't mine." He puts it down inside the camper. "It ain't been fired." His voice is hoarse, and he has grown pale though his skin is like tanned leather. "And I didn't hear no shot."

"Not yours? It's the kind the Army issues, Steve."

"Banged against the truck. Middle of the night. Found it there by the front wheel." He kicks into ragged jeans. "Why here?"

"It's not your lucky day," Bohannon says. "Come on. Have a look at him."

"I don't see what for," Belcher says.

"So I can see your face when you say you don't know who he is. I've always trusted you. I want to see if I still can."

Belcher grunts and comes loose-limbed down the trailer's little metal stairs. His feet are dirty. "I don't want to see no more floppies. I seen enough. I told you that. Hell, Bohannon, I killed enough. Too many. Drives me crazy dreaming about it. I'd never kill again."

"You still keep your pistol," Bohannon says.

"I would," Belcher says, "if it would kill ghosts. It's not mine, Bohannon, I told you that. I hate the goddamn things."

"Come on." Bohannon turns away and starts downhill. "You know Lieutenant Gerard is going to home in on you. You're the obvious suspect." He goes quickly. The underfoot is slippery with morning dew, and he almost falls. "He and I were partners once, and if I tell him I'm sure it wasn't you, it might help." He looks over his shoulder.

The truck's cab door slams. The starter whinnies.

Bohannon turns back, loses his footing, falls to hands and knees. "Wait. Steve—don't do this."

The truck engine roars. Belcher looks out the window. "Forget it, Bohannon. You know what Gerard will do. I'm a homicidal maniac. He's been waiting years to prove that." He lets the parking brake go, the truck rolls backward about a foot, then springs forward. "So long." With old gray tires kicking up duff, Belcher weaves the truck away fast, in and out among the trees.

Bohannon struggles to his feet. "You're only making it worse," he shouts.

But maybe not. Maybe there's no way Belcher could do that.

He sits on a stump, lights a cigarette, and waits. He can't leave the body. If instead of riding Buck up here, he'd come in the truck, he could radio the sheriff station. He's just stuck, is all there is to it. Until somebody comes along. And Rodd Canyon is not known for heavy traffic. Whole damn day could pass without a single car. Sure as hell won't any horses be coming by. Not till he gets back down to his place. It's the only rental stable around. He stands up. This is a hell of a note.

It remains that for forty minutes (he keeps checking his watch), and then he hears an engine, the loose tool rattle and spring squeak of a vehicle. It's a red pickup. Fire patrol. He steps into the road. The driver is Sorenson, whom he's known for years. Sorenson stops the truck. He stares through the windshield at the body on the road.

"What does that mean?" he asks Bohannon.

"Means you can use your two-way," Bohannon says, "to let them know down at Madrone, and they can come pick him up. Shooting victim."

"Get in." Sorenson stretches across and opens the door on the passenger side of the cab. "You know how to use the thing."

"Do it for me," Bohannon says. "And lie a little, will you? Tell T. Hodges you found him. Leave me out of it."

Sorenson, blond and sunburned, looking twenty years younger than his age, wrinkles his brow. "What for? You don't want her to know you were riding your horse up the canyon? Why not?"

"Just do it," Bohannon says.

"Hey." Sorenson half lies across the seat, craning to see up the slope. "Where's Steve Belcher? He had his camper up there."

"Did he?" Bohannon says. "Not here now."

"I wonder why?" Sorenson says. "You've protected him time and again, Hack. But for a shooting? A killing?"

"Don't drag Belcher into it," Bohannon says. "Just tell them about the body, okay?"

Sorenson takes the part of the two-way radio you talk into from its hook and puts it to his mouth. There are noises, cracklings, sandpaper voices, indistinct words. He switches those off and talks into the mike. "Sorenson, up here in Rodd Canyon, trail that drops off the main road at the stand of big old eucalyptus trees on the left? Dead body of an older man lying in the road. Shooting victim, looks like." An answer crackles, and Sorenson says, "Ten-four," and hangs up the microphone.

"Thanks. Really appreciate it." Bohannon is already astraddle Buck and headed back for the main road. "Got to get home. Lost my stable hand again. Work enough for three men waiting for me."

For an answer, Sorenson gives a short hoot on his siren.

"As a licensed private investigator," Gerard says, "you can't encourage a suspect to flee. You can't aid and abet—"

"Shut up, Phil," Bohannon says, grinning. "This is my house, and I don't have to listen to you rave. Not here. Sit down. Have a drink."

Red-faced, Gerard yanks a chair out from the round deal table that stands in the middle of Bohannon's big pine-plank kitchen and drops onto it. He bangs his helmet down on the table. "Naw, I'm serious, Hack. You just stood there and watched him take off. And you let us think you weren't even up there." Bohannon hands him a glass with Old Crow in it. "I can't understand you."

"Was the man shot with a nine-millimeter Browning?"

"Nine-millimeter something." Gerard takes a swallow from his glass and makes a face. "How can you drink this stuff?"

Bohannon chuckles. "I manage. You find any ID on the body?"

"Robbery," Gerard says. "That's what Belcher wanted it to look like. Anyway, no wallet. But that's a good suit, and the labels are in it. Expensive, maybe even tailor-made. We'll check the shop out tomorrow."

Bohannon grunts. He has his glasses on and papers spread out in front of him. He pushes them into a raggedy stack and pokes the stack into a manila envelope. This was George Stubbs's job. Bohannon can't do paperwork and drink. Hell, he hates paperwork at the best of times. And this is not the best of times. He's worn out from rubbing down horses, picking gravel out of hooves, mucking out stalls, raking gravel, hauling water, pitching hay, writing receipts, answering damn fool phone calls, trying to collect overdue board bills, walking little kid riders around the railed oval he had built for that back when Rivera was here.

"There was nothing on the soles of his shoes to indicate a hike. He drove there."

Gerard studies him. "No car around. One car brought him and his killer both? And the killer drove it away afterward?"

Bohannon nods. "Which leaves out Steve Belcher."

"How?" Gerard says. "His camper was within yards of the victim. Why didn't Belcher bring him up from town for some kind of meeting? And it went sour, and Belcher lost his temper and shot him? He's got a mad dog temper, Hack. You've got to admit that."

"Maybe, but he's only a little bit crazy. He wouldn't leave the body lying there. He'd take it someplace else. Come on, Phil."

Gerard makes a skeptical sound, picks up his helmet, and gets to his feet. "We'll see what turns up in that camper."

Bohannon stares. "You've got it?"

"It's not hard to spot," Gerard says. "He hadn't got

to Fresno yet when the CHP pulled him over. On our APB."

Bohannon switches on the lamp in the middle of the table. There's still some daylight outside, but the kitchen doesn't get a lot of it. The lamp is an old kerosene lantern fitted out for electricity and enameled red. Linda's idea—his wife, who is in a private mental home just over the ridge, has been for a long time and looks like being there forever. Gerard walks to the open door.

Bohannon tells his back, "You're going to find the dead man's car up the canyon someplace. What? Mercedes? BMW? Jaguar? Abandoned in a ditch. Wiped clean of fingerprints."

"I know how to do my job," Gerard says, and pushes open the screen door.

Bohannon says, "Oh, and find a kid named Kelly. Hold on a second." He walks to the sideboard and takes a slip of paper from a drawer. He puts on the damn reading glasses again and peers at it. "Kelly Larkin. Hails from San Bernardino. Jockey-size, shaved head, tattoos. He'll likely be on foot, doesn't own a car. He was my stable boy till this morning very early. Maybe about the same time the man in the expensive suit got so fatally shot."

"We've got the nut who shot that man," Gerard says, "and you know it. Steve Belcher has been a disaster waiting to happen for years now. You always took his side. Don't make that mistake this time. You're already in deep, letting him get away this morning."

"What was I supposed to do? He had a gun. I didn't. He had a car. I didn't."

"Right. So why not admit right away that you were there? Way you handled it, anybody can think anything they want."

"They'll do that anyway." Bohannon walks to the door, steps out, watches Gerard go off along the porch to his brown sheriff's patrol car. He calls after him, "Did you find the bullet up there? It went right through him."

"Not yet," Gerard calls, "but we'll find it. Don't get your hopes up." He starts the car, slams the door, and takes off.

Bohannon can't understand it. He comes from his bedroom down the hall to the kitchen, following bacon smells, coffee smells. Hair wet from the shower, he stands barefoot in jeans and T-shirt, blinking in the lamplight. It's not daylight yet. The old schoolroom clock on the kitchen wall reads 5:10. And beside the monster nickel and porcelain stove stands T. Hodges, the slim, dark young woman deputy who is Bohannon's prime friend. She is beating up eggs in a pottery bowl that has Indian designs on it. She throws him a smile. "Good morning."

"I'll say. What's the occasion?"

"The lieutenant told me Kelly's left you," she says. A pitcher of orange juice is on the counter. She pours him a glass and holds it out for him. He limps to her and takes it. "That you're trying to do it all here. Stubbs's work, Rivera's work, and yours."

Bohannon nods and swallows some orange juice. "True, but—"

"So, I thought at least I could fix breakfast for you," she says.

"Mighty nice. Pretty early for you to get up,

though." He sets the orange juice glass on the table and goes to take the old speckled blue enamel pot off the back burner on the stove and pour himself a mug of coffee. He raises the pot to her. "Pour some for you?"

"Not yet, thanks. Go sit down and enjoy that." She examines an iron skillet, turning it in the light, finds it acceptably clean, sets it on the stove, and cuts butter into it. "There's news. The dead man's name is Lubowitz, Cedric. A stockbroker. Beverly Hills. Age sixty-five. Newly a widower."

Bohannon lights a cigarette and squints at her past the light of the table lamp. "How'd they come by all this?"

"His picture on the news," T. Hodges says. "Seems he used to appear now and then on *Wall Street Week.*"

"Nobody in your department watches *Wall Street Week.*"

She laughs. "Picture it if you can," she says.

"And what was he doing in Rodd Canyon? What did he want up this way at all? Only stock up this way is livestock."

"And commodities were not his line," T. Hodges says.

The coffee is hot and strong. He douses it with cream. "And Belcher. Did Belcher know him?"

"Belcher watches *Wall Street Week* even less than Gerard." She brings a plate of bacon, eggs, and hash browns and sets it in front of Bohannon. "Eat hearty."

"What about you?" he says.

"Coming up," she says, and it is. In another minute, she has taken the pressed-wood chair opposite him. Now there's a stack of toast on the table, too. She

tucks in a gingham napkin, picks up her fork, then
looks at him. Very seriously. "Hack, you can't let
Gerard do this to Steve Belcher. He's the gentlest,
sorriest creature in the world. But everybody is ready
to believe the worst, you know that."

Bohannon piles guava jelly on a slab of toast. "So
does Belcher. Nothing I can do about it. He'd have
been better off it he just hadn't—"

"He didn't kill that man!" T. Hodges says hotly.

"I guess not," Bohannon says. "But I'm not the
jury."

"You mean you're going to let it happen? Just sit
back and—"

"Teresa," Bohannon says gently, "you've already
told me I'm trying to do three men's work around
here. It's my living. I can't play detective anymore.
Even if I had the energy, I haven't got the time."

"I'll do the leg work for you," she says. "You just
tell me what needs to be done, and I'll do it. Kelly.
Gerard says you think Kelly might have done it. I'll
find him and bring him here."

"You have a job, love," Bohannon says. "Eight
hours a day and sometimes more. Anyway, Gerard
wouldn't tolerate you working the case against him.
Behind his back. Don't think about it." She opens her
mouth to argue, and he says, "Eat your beautiful
breakfast, kid, and listen to your old man. Things
happen every day that are at least as unjust as what's
happening to Steve Belcher. All over the world. We
can't stop them, no matter how much we'd like to."

"Oh, rubbish," she says. "Honestly, Hack. 'Old
man,' indeed. I repeat: You tell me where to go, what
to look for, who to talk to, and I'll do it. Yes, I have a

job, but I have a lot of time away from that. Besides, Gerard is sexist. He never lets me have a case. Closest I get is tracking down lost children. A case like this is man's work, right?"

"That's Phil." Bohannon grunts. "These are better hash browns than Stubbs ever made. What's your secret?"

"Don't boil the potatoes first. Grate them up raw." She gives her head an impatient shake. "Don't change the subject, damn it. Hack, Fred May says it's hopeless; he can't win without you."

May is the local public defender, those rare times when a public defender is needed around here. Fat and amiable, he devotes most of his time to his wife and kids, and to protecting the whale and the wolf and the wilderness. Bohannon has often acted as his investigator.

"Don't look at me that way," he says. "I can't do it, Teresa. I have horses to look after. They can't feed themselves and clean up after themselves. You know that. Be reasonable."

"Reasonable won't save Steve Belcher." Tears are in her eyes. "The town can't wait to get rid of him. You know that."

"And I can't stop them." Bohannon stands, picks up his plate and hers—she's hardly eaten—and carries them to the sink. He brings the coffee pot back and refills their mugs. When he sits down, it is a gesture of disgust. "What the hell was Cedric Lubowitz doing here, anyway?"

"I thought you'd want to know," a tart voice says from the doorway. Belle Hesseltine stands there, backed by the first faint light of sunrise. She is a doctor who moved up to Madrone to retire many years ago now, and instead got busier than she'd ever been before. A lean, tough old gal, she's a mainstay of hope and courage and caring for many. For Bohannon, too. "I went past the substation to tell the lieutenant, but he hasn't come in yet." She walks toward the table, pulls out a chair, seats herself, looks at T. Hodges. "You weren't there, either." She sets her shoulder bag on the floor. "So I thought the one to tell was you, Hack."

"Well, you're wrong about that," Bohannon says. "But I'm happy to see you, all the same. Coffee?"

"I'll get it," T. Hodges says, and hops up and goes away into the shadows. "You persuade him he's got to help poor Steve Belcher."

Belle Hesseltine scowls at Bohannon. "Persuade? What's that mean? You aren't going to—? But the man's doomed unless somebody intervenes. He hasn't a chance. He can't rely on himself. He can't put his thoughts together. He can't fight back. Hack, I'm shocked."

"I'm stuck, Belle. I have to run this place alone. Time a day is over, all I'm good for is to sleep."

Belle watches T. Hodges set a coffee mug down for her. "What happened to my tattooed angel?"

"Kelly? Spread his wings yesterday morning and flew away. I told Gerard, it could have been the same time Lubowitz was shot. Phil doesn't see any connection. If I know him, he won't even bother to check." It is risky, and he knows it, but he lights a cigarette anyway. The old woman glares disapproval, but this time she doesn't bawl him out. And he asks, "So . . . what's Lubowitz's connection to our little township?"

"His sister-in-law," Belle says, and tries the coffee. "Ahh!" She holds the steaming mug up for a moment, admiring it, then sets it down with a regretful shake of her head. "Why is it that everything that tastes so good is so bad for us?"

"Sister-in-law?" T. Hodges wonders.

"Mary Beth Madison." Belle Hesseltine leans toward the table's center, peering intently. "Is that some of George Stubbs's guava jelly? Hack, push that toast and butter over here. That wicked old man made the most sinfully delicious preserves." She steals Hack's knife and goes after the toast and jelly as if the world had stopped for her convenience. When her mouth is jammed and her dentures are clacking happily away, when she is licking her fingers, slurping coffee, she notices their strained faces and makes an effort to swallow so she can speak. She sets down the coffee mug. "Very good Pasadena family. It was Mary Beth's older sister, Rose, that Cedric Lubowitz married. There was a scandal and talk of disinheriting Rose for marrying a Jew, but that blew over."

A corner of the old woman's mouth twitches in a smile.

"The Lubowitzes were neighbors, after all, and their house was just as splendid. The girls and young Cedric had spent their childhoods together, very close. I also suspect some Lubowitz financial advice had helped stabilize the Madison fortune. It was shaky. Henry Madison III had not been clever with his inheritance. Among his lesser follies was buying land in Madrone and Settlers Cove. Worthless at the time. That's how it happens that Mary Beth settled here. And"—she looks at first one, then the other—

"the reason I retired here. My father, the Madison family doctor, had accepted a lot up here to settle a bill when times were bad."

"And that's how you know all this dishy stuff," T. Hodges marvels. "But doesn't Miss Mary Beth Madison live with Dr. Dolores Combs? The Chamber Symphony? The Canyon Mozart Festival? The Gregorian Chant Week at the Mission?"

Belle Hesseltine nods. "And much else as well. Yes, that's Dolores. Hard to believe that as a child she was scarcely more than a foundling, isn't it?"

T. Hodges's jaw drops. "Are you serious?"

"The Madison girls took to her, brought her home from the park one summer with them, and after that she was in the Madison mansion almost constantly. The family soon accepted her. After all, what she lacked in breeding and background she made up for in brains and talent."

Bohannon says, "She cuts quite a figure these days."

Belle Hesseltine smiles. "Her people were poor, uneducated; the father drank. They had no idea they had a musical prodigy on their hands. It was the Madisons who bought her a piano, got her lessons, sent her to university."

"And so," T. Hodges says, "when it came time for Cedric Lubowitz to marry, and he chose Rose, Dolores Combs and Mary Beth Madison soldiered on alone together?"

Bohannon is laughing.

She frowns at him, startled. "What's so funny?"

"You never told me you liked love stories." He grins.

"Well—well, I don't," she protests. "But this is

about a murder case, Hack. It's straight out of the training manual. The most important person in any murder case is the victim. And the most likely killer is someone the victim knew well. Right?"

"Sounds more like Agatha Christie to me," Bohannon says.

"Well—" Belle Hesseltine unfolds her tall, bony frame from the chair and picks up her shoulder bag. "I have patients to see."

"Wait," Bohannon says. "Was Cedric Lubowitz up here to visit Mary Beth? Is that what you're saying?"

"Oh, I don't suppose so, really. He owned one of those lots his father-in-law bought so long ago," the old doctor says. "He may have planned to build on it and settle down here to live out his sunset years in quiet. Hah! I could have told him a few things about that, couldn't I?" She opens the screen door and pauses to look back. At T. Hodges, really, so maybe she's teasing. "Then again, perhaps having lost dear, pretty Rose and feeling lonely, he came to renew acquaintance with Mary Beth, who is every bit as pretty. I suppose, if you like love stories, you're free to think that."

And with a bark of laughter, she marches off.

Tired as he is, he goes to see Stubbs. It's a long drive to San Luis, but he skipped last night, and it's not fair. The old man is lonesome as hell. Anyway, Bohannon misses him. If there's nothing to talk about, they play checkers or watch horse racing or bull riding on television. Tonight there is Steve Belcher to talk about, and Cedric Lubowitz. Stubbs regards Bohannon from his narrow bed with its shiny rails, where he is propped up with his wooden drawing kit and drawing pad beside him on the wash-faded quilt. When the pain isn't too bad, he can still draw.

He says reproachfully, "You ain't gonna help him?"

"Stable boy left me. No time, George."

"Oh, Kelly." Stubbs grunts. "Yeah, I know. He come by here real early yesterday. Says will I tell you. Gotta go home. Ma needs him. Runnin' her out of the mobile home park. Fightin' with the boyfriend."

"He could have left a note," Bohannon says.

"Nothin' to write with," Stubbs says. "Nothin' to write on."

"On the kitchen table," Bohannon says. "He knew that. Knew where I sleep, too. He could have wakened me and told me. He woke you."

Stubbs waves a gnarled hand. "Had to see me. Had one of my drawings. Took it down off the tackroom wall. Wanted it for his room at home. Wouldn't steal it. Offered me five bucks for it. I give it to him."

"How did he get in here so early?"

"It was warm." Stubbs nods at the window. "Come in there."

Bohannon says, "Didn't say anything about the killing, did he?"

Stubbs frowns. "How would he know about it?"

"Just asking," Bohannon says.

Stubbs squints at him, surprised. "You don't think he'd have killed this Lubo—what's his name. Why?"

"I'd like to ask him," Bohannon says.

"He'd need a gun," Stubbs says. "Where would he get it?"

"A Browning automatic. I don't know. Someone got hold of one. Threw it away after the shooting."

"And Belcher just picked it up?" Stubbs says.

"That's his story. I doubt they'll find a record of it.

Bought on the street, most likely. And the tattoos suggest Kelly knows the streets."

"Ballistics report in already?" Stubbs's white, tufty eyebrows are raised. "They know it was the Browning?"

Bohannon shakes his head. "They can't find the bullet," he says. "But a paraffin test says Belcher shot the gun lately."

"Oh, hell," Stubbs says.

"He told Gerard it was to scare off a prowler," Bohannon says, "but he told me earlier it hadn't been fired."

"You see why you have to pitch in and help him?" Stubbs says. "The fool's his own worst enemy. Always has been."

"Not always," Bohannon says. "Once it was Uncle Sam."

"Just a minute." Stubbs massages his white beard stubble thoughtfully. "Could the prowler have been Kelly?"

Bohannon blinks surprise. "Well, I'll be damned," he says. "Good thinking, George. Why not?"

He swings into the ranch yard and in the headlights sees a brown sheriff's patrol car. Lights wink on top of it. Two doors stand open. Two people struggle beside it. He drives on hard toward them. One is T. Hodges, her helmet on the ground. The other is Kelly Larkin. He pushes T. Hodges backward so she falls. He turns and comes running directly at Bohannon's truck. From one wrist dangles a pair of handcuffs, glinting in the light. His shirt is torn down the back and slipping off his shoulders, showing his tattoos. Bohannon jams on the Gemmy's brakes, jumps down with a yell, and grabs the boy. Who twists and hits out with the handcuff-dangling fist. It knocks Bohannon's hat off.

"Stop it," he says. "Stand still, damn it, Kelly."

"Aw, let me go," the boy says. "I didn't do nothin'."

"Then don't fight," Bohannon says. "There. That's better." He calls to T. Hodges, whom his headlights shine on. "You all right?"

"Kelly . . ." she says in a menacing voice, and comes toward them.

"I'm sorry," the boy says, hangdog.

"I should think so." She is wiping dust off her helmet with her sleeve. "I was taking the cuffs off him. I told him I was sure I could trust him. And look what happened."

"We'll just put them back," Bohannon says, and clips the cuffs on him again. "There." He picks up his hat. "Now, let's go into the kitchen, sit down, have some coffee, and talk this over civilized. All right?"

"I don't know anything to talk about," Kelly says, stumbling along, Bohannon holding his arm. "This is crazy."

They step up onto the long covered walkway that is the ranch-house porch. Bohannon looks over Kelly's head at T. Hodges. "Is it crazy?"

"I don't think so," she says. "Not when you consider that his last name isn't Larkin—"

"It could be," Kelly says. "It was my mom's name."

Bohannon pulls open the kitchen screen door, they walk inside, and he hangs up his hat. The lamp on the table glows. "It's Belcher, right?"

Kelly stares. "How did you know?"

"Sit down," Bohannon says. He goes to the looming stove and picks up the speckled blue coffee pot. But T.

Hodges comes and takes it out of his hand. "I'll do it," she says. "You talk to him."

"This is going to get you into a mess with Gerard," he says.

"We'll deal with Gerard later," she says.

Bohannon drops onto a chair at the table and, as he lights a cigarette, studies the sulking boy. "You didn't happen in on me by accident, looking for work. You found out your father was here, and you wanted to see him, talk to him."

"He left when I was four," Kelly says. "Walked out on my mom and me. Beat her up and walked out and never came back."

"Which broke your mother's heart?" Bohannon asks.

"Not exactly. She couldn't take it anymore. He was so mixed up and half out of his gourd from the war, all that killing, those nightmares, the way he'd scream and hide . . ." Tears shine in Kelly's eyes, and he drops his head and sniffles hard and wipes his nose with the back of one cuffed hand. "It wasn't his fault. I knew that. She knew it, too, but he wouldn't get help. The veterans, they're entitled to help, and he got some before they got married, but then he was happy, and it was all right for a while, but the horrors came back, you know? It started all over again. He couldn't keep a job, he started boozing all the time, throwing stuff, smashing stuff, hitting her—" The boy's voice breaks, and he shakes his head and looks at the floor.

"And you came to get him to come home?" Bohannon asks.

The boy nods, lifts his tear-shiny face. "It was years ago. And she needs him. She's always getting new men. And they're none of them any good. Highway trash. She's a waitress, works hard, they just take her money and lay around watching TV all day."

"You think he's cured now?" T. Hodges brings coffee mugs into the light and sets them down for the two men. "Kelly, he doesn't work, either. Lives off his disability check."

"Yeah." Kelly touches his coffee mug. "And hates everybody."

"You talked to him?" Bohannon says.

Kelly makes a face. "He wasn't happy to see me. It wasn't a good talk. Nothing like what I expected."

"'Dreamed,' you mean." T. Hodges sits down with her own coffee in the circle of lamplight. "Kelly, some things just aren't meant to be."

Kelly blows steam off his coffee and gingerly tries it. "I wasn't giving up. I was going to take him back. I promised my mom. Take him back with me, and we'd be like we were in the seventies, a family. We had good times. He was okay then. Steady. Cheerful, even. A good dad. I really have missed him. Twenty years is a long time."

"Granted," Bohannon says. "So you tried talking to him again?"

"Three, four times. He ordered me off, told me to leave him the hell alone."

T. Hodges hasn't done this for a long time, but now she reaches for Bohannon's Camels on the tabletop and lights one. In the slow-moving smoke that circles the lamp, she says, "And night before last?"

"I couldn't sleep. I kept arguing with him in my head. Yeah, I went up there." Kelly doesn't look at her or at Bohannon. His voice is almost too low to be heard. "He took a shot at me."

"You sure he saw you, knew who you were?"

"Well, hell, how do I know?" Kelly says. "Think I stayed around to find out? He had a gun. You don't know how fast you can run till somebody shoots at you."

"Uh-huh," Bohannon says. "And what did you stumble over?"

"What?" Kelly sits very straight, eyes wide. "What?"

"You were running scared, and you didn't watch where you were going, and you stumbled over the body of a man down on the road."

"Hell," Kelly says. "How did you know?"

"Your hands are scraped and scabby from falling on pavement," Bohannon says.

"And I'm afraid," T. Hodges says, "the thought that jumped into your mind was that your father had killed that man, and that he'd changed more than you'd thought in those twenty years, and you were suddenly very much afraid of him."

"And didn't want to stay anywhere near him anymore," Bohannon says. "You were on your way. Which is why you didn't take time even to write me a note."

"I stopped to see Stubbs," Kelly says defensively.

"Sixty-five miles down the road," Bohannon agrees. "And George didn't describe it as a long visit."

"What will they do to my dad?" Kelly asks anxiously.

"You love him in spite of everything," T. Hodges marvels.

"Don't worry about him," Bohannon says. "I don't think he killed the man. But it would help if I knew who did."

T. Hodges puts out her cigarette. "You didn't see anyone around there? An expensive car, maybe?"

Kelly laughs, but there's no humor in it. "I was so scared I didn't see nothin'. Man, I was outta there. I mean, we're talkin' roadrunner here." They watch him without comment, and he pauses and blinks to himself seriously. "Wait. No. You're right. There was a car. Other side of the road. Mercedes. Parked wrong way."

"No driver?" Bohannon says.

"Not that I saw." Kelly turns pale. "The killer, you mean?"

"The killer, I mean," Bohannon says.

For a long time, he didn't want and didn't keep a phone by the bed, but when Stubbs got to the wheelchair stage, it helped to have it there in case of emergencies. After Stubbs went to the nursing home, Bohannon just kept the phone. And now it rings. Early morning. He's overslept. He groans, gropes out, gets the receiver, and mumbles "Bohannon" into it.

"The gun was the proud possession of the deceased," Gerard says. "Cedric Lubowitz. But the only fingerprints on it were Steve Belcher's."

"The good news," Bohannon croaks, "and the bad news all in one package?"

"No, the bad news is I know all about Teresa's activities last night, and she is on leave till this case is over with. I'm holding Kelly for at least seventy-two hours. The provenance of the gun suggests he could have been the killer. Motive, robbery. The vic's wallet hasn't turned up."

"Kelly got money on him?"

"Not very much," Gerard says. "You should pay your help better."

"I'd have thought a man like Lubowitz would keep a couple hundred bucks cash on him." Bohannon throws off the blankets and sits on the edge of the bed. "Well, since you haven't got the wallet, that means it wasn't in the camper. And that clears Steve, anyway." He reaches to get a cigarette from his shirt which hangs on a painted straw-bottom Mexican chair. "Of course, you checked to see whether the killer threw the wallet away along the roadside."

"That's what the citizens pay me for," Gerard says. "Me, not you, Hack. Will you stay out of this now?"

"I keep trying," Bohannon says. "Don't worry. I haven't got time. Not with my stable hand in jail." And he hangs up.

"He didn't tell you about Lubowitz's car?" T. Hodges says. She is at the stove cooking breakfast for him again. Earlier, she cleaned out the box stalls, fed, watered, and groomed the horses while he slept. Now she puts plates of ham and eggs and fried mush on the table. "They found it at the Tides Motel on the beach where he was staying."

Bohannon raises his eyebrows. "Not in the guest room at the beautiful home of his sister-in-law and her eternal friend Dr. Combs?" Bohannon pitches into his breakfast. Mouth full, he says, "So much for the love story motive."

T. Hodges quietly pours syrup on her slabs of fried mush. "Don't jump to conclusions," she says. "His first night, they all had dinner together at the Brambles. Very pleasant. Fresh salmon, champagne. Lots of laughter and jokes about him sweeping Mary Beth off to Paris on the Concorde. The check went on his credit card."

Bohannon chews a chunk of ham. "And afterward?"

"The waiter at the Brambles said they took Mr. Lubowitz home with them afterward, for dessert, and to listen to some new Mozart CDs on the stereo. The motel says he didn't get back there until midnight."

"Mozart. You remember when Steve Belcher camped up in the Mozart Bowl?" It's a little natural amphitheater among the pines in Sills Canyon. "Dr. Combs got on his case hot and heavy for that."

T. Hodges laughs. "She'd taken some possible large contributors to the Canyon Mozart Festival up to see the place in all its unspoiled loveliness. Sasquatch was not what she'd expected to find. She could have killed him."

"You don't mean that," Bohannon says.

She wags her fork in denial. "Figure of speech. When our team examined the Lubowitz Mercedes," she says, "it had no fingerprints on it. Inside or out. Not the victim's, not anyone's."

"A careful murderer," Bohannon says, and tries his coffee. "A schemer, a planner-ahead. Wore gloves. Nothing spontaneous about this killing, Teresa." He sets his cup down and lights a cigarette. "Nobody at the motel saw who returned the Mercedes?"

She shakes her head. "Not the day man, not the night man. None of the guests Vern could find to question."

"Yup," Bohannon says, looking across at the sunlit kitchen windows. They are open. Smells of sage and eucalyptus drift in on a cool breeze. The sky is clear blue above the ridges. "Craftily plotted. An organizing mind, used to managing people and events."

"But insane," she says. "Cedric Lubowitz was a gentle old man."

"Yup." Bohannon scrapes back his chair and goes to stand looking out the door. "Nobody's given me the medical examiner's findings. No, don't say it. Let me guess. He was shot at close range, right? Only a few feet. And through the chest. He was facing his killer. His killer was a friend."

"He must have thought so." T. Hodges gathers up the plates and carries them to the sink. "What a horrible way to die."

"Sure as hell too late to learn anything from it."

Water splashes in the sink. "You go along and find out what you want to find out," she calls. "I'll look after things here."

"On a day like this," he says, "there'll be lots of people wanting to go horseback riding. You'll be run off your feet."

"Be careful," is all she says.

And he takes down his hat and goes.

Steve Belcher sits on the bunk in his cell and glowers. Outside the windows, towering old eucalyptus trees creak in the breeze. Fat Freddie May stands leaning against the sand-colored cinderblock wall. Bohannon leans back against the bars. Down the way, someone is softly playing a harmonica. A hard song. "I'm comin' back, if I go ten thousand miles . . ." A dimestore mouth organ can't handle it, but the player keeps trying.

Bohannon repeats his question: "You said there was a prowler, and you shot the gun to scare the prowler off. What did the prowler look like, Steve?"

"How do I know? It was midnight. It was pitch dark."

"Tall, short?" Bohannon says. "Thin, fat? Wearing what?"

"I only heard him tramping around," Belcher says.

May says in his gentle voice, "It was Kelly, wasn't it? Your son, Kelly?"

"Oh, hell," Belcher says, and runs a hand down over his face. "Is he messed up in this, too, now?"

"Since last night," Bohannon says. "He went up there, and you shot the gun off. So it was after Mr. Lubowitz was killed, after the killer threw the gun at your camper."

But Belcher is shaking his shaggy head. "It wasn't him. This one was bigger. Taller. Heavier. Kelly's head is shaved. This one had hair."

"That's all?" Bohannon asks. "Clothes? Voice? Anything?"

"Went crashing down through the trees." Belcher grins. His teeth are in poor shape. "Maybe it was a bear."

"You don't want to help us get you off the hook? Okay." Bohannon sighs, straightens, peers through the bars. "Vern?"

Fred May says, "And Kelly. You don't want to help him?"

A guard with a big gun in a holster on his hip comes and unlocks the cell door. Bohannon goes out, May after him. The door closes. They follow the guard along the hallway.

And Belcher calls, "It could have been a woman."

Bohannon doesn't break stride, but he smiles and says, "Ah!"

He noses the green pickup truck into a diagonal slot in front of the drugstore. A pair of sleepy old huskies with pale eyes look at him as he passes. One of them sniffs his boots. He pushes into the gleaming shop and stands looking for Mrs. Vanderhoop. There she is, at the back, by the prescription counter. When he nears, he sees she is talking with a bald little man who plays cello in local music ensembles. Mrs. Vanderhoop, wife of the pharmacist who owns the only drugstore in Madrone, is a busy part-time musician herself. Piano. Though Bohannon seems to remember she once sang. She sees him and gives him a smile, excuses herself to Mr. Cello, and comes to him, gray-haired, thin, running to homespun skirts, Navajo blouses, Indian jewelry.

"Mr. Bohannon?" Her expression is concerned. "Isn't it terrible about that poor man, Liebowitz?"

"Lubowitz," Bohannon says. "Listen. You can correct something I heard. That he came up here to see his sister-in-law, Mary Beth? Wouldn't he have seen her at her sister's funeral, his wife's funeral?"

"Oh, no." Mrs. Vanderhoop shakes her head firmly. "Not that Mary Beth did not love her sister. But Dolores wouldn't allow it. They had a terrible argument about it. I came back for something I'd forgotten after a rehearsal. Mary Beth was in tears."

"I don't understand." Bohannon pushes back his hat. "I heard they were all close friends together when they were young."

Mrs. Vanderhoops's smile is bleak. "Yes, well, for some of us, young was rather a long time ago. No, there was no love lost."

"But they had dinner with Mr. Lubowitz only the night before he was killed," Bohannon says. "Very friendly and good-humored, I'm told. Laughing over old times."

"Did they? Really." Mrs. Vanderhoop blinks thoughtfully to herself. "Do you know, if it wasn't you telling me, Mr. Bohannon, I wouldn't believe that. Dolores Combs despised Mr. Liebowitz. And once her sister Rose took sick, she wouldn't let Mary Beth near him."

Bohannon circles the house, a sprawling redwood place with windows that stare at the ocean. It's isolated on its hill, land once owned by Henry Madison III. Big pines shelter it. Nobody is around. Cars? The garage doors are closed. He parks his green pickup truck, gets out, and looks down the road. Only a short walk to the beach, only another short walk to Cedric Lubowitz's motel room. You could do it in ten minutes. He hikes up through the trees around the back of the house, where he spots the structure he wants and goes toward it, waiting for some reaction if he's been seen. He doesn't hear or see any. The enclosure of redwood plank fencing he has had his eye on has a gate, but it isn't locked. He works the latch quietly, opens the gate, and sees inside what he expected. Trash barrels. Two are filled with yard trimmings, and their lids are propped against the enclosure, but the third has its lid in place. Heart beginning to beat fast, he pries the lid off. Inside is a large green plastic bag. He undoes the wire twist that closes it, pulls the bag open, reaches inside, and a voice behind him says: "What the hell do you think you're doing?"

He turns. It's Gerard. He looks stern.

Bohannon says, "Collecting trash? Is that against the law?"

"You haven't got a license to collect trash," Gerard says. "What you are doing is breaking and entering, conducting a search of private property without a warrant."

Bohannon pulls a white cableknit sweater out of the bag and holds it up. It has bloodstains on it. And next, a brand new pair of women's jeans, also splashed with blood. "Hundred to one," he says to Gerard, "those will match Cedric Lubowitz's blood type. And his DNA." He brings out a pair of expensive low-heeled women's walking shoes. Turns the soles up. "More of same off the road." With a fingernail, he pries out scraps of oak and eucalyptus leaves, pine needles. "Stuff like this lay all around the body." He looks at Gerard, whose face is expressionless. "What you're saying is that I've made this inadmissible evidence."

"It would be," Gerard answers, "except when I learned you were out and around, talking to prisoners behind my back, checking out the tires on Lubowitz's car at the impound, generally acting your usual hot-dog self, I got a warrant." He pulls the folded paper from inside his uniform jacket. He edges Bohannon aside and rummages in the trash bag for himself. "The wallet," he says, and holds it up.

"Isn't it disgusting," Bohannon says, "how right I always am?"

Gerard starts off. "Bring that stuff. Let's go arrest her."

He presses a bell button on the wide, redwood-beamed porch. Handsome stained glass frames the doorway. The motif is California wildflowers. Yellow poppies, blue lupine, white yucca. Suddenly, the door flies open, and Dolores Combs stands there angry, a big-boned woman, white hair cropped handsomely. Arty women in Settlers Cove run to sweatshirts, but not she. A shirtwaist of brown shantung. Tailored slacks. A jade necklace. From Gump's, probably.

"I warned you," she begins. "It's you, Lieutenant Gerard. Forgive me. I thought it was more news people. They've been pestering the life out of us."

"Morning," Gerard says. "We're here about the death of your friend Cedric Lubowitz. This is Hack Bohannon, investigator for the public defender's office."

She glares at Bohannon. "You're defending that animal Belcher?"

Bohannon tugs his hat brim. "Ma'am."

"These things belong to you?" Gerard takes sweater, jeans, and shoes from Bohannon and holds them out to her. She blinks at them and turns pale. "N-no. Certainly not. Where did you get them?"

"Out of your trash barrels back of the house," Bohannon says.

She acts indignant. "You had no right to—"

"We have a search warrant." Gerard hands her the sweater, jeans, and shoes and produces the paper again, unfolding it, holding it up for her to read. "It covers the grounds, the house, and all outbuildings."

She eyes it and seems to shrink a little. But she braves up in a second. "I have no idea how these got there. No idea." She drops the clothes and snatches the paper, reading it closely. Her head jerks up.

"Harold Willard? Why—why—Judge Willard is a close personal friend. He's one of the principal contributors to—" She thrusts the paper back at Gerard. "Why would he sign such a warrant? What lies did you tell him about me?"

"It's not going to be hard to prove those are your clothes, Dr. Combs, your shoes. And they have blood-stains on them. We can trace the clothes to where you bought them. We can trace the bloodstains to Mr. Lubowitz. And"—he flashes it—"Mr. Lubowitz's wallet."

"Dolly? What's wrong?" A dainty pink and white woman appears behind the doctor of music. *Fluffy* would describe her. Curvacious once, now pudgy. Her voice is little-girlish. "Who are these men?" Her blue eyes widen, looking at them. "What do they want? Is it about poor, dear Cedric?"

"Go away, Mary Beth. Let me handle this."

Mary Beth Madison sees the clothes. She stoops and picks up the sweater. "Why, where did you find this? I've been looking all over for it. I was going to take it to the cleaners days ago." She draws in her breath. "Why, just look at those stains. Now, those were not on it when I—"

Dr. Combs tries to kill her with a look. "Will you be quiet?" she says. "Do you have to rattle on and on constantly?"

The plump little woman is amazed. "But, Dolly, I only—"

"Shut up, can't you?" The Combs woman is trembling. "Mary Beth, please go away, now. You're only making things worse." But Mary Beth simply stands, holding the sweater, totally bewildered.

Gerard asks her, "Is that Dr. Combs's sweater?"

"Oh, yes." Mary Beth nods. "Hand-knitted. From Ireland. We were there two years ago." She looks adoringly at her big friend. "Dolly played an organ recital in Dublin. Beautiful old church." Her small hands are stroking the sweater. She looks at it again. "Dolly, what are these awful splotches? Will they ever come out?"

Her lifelong friend lets out a snarl and strikes Mary Beth Madison hard across the face. The little woman staggers backward, appalled, holding her bruised cheek.

"Dolly." She gasps. "You hit me. What's happened to you?"

Gerard steps forward, taking handcuffs off his belt. "Dolores Combs, you are under arrest for the murder of Cedric Martin Lubowitz." He reaches to turn her around, but she swings at him, too. He dodges the blow, but she is running away, down a long living room where a Bösendorfer grand stands glossy in stained-glass gloom. Bohannon takes after her. Oriental carpets slide under his boots. She has reached French doors at the end of the room and is tugging at the latches before he can grab her. She is strong and flails and kicks, but he gets her arms behind her, finally, and swings her—she's a good weight, is Dr. Combs—back toward Gerard, who now manages to cuff her wrists. Behind her, as if she were some L.A. street tough.

He half nudges, half lifts her down the room, toward the front door, droning the Miranda warning, grunting with the effort she is costing him. Bohannon goes ahead to gather up the jeans and shoes from the floor. He reaches out to Mary Beth for the sweater.

She hands it to him, but she is listening to the outraged Dr. Combs.

"This is grotesque," the big woman says. "Why would I kill Cedric Lubowitz? Why would I kill anyone? No jury in the world will believe Dr. Dolores Combs is a murderer. When Judge Willard hears—aah! Let me go. You're hurting me."

Mary Beth begins beating on Gerard with her little fists. "Stop it," she says. "Stop hurting Dolly." Bohannon pulls her off the lieutenant. She clutches his arms. "Where are you taking her?"

"Just down to the sheriff station." Gerard grunts, wrestling the large woman through the doorway, out onto the porch. "For a nice talk."

"I'll come, too," Mary Beth says. "Dolly, what shall I wear?"

"No, dearest," the handcuffed woman says. "You stay here and feed the cats." And she goes with Gerard down the plank steps to the path, no longer resisting, lumpish, defeated.

The little pink and white girl of sixty gazes wanly after her. "When will you come home, Dolly?" Her question drifts off into the noon silence of the woods, as sad a sound as Bohannon has ever heard.

It is sundown. T. Hodges is washing down Twilight, while Mousie stands by, reins loosely knotted to a post of the long stable walkway. Before Bohannon has fully stopped the truck, Kelly is out of it, running to help the deputy. She smiles at him, hands him the sponge, walks toward Bohannon, wearily brushing a strand of hair off her face.

"Boy, am I glad to see you." She gives him a hug.

"You okay?" he says.

"I think," she says thoughtfully, taking his hand and walking toward the ranch house, "you work much too hard for a living."

"I'm sorry I stranded you here." They go along the house porch and in at the kitchen screen door. "I didn't know so much would happen so soon. And Gerard wanted me there for the interrogation."

"It was Dolores Combs, then?" She drops onto a chair. "Oh, am I going to be sore tomorrow."

"It was Dolores Combs." Bohannon fetches Old Crow and glasses and sits down opposite her at the table. "She thought we'd never guess, so she didn't bother to hide her bloodstained clothes." He pours whiskey into the glasses and hands her one. "She just threw them in the trash."

"How did she get him to drive her up the canyon?"

"Some romance about Mary Beth being stranded up there. I don't know why he believed her. But he did. And took along his gun."

"Odd." She frowns. "A man like that carrying a gun."

"One of his fellow stockbrokers got mugged and badly beaten recently. It upset the firm, and Cedric Lubowitz not least. Another lesson for society. Leave the guns to law enforcement. But they won't learn."

She tastes the whiskey and again reaches for Bohannon's cigarettes on the table. "And the prowler Steve Belcher shot at?"

"Combs. After she'd driven halfway down the canyon, she worried whether he'd find the gun and pick it up. She turned the car around and drove back. Well, he'd found it all right, hadn't he?" He gives his head a

76

wondering shake. "She and Kelly must have missed each other by inches, running away in the dark."

She laughs briefly, grows somber again. "We know why she hated Steve. Why did she hate Cedric Lubowitz?"

"Fear is the word you want." Bohannon stretches an arm and switches on the lamp. "She was convinced, as Mrs. Madison, the girls' mother, had been, that that Jew scoundrel only married Rose for her money."

"Please, Hack. Belle Hesseltine says the Lubowitzes were rich."

"If you want to hate Jews, sweet reason is meaningless, Deputy."

She sighs. "I guess so. So . . . Dolores was convinced once Rose was dead, and Cedric came up here, and immediately started wining and dining Mary Beth, he meant to marry her and take over her fortune, too?"

Bohannon nods. "And put Dolores Combs out to starve and freeze in the cruel world. And she didn't want to give up the beautiful house, the antiques, the jewelry, the Cadillac, the parties and banquets. And most of all the power. Money is power, Deputy. Ever hear that before?"

"Mary Beth's love didn't count for anything?"

Bohannon shrugs, sighs. "Who knows? Maybe once long ago. But Dolores learned how nice being rich was, and, face it, she didn't do much with all that talent she kept raving about this afternoon." He adopts a plummy elocutionary voice. " 'I could have been an international star. But I gave that up for Mary Beth. Stayed here in this backwater . . .' et cetera, et cetera." He resumes his normal voice. "Hell, a backwater was what she needed. Organizing her little ensembles, festivals, concerts. She swayed around here like a duchess. You've seen her."

"And she thought Cedric Lubowitz would end all that?"

"Thought so enough to kill him," Bohannon says.

T. Hodges sits studying her hands around the glass for a long minute. "It's pitiful," she says. She raises her head, looks into his face. "And Mary Beth? Mary Beth worshipped her. What will she do now?"

"Wait for her to come home," Bohannon says.

All You Need
Is Love

Sarah Shankman

T

he whole thing was my mother's fault.

If she'd said it once, she'd said it a million times: "Georgie Ann, you're thirty-five years old. If you don't get out and find someone soon, no one's going to have you."

I tried not to snap back at her, to remind her that she'd been married plenty enough for the both of us. Most of the time, I succeeded. Not always. Everyone has their limits beyond which they ought not to be pushed.

Look, it's not as if I didn't have good reason for being love shy. Why, I'd been nearly destroyed by the flames of passion. But Mother has a convenient memory, the ability to forget that awful day at St. Philip's when William detonated my heart. Tiny bits of it stuck to the front of my wedding dress like scarlet polka dots.

Doomsday. That's what I called it, that gorgeous, full-throated spring day five years earlier, when I was left at the altar. You think it never really happens, that old cliché. Well, I'm here to tell you, it does.

I had met William in the most romantic way possible. It was a rainy October afternoon here in Nashville, my thirtieth year, the day after Falstaff, my sweet old pussycat, had passed over to his reward. I'd taken my grief out for a walk, was blindly weeping through neighborhood lanes. I'd missed a curb and fallen, therefore was both damp *and* lame.

William came motoring along and spotted me snuffling and shuffling, rather like a character in a country song. He leaped from his car and unfurled his handkerchief, pressing it into my hand. "How can I help?" he asked. "I can't stand seeing a beautiful woman cry. It breaks my heart."

Any beautiful woman? *All* beautiful women? I should have asked. But who thinks beyond the end of one's nose when the compliments are falling like a fine warm rain?

Besides, William was quite dazzling. Wonderfully charming. Incredibly intelligent. Not to mention sweet. And a good deal more handsome than a man has a right to be. Did I say he was tall? I'm only a hair short of six feet in my stocking feet. You might have mistaken us for brother and sister, with our long limbs, blue eyes, and honey-colored ringlets.

The main thing about William, the architect, was that he made me feel safe. From the moment we met, he felt like home. Not the houses I had skimmed through as a child, barely getting my toys put away before my hummingbird of a mother was packing us up for the next perch, the next husband. William was the home I had always dreamed of. A home whose windows at twilight framed golden Norman Rockwell scenes. A cozy kitchen with soup on the stove. An open book resting on a hassock before an easy chair. A man and a woman chatting across a table, the tips of their fingers touching.

I should have noted that William designed mostly highrises. You can see his work in major American cities, sleek and phallic and filled with men in suits massaging cash.

On our aborted wedding day, when William finally called—two hours after the guests had gone, stuffed with crab sandwiches, lubricated with champagne, Mother having seen no reason to waste a perfectly good party—William said that he was sorry, very, very sorry, horribly sorry, but did I remember the Atlanta insurance mogul whose offices he'd been designing? Well, it seemed the man had suddenly dropped dead, and his really quite lovely, much younger widow was terribly distraught. "You know I can't stand seeing a beautiful woman cry," William had said. "It breaks my heart. So I offered her my handkerchief, and then . . ."

I hadn't thought that a person could endure such pain. Every cell of my body cried out. My lungs grieved, my skin, my cuticles. Sorrow filled my nights as well as my days, jumped at me from photographs, from letters. A single golden hair of William's ambushed me from a sweater.

The hands of every clock in my apartment stopped at the hour of my abandonment. If they ever moved after that, I never caught them at it. Each hour was one hundred slow, murderous years on the rack. Yet rising from my bed of nails was impossible. Diversion, Mother said. I needed diversion. I needed to get out. But how could I?

I was blind with weeping, but I could still hear the whispers: *Georgie Ann, the poor thing. Deserted. Altar. Pitiful. Would die, myself.*

I resigned my job by telephone. "Dr. Wilson," I croaked at the head of the English department, "the worms are at me. I won't be back again."

He protested, of course, but to no avail. How could I stand before a classroom of sweaty undergraduates to explain the sexual imagery of *Love's Labor's Lost?* Navigate the crannies of the heart with Byron, Shelley, Keats, the Three Musketeers of Romanticism?

I couldn't. For quite a long time, I could do nothing but contemplate my own demise.

I lay upon my bed and considered my father's old hunting rifle. I pulled it from the back of my closet, loaded it, racked it back and forth. I became enchanted with that racking. It called to me like a siren. But, my mother's daughter in that regard, I couldn't bear the thought of blood and brains and teeth and bone splattered across my snowy ceramic tiles.

I dreamed of Virginia Woolf and one gray afternoon found myself swaying for hours at the edge of Percy Priest Lake, my pockets filled with stones. But my imagination showed me my pale, bloated face, nibbled by perch, and I had too much pride ever to let anyone see me like that. So I trudged back home to pore over the labels of ant killer, rose dust, ammonia, to count the sleeping pills my family doctor had scrawled a prescription for, pressed into my hand on the steps of St. Philip's on Doomsday. He'd had a crumb of crab sandwich on his lip.

Then, of course, there were the days when my agony would flip-flop and point itself outward, full speed ahead, like a divining rod, toward William. And I would recite a rosary of palliatives: guns, knives, ropes, bombs. But those thoughts passed, and in the end I opted for seclusion, solitude, retreat. I took a very early retirement from the world.

Rilke said it best: ". . . your solitude will be a hold and home for you . . . and there you will find all your ways."

I withdrew into my home. I lived quite comfortably in a rambling top-floor apartment in one of Nashville's oldest apartment complexes, a gray elephant of a place shingled in softly silvered wood. I had two huge bedrooms, an L-shaped living room with French doors opening into a high-ceilinged dining room, closets galore. I'd moved in when I returned to Nashville right after graduate school and had never had any reason to leave.

Now, I thought, I never would. I had a little money from my father. Invested wisely, it would see me through to the grave. I would never have to leave my apartment again. Not alive, anyway.

Five years passed, and I didn't set foot across my threshold with the sole exception of annual visits to the dentist and doctor. The pansies and petunias in my window boxes came and went. I cooked. I read. I cut my own hair. Catalogs, mail order, groceries by phone, books, magazines, newspapers, everything I needed came to me. I didn't desire the world. I didn't miss it. I was perfectly content.

Mother, of course, wasn't. She called me noon and night. "Georgie Ann, this isn't natural. You must go out. You must have a life."

"I do, Mother. *My* life."

She tried every subterfuge known to woman. She said she was dying. I waited, and she didn't. She proffered a first-class trip around the world. I demurred. The president of the United States was in town. He was coming for dinner. "Really, Mother," I said.

The next day, there it was in the Nashville *Banner*. The president and first lady and the president's most attractive, not to mention single, campaign adviser, had indeed dined with my mother and stepfather, Jack, a major fund-raiser here in Tennessee.

"I *am* sorry I missed that," I allowed. And I was. I would have horsed myself out for the first couple.

I shouldn't have admitted it. Mother saw a chink in my defenses, and she went hog wild.

What she did, precisely, was she burned me out.

She would never admit it, of course, but the very next night after the president's visit, *someone* started a fire on my service porch. It gobbled the whole apartment—filled with overstuffed furniture, old lace, gauzy curtains—in twenty minutes flat. Thank goodness it didn't spread to other units. I had time to grab only a few clothes, the sterling flatware handed down from Gram, and Wabash, my cat.

Now where was I to go? To Mother's, it seemed, as she and Jack showed up so conveniently, Stepdad Number Five wheeling his big old Mercedes through the fire trucks. My neighbors had called, Mother said.

"Bullshit," I spat. "You torched my home."

"Oh, Georgie Ann," she said. "Don't be ridiculous. Come stay with us in Belle Meade. You can have the whole guest wing. You'll never even see us."

Having no other choice, I took her up on it, I'd

squat in their red-brick mansion on the very best street of Nashville's very best neighborhood, but only for a bit. Seeing that she had to work fast, Mother was parading prospects past my door before I'd washed the smoke from my hair.

"Mr. James here is just stopping by to talk about our portfolio."

"Mr. Jones is helping Jack with his will."

"I don't believe you've met Mr. Smythe. He's down from New York developing that new shopping center."

There was nothing palpably wrong with any of these men. No two-headed monsters. No machetes secreted behind their backs. Not even a single pot belly.

But I wasn't interested. I would never be interested. "Look, Mother," I said, "all I want is to collect my fire insurance and get myself relocated."

"And lock yourself up again?"

"I can't see why not."

It was then that Mother actually rolled on the floor. It was a scene from a bad novel. She screamed and, furthermore, rent her clothing, a perfectly lovely violet-sprigged afternoon dress.

I was impressed. "Oh, all right, Mother." I relented. "I'll go outside, occasionally, if you will promise never *ever* to try and fix me up again."

Mother clapped her hands like a little girl. "I'm so delighted, Georgie Ann!"

"Are you delighted enough to call Jack off the insurance agent so I can collect my money and set about finding another place to live?"

She was. She did. And, miracle of miracles, not only

did I collect from my renter's policy, but the owner of the building had coverage also, and I ended up with quite a tidy little sum.

Why, I thought, I could *buy* a place. I could become, within my modest means, a home owner.

Mother wasn't crazy about the idea, but she did suggest a Realtor for me to call, one C. Burton Wylie. I was certain that Mr. Wylie would be single or about-to-be-single, so I phoned Charlotte Dillon.

I'd known her since grammar school. "Charlotte," I said, "it's Georgie Ann Bailey. I'm looking for a little house, nothing fancy, close in to town. Something with some privacy."

Charlotte didn't skip a beat. She didn't say, "Where the hell have you been the past five years?" but rather, "Give me a couple of days."

And she was as good as her word. "Meet me at my office at ten," she said two days later. "I have four or five things I think you might like."

I was as excited as a new pup. Got all dressed up, the way I used to for men. Well, after all, I told myself, this *was* a first date. Between me and my new home.

Imagine my dismay when I walked into Charlotte's office to be greeted by one Alexander Persoff. Tall. Lean. Dark. Black eyes flashing with fire. Ruby-lipped. The man was something one of those romance writers would have dreamed up. In any case, Alexander Persoff was *far* too handsome to be taking my hand and telling me that Charlotte had fallen down her stairs that morning and would be out of commission for at least a week.

"But I'll be delighted to help you," he said. He was a tenor, surprising in a man his size, but the voice was hardly unpleasant.

"No," I said, back-pedaling, putting one black pump neatly behind the other. "I don't think so. No. No."

"But, Ms. Bailey, I'm sure . . ."

I didn't wait to hear what he was sure of, for *I* was certain that Mother had had a hand in this. Charlotte had no more somersaulted down her stairs than she'd grown two extra toes. Well, good luck to them, and hallelujah. Charlotte Dillon and Alexander Persoff were not the only two Realtors in Nashville.

Five minutes later, I was stopped at a traffic light, muttering to myself. *Granted, some of my decisions might seem eccentric to other folks, but so what? It's none of their beeswax.* Just then, a long black car pulled up beside me, with Alexander Persoff behind the wheel. The next thing I knew, he was leaning into my window.

"Ms. Bailey," he began, "you must tell me how I've offended you."

"Mr. Persoff, you are going to get run over."

"No, please, I insist. I must know." Then the light changed. Horns bleated behind us. Alexander Persoff, down on one knee on the pavement, ignored them. "You must give me another chance."

"Oh, for Pete's sake. Get up and pull over there." I pointed to a parking lot.

Watching Alexander disembark from his car was like witnessing a mighty oak growing in fast-forward. Do you know the tree I mean, the kind they grow down in Louisiana, a noble king of a tree but a kindly king you're just dying to climb, with cozy places you'd love to snuggle into?

If you were interested in trees—or men—that is.

I was only interested in the former.

Alexander, fully unfolded, stood, the toes of his soft brown loafers edging on the white line between our cars, close but not too close. He must have sensed that if he crowded me, I would jump back into my car and be gone.

I stared up at him. But it was my nose that took him in, for suddenly there was something citrusy in the morning air. Lemons, fresh lemons, heated by the sun. I blinked, and I was standing on a high and rocky coast. The dark sea crashed into the pebbly beach below. Back from the lacy edge of the water, a man and a woman lay on a straw mat, their bronze arms entwined. Their legs. Unfamiliar desire tugged between my own. I willed it to be gone.

Meanwhile, Alexander waited silently for me to speak. He would stand there for eons, I could feel that. He had the tenacity of Penelope, warding off suitors while Ulysses wandered the earth. Patience was not one of my strong points, though I admired it in others.

"You don't look like a Realtor," I said finally.

"I'm not, really."

I stepped back. I didn't want to get entangled in his smile, bright with invitation and promise.

"Then why are you posing as a Realtor?" I demanded. "My mother called you, didn't she?"

Alexander frowned, and I heard the crash of boulders rolling down a steep peak somewhere in the Caucasus. If he were *truly* angry, I thought, the avalanche of his passion would burst my eardrums.

"Your mother?" he said. "I don't know your mother. What I meant was, I sell real estate to keep body and soul together, but my passion is my painting. Portraiture is my true love."

"Ah." I felt more than a little foolish.

"So. Will you let me show you some houses? Charlotte said that you were very much in need of a home."

Yes. Yes, I was. And before I knew what was happening, I had allowed Alexander to seat me in his black chariot, and he was driving me to a house he was certain I would love.

On the way, he told me that his father had been a portrait painter, as had his grandfather, who'd escaped from St. Petersburg with a greatcoat, its lining stuffed with the family silver. We Southerners are pushovers for stories that involve sterling flatware. Many of us ate with forks our great-great-grandmothers had hidden from the Yankees.

I sallied forth. I told him about the fire in my apartment, how I'd grabbed my own Grand Imperial along with the cat.

"You don't say! That's my family's pattern, too. What a coincidence."

Then, in my mind's eye, I could see a long table set for twenty-four, Alexander's silver and mine intermingling. Wedding cake would taste the same from both.

But then a bright red flag of danger unfurled. For, it warned, this was not only a man but a handsome man, and a Realtor to boot. Worse than lawyers. More devious than used-car salesmen. Lower than pond scum, even architects.

I stared out at bowered Whitland Avenue, flush with fine old homes. "Let's go back," I said. "This neighborhood is far too rich for my blood."

Alexander raised his right hand from the wheel and held it out like a traffic cop. "Wait," he said, then pulled into a driveway opening through a tall green wall of hedge like a secret door.

A long, looping drive cut through grass that grew ankle-high, old grass, sedge, grass that had never been cleared by the bulldozer, never plowed, ungrazed native grass, grass that had been there before the first English settlers. The apple trees were more than a century old. Plums. Pears. And at the end of the drive, a stone house that looked as if it, like the grass, had simply sprung from the earth.

"What *is* this place?" I wondered.

"It was part of a farm." Alexander pointed with long arms in either direction. "All the rest of it was sold off, but this has remained, the house and three acres. The owner died a few months ago, one year shy of a hundred. The place needs work, of course, but it has very good bones. Shall we go inside?"

I couldn't. Out of the car, I plopped down on a stone step, oblivious of my good black skirt. I was dizzy with longing and damp with fear.

This cannot be good, the voice inside me said. *You didn't emerge from your cocoon after five years, simply to say* I want, *and have your heart's desire handed to you on a plate by a Russian portrait painter, no less, with a cleft in his chin that your little finger would fit perfectly.*

"Are you all right?" Alexander frowned with concern.

"I'm overcome."

"Ah." He sighed and sat down beside me. "I thought you'd love the house. What are you afraid of? Tell me."

Well, now. That was the question, wasn't it?

I was afraid of love. I had loved William and lost him. I had loved my apartment, and it had burned. I had loved Mother, and she had tossed me like a throw pillow through her many marriages. If I allowed myself to fall in love with this house, and something were to happen to it, well, I didn't think I could go on. I simply couldn't. Even now, I could hear Father's rifle racking like distant thunder.

Finally, Alexander broke my long silence. "Do you tango?"

"What?"

"I bet you do."

He stood and drew me to my feet, placed a hand at the small of my back, and, humming a familiar Latin tune in my ear, danced me into the house of my heart's delight.

I couldn't afford The House. The asking price was exactly twice my budget, twice what I'd received from the insurance company.

Alexander said, "You don't have to pay cash for the whole amount, you know. All you need is a down payment. We'll get you a mortgage."

"Well, that's a grand idea," said Jack, Stepfather Number Five, "if you can make the payments."

"What do you mean? Isn't it like rent?"

It was, except it was considerably more, my rent having been a pittance. Besides, what bank was going to give a mortgage to an unemployed hermit?

"We could lend you the money," said Mother, "though if you went back to work, you could easily qualify on your own."

"I wasn't planning on that, Mother."

I can hear you thinking, *What a lazy woman.* But it wasn't indolence. I just couldn't. I wasn't yet ready to go back into the world.

"Welllll," Mother drawled. "We'd love to help you, you know . . ."

I hated it when she used that tone. My anger got the best of me, and I flung words at her. "Alexander said I could get a mortgage, so I'm sure I can."

"Alexander?" Mother's ears perked like a collie's.

"Alexander Persoff, my Realtor."

"Alexander Persoff the portrait painter? The one who did Mimsie Stovall's portrait? And Sally Touchstone's?"

"Probably," I allowed.

"Oh, Georgie Ann." Mother swooned. "He is quite the rage. And *very* handsome, I understand."

"I suppose," I said. "But why did he lie to me about getting a mortgage?"

Confronted, Alexander said, "I didn't quite understand that you're not employed. And now I see that the income from your investments is not really enough. But don't worry, Georgie Ann. We'll find you another house."

I didn't want another house. I wanted the stone house hidden behind the tall hedge, The House that Alexander had tangoed me into. The House with the center hall, the big square living room off to the right, behind it a mullion-windowed dining room. I could close my eyes and see the silver dully glinting. Behind that stood a kitchen that needed a godawful amount of work. On the other side of the hall were a library, two tiny bedrooms, one bath. You had to climb the steep-pitched stairs to see the best part. The master suite took up the whole second floor. I'd replace the fixtures in the bathroom, tear out the mingy closets, make a dressing room. *And* there was a huge skylight on the north side.

The old lady had been a painter, according to Alexander. Yes—I sniffed—there was still a hint of turpentine in the air.

I wanted this house, oh, how I wanted it. It was *meant* to be mine. I could feel that in my bones.

Nevertheless, a-house-hunting Alexander and I went. Suddenly, Georgie Ann, the recluse, was out and about every day. Alexander and I looked at tiny split-timber Tudors, redwood ranches, a dozen white bungalows with green shutters. We trod scores of sagging porches, inspected rows of sad little fixer-uppers. I became familiar with every nook and cranny of Nashville, with zoning, with the ebb and flow of neighborhoods, with furnaces and air conditioning and basements and easements.

But all of it was bootless. For I was not a child who could be placated with a cherry-flavored lollipop when my heart was set upon a hot fudge sundae.

At the end of each day, I sank into my own personal slough of despond.

Then Alexander would cock an eyebrow. "Shall we?"

"Oh, yes!" I implored.

And then we'd fly through Music City's streets and make that quick turn through the tall hedge like fleeing bank robbers. We'd jump from the car, tango down the walk, onto the front porch, through the door, and up the stairs, where we would circle through the master suite before settling down to my portrait.

What portrait?

The portrait of me that Alexander was painting, of course.

The notion had come to him that very first day as the two of us wheeled around that glorious second-story suite.

"I *love* this north light," he'd said. "And it loves you. Be still, yes, there, just for a moment. Let me look. Oh, yes, it's a match made in heaven, this light and you. If I could just capture what I see, I know my life would be forever changed."

Who could say no?

So I posed for him under that wonderful north light two or three afternoons a week. He stashed the portrait in one of the dark closets upstairs. None of the other Realtors ever found it.

For that, I was very glad.

It wasn't that the painting was shameful. It was art. The thing was, Alexander had chosen to paint me nude to the waist, or almost. The top of my right breast was covered by my long blond hair. Then, around my middle, there was the drape of a white dressing gown, which seemed, in the narrative of the painting, to have slipped from my shoulders. Behind me, out the window, were the apple trees, the plum, the pear. They were in bloom when Alexander began the portrait. There was fruit before he finished. One glorious afternoon, when I was done posing, Alexander fed me a handful of sun-warmed plums, the color of bruises.

The next day, as I sat for him, I imagined what it would be like if Alexander grasped me hard enough to leave such bruises on my upper arms. Not that he had ever touched me, you understand, except for our tangos up the steps and then the occasional adjustment of a curl here, a limb there.

I cannot describe to you what it is like to sit, day after day, half naked before a man who considers you with total concentration but does not, as far as you can tell, desire you. After a while, I began to hear a ringing in my ears that I finally recognized as the chanting of cloistered nuns raised in endless adoration to their Lord. Brides of Christ, deprived of those most elemental of human needs.

As the painting neared completion, Alexander grew more enthusiastic. "This is going to knock them dead," he crowed. "I can't *wait* to see their faces. After this show, just you wait, Georgie Ann . . ." He paused, and my heart stopped, waiting for the next words. "I'll never have to sell another house."

That was not exactly what I longed to hear.

For, by now, of course, as you know, clever reader that you are, I was completely besotted with Alexander.

I could spend a day on a consideration of any single detail of his person. Take his hair. The heft of those dark strands, the way they whorled back from his temples like lifted oars. The sweet feathering at the nape of his neck. The glistening of clean pink scalp at the part which I longed to taste. The warm, sun-baked smell of the dark locks that brushed against my cheek when we tangoed.

Mother had been right, damn her. She'd promised if I went outside I would find diversion. I had, and now I was not only diverted but distracted almost beyond bearing. I had Alexander, I had The House, and I had neither.

Yet, in my mind, I held them close, the two inextricably bound. I filled hour after happy hour imagining life with Alexander in The House. He would paint in our second-floor aerie while I sat and read. I could see us in the kitchen preparing dinner together. I chopped neat little mounds of onions and peppers and garlic while he sauteed and stirred and tasted. There we were, sitting side by side in matching chairs in the living room. I read the front section of the paper, he the last. Upstairs, on a night drenched with rain, we embraced, and the room rocked with love, threatened to lift off, to take flight, to soar out above the apples and pears, to knock the plums into jam.

I carried one of Alexander's handkerchiefs in my pocket at all times. I had stolen it, of course, when he wasn't looking. I caressed the fine lawn with my fingers, read like Braille his block-lettered monogram.

Once, a lifetime ago, back when I was an assistant professor of English, my department chair, an old roué if ever there was one, reached into his pocket in the middle of a department meeting and pulled out a pair of black lace bikini underpants upon which, unseeingly, he blew his nose.

I tried to think that I wouldn't titillate myself in my solitary hours with a pair of Alexander's briefs, but, had I the chance, you never know.

It was about this time that Mother began saying, "You know I love having you here, Georgie Ann. Hope you stay forever." When I didn't respond, she said, "Dear, are you really looking for a house, or is there something else going on?"

As I watched Mother's mouth, it transformed itself into Alexander's. You could take a walk upon his bottom lip, it was that generous. The curves of the upper lip were like the fenders of a '55 Buick. I traced it in my dreams.

Mother said, "Whatever you're up to, you have to move forward or backward, darling. Forward, preferably."

"Yes, Mother." I smiled.

Then came the August day when Alexander announced, "Tomorrow the painting will be finished." The heat had made a damp cap of his hair, waving it close to his head. He looked like Julius Ceasar. "And," he added solemnly, "I think you ought to know, there's someone interested in the house."

The temperature plunged sixty degrees in an instant. I froze.

"My House?"

"I'm afraid so, Georgie Ann. Now, as I said, if you would only go back to work, we could get you a mortgage. Have you thought about it?"

No. Of course not. I had convinced myself that a miracle would occur. My portrait would bring enough for the down payment on The House. Then Alexander would propose. We would live happily ever after, in The House, of course.

Alexander said, "School's about to start soon. Could you ask the university to take you back on? Even part-time, that would be a show of faith for the mortgage company."

Go back into the classroom? Speak to sweaty youths about the marriage of true minds? Why, I could no more do that than I could ankle into Kroger's for canned peaches or plums when all the sweet bounty I ever needed awaited me at The House.

"No." I choked. "I can't."

"You ought to think about it, Georgie Ann."

Then, before I had time to absorb what Alexander was telling me, August was over, and Labor Day fell quickly behind it, early that year. Sharpened pencils. Back to school. The season had opened. Mother began planning for her annual opera pilgrimage to New York. Alexander was frantically preparing for his upcoming triumph in Atlanta. When he called, barely once a week now, it was to try to persuade me to come to his show. The Callendar Gallery attracted serious collectors, he said. My portrait would be the center-piece. Everyone would want to meet the model.

That was out of the question, of course. Step not only into the world but into the spotlight? All those eyes . . . the very idea was preposterous.

The night of the opening, I drove over to The House. I would sit on the steps and imagine Alexander in his glory. But when I pulled into the drive, the first thing I saw was a little strip attached to the For Sale sign. "Sale Pending." I saw red, the blood flooding behind my eyes. My head threatened to explode. I uprooted the sign and tossed it into the trunk of my car. It would suffocate there. It would die. There would be no sale pending.

Nor would I deign to give the matter further consideration. I could control my thoughts and my actions. Hadn't I proved that, long ago? I had come *that* close to doing away with myself, but I hadn't. I hadn't killed William, either. I had withdrawn and, with that, had overcome.

So, calmly, I sat at the top of the stairs, just outside the door of the master bedroom where Alexander and I had passed so many happy hours. I thought of well-barbered men in dark suits, women in small-shouldered dresses of black and gray and taupe three hundred miles away in Atlanta, staring at my breasts. They would do it ever so politely, of course, with the soft murmurings with which well-bred people communicate. I imagined their eyes going wide as they looked, and their mouths making little O's.

I pulled a plum from my pocket. Mother's housekeeper had brought it home from the store. I bit into the purple flesh. The juice filled my mouth, not with the nectar of summer but with a tart, thin syrup.

I sat at the top of the stairs until there was no more light, and then I felt my way out, the details of The House familiar as a lover's bones. Back in my bed at Mother's, nightmares stalked my sleep. The next morning, I couldn't remember much of them, but I felt queasy, as if a buzzard's wing had brushed me.

I held my breath for Alexander's call. Three days later (three years, three millennia), it came. The show had been a great success, all the work sold. My portrait had gone for its extravagantly hopeful asking price. A Japanese automotive executive was taking it back to his home near Kyoto. I closed my eyes. I could hear temple bells and people murmuring in a foreign tongue.

"However," Alexander said, then paused.

I didn't wait to hear his next words. I knew what they would be, couldn't bear to hear them from his lips. I hung up and dialed Charlotte. Then I drove out to The House once more.

Even though I'd been forewarned, the new sign, with its red banner, "SOLD," was a shock. But not for long. I uprooted it and buried it, along with the earlier sign, in my trunk.

* * *

I was sitting at the top of the stairs when Alexander found me, just outside the master suite with the wonderful northern light which I had hoped would someday awaken the two of us, entwined in each other's arms.

"I knew you'd be here," he said.

"And I knew you'd come."

"Georgie Ann, I'm so sorry. But it's over. You wouldn't do a thing to stop it, you just sat, frozen, and now the house has been sold." He dropped a hand to my shoulder. I shrugged it off. He frowned. "You must let it go."

I didn't say a word.

Alexander sat down beside me. He took my hand. His touch was cold. I could feel the lies that he'd so carefully rehearsed coursing through his blood. They fell from his mouth like little red ice cubes out the refrigerator door.

"I warned you," he said, "that someone was seriously interested in the house."

I raised my hand and stopped his words with my fingers. Then I stood. "Let's dance, one last time," I said, and stood upon the hardwood of the upper hall.

"Yes." He smiled. "Let's." I could feel his relief. I was going to be a good sport.

He'd feared, of course, that I would go mad. That I would foam at the mouth. That I would scream and roll on the floor. That snakes would sprout from my head and strike at him. And well he should fear. Had he thought I wouldn't know?

That one call to Charlotte was all it had taken to confirm my fears. First Alexander had stolen my image with his paints and brushes and sold it into geishadom. Then he'd used that boon to buy The House. It was that magical north light, he'd told Charlotte. It had changed his life. He simply had to have it for his own.

Would Alexander be living in The House alone? I'd asked.

Yes, she'd said. At least, she thought so.

She was lying about that, I could tell.

And so, I slowly raised my arms to Alexander's for one last tango. He held me close. I smelled lemons. I heard the crashing surf. My breasts pressed against his chest, unwanted, unloved. We marched in slow Argentine splendor across the hardwood floor. Then back. Then forth again.

The third time, as he spun me out away from him, his heels came very, very close to the lip of the top step. I had been watching carefully for this angle, this moment. Then I simply let go, and the centrifugal force of our swing propelled Alexander backward as surely as if he had been pulling on a rope that had snapped.

He tumbled down, step after step, head over foot, and landed with a sharp crack of his head and neck on the old oak flooring below.

I swooped after him. Leaned over him. Pressed my face close as if for a kiss.

"Help me" were his last words.

"No" was mine.

Once he was gone, I brushed my lips across that place at his nape where the dark curls feathered so sweetly, then headed for the door and the nearest phone to call 911. A terrible accident, I cried. Please come.

Too bad. So sad. Such a handsome man. And poised on the brink of fame. The murmurs came from every quarter.

But that didn't bother me at all. No more than did that last image of Alexander, his neck askew, lying at the bottom of my stairs.

I step over that spot twenty times a day now, with nary a quiver. As I told you before, my self-control is as strong as granite. You could erect a gravestone of it; it would last a millennium.

Besides, I have so many other things on my mind these days. My new job keeps me hopping. Charlotte says she's never seen anyone catch onto real estate so quickly. She's forgotten all those months I spent house hunting. And Alexander was a very good teacher.

But, wait, wait, you say. How could I so blithely jump back into the world, bypass the cloister of academe for the rough and tumble of commerce as easily as if I were changing my clothes?

The answer's simple. The winning, and then the renovation, of The House—my passion, my heart, my soul—required heroic measures, not to mention oodles of cash.

One does what one has to do, for love.

Afraid of the Dark

Nancy Pickard

S
Friday, September 19

he thought she'd already used up all of her courage.

Simply by stepping into the doorway of the abandoned tunnel underneath the Kansas prairie, Amelia felt as if she'd called upon every ounce of nerve she possessed. She had just enough left, maybe, to help her walk farther into the underground rooms. And after that? Then her entire lifetime's supply of bravery would be depleted, Amelia felt quite sure.

Yes, there was a bare electric light bulb hanging from the deteriorating ceiling. Yes, it glared forth a naked illumination, powered perhaps by some old generator left behind to rot. And, yes, it lighted the underground room for the first few yards that Amelia could see, as she held her breath and tried to work up enough gumption to get her legs to move forward. But she couldn't see beyond the light.

An improbable scene lay before her.

An antique barber shop. Underground. Chairs and all.

It was all revealed for the first time in who knew

how many decades, by the bare light, to her astonished eyes.

The walls of the barber shop in the tunnel had been plastered, once upon a time, but she wouldn't want to touch the slime that glistened on them now. Amelia couldn't tell what color they might have been painted when the underground chambers were constructed seventy-five years ago. Fifty years before she was even born. She knew there wasn't merely this tiny barber shop but also a mercantile store, a church, and a town hall. Amelia felt there was no way she could work up the nerve to explore all of it, not now, not ever.

The decaying wood floor revealed earth beneath her feet.

It had all been a clever idea, a cool commercial and civic venue dreamed up by the citizens of Spale, Kansas, population 956 men, women, and children in the year 1922. *It's still as cool as a grave,* Amelia thought as she stood shivering in the doorway. *Just emptier.* Unless she counted herself, which in that context she didn't want to. The decrepit roads and buildings above her head were a ghost town now, with all the former residents fled to cemeteries or to other destinies.

In seventy-five years, everything made by the hand of man in Spale had changed. Not much in nature had, Amelia guessed. She imagined that the heavy heat of Indian summer hung as heavily on this day as it had all those many days ago. The humidity was probably just as high as it had ever been, and the falling leaves were no doubt just as golden as they used to be. They had escaped the heat and mosquitoes of their Kansas summers by coming down here to do their business and say their communal prayers, and they'd used it to escape cyclones and bitter winter days, as well. Thirty-two couples were married in the underground chapel. Countless whiskers were shaved in the barber shop.

Amelia knew all those facts and more.

What she didn't know was what lay in the darkness ahead of her.

At least there was light. She believed she could stand almost anything as long as there was even a glimmer of light. It was total darkness she feared more than anything on earth.

Amelia stepped reluctantly forward, until she could rest her left hand on the filigreed silver arm of the closest barber's chair. There was a badly cracked and distorted mirror behind it. She looked and saw herself. As if she were a distant observer, Amelia took in her own widened brown eyes, the disarray of her short brown, curly hair, the sweat stains on her red T-shirt, and the streaks of dirt on her jeans, and she thought, *I look scared.* Unnerved by the visual evidence of her fear, Amelia glanced away and down into the further darkness at the other end of the shop. As dim shapes revealed themselves, she realized there was a third barber chair and that someone was seated in it.

"Oh, there you are!" she exclaimed.

Several events seemed to happen at once.

Close enough now to the last chair to see who was in it, Amelia suddenly felt a deep, deep coldness. The man in the chair was dead. At the sight of his wide-eyed face, she was pierced by such unexpected sorrow that it temporarily submerged her shock.

Briefly lifting her gaze to a mirror behind the third

chair, she then saw another man's face appear in the doorway behind her, and she—gratefully—recognized that man, too.

"Look!" she cried, whirling to face him. "Oh, look at what's happened—"

But instead of walking into the room to join her, he reached in with one hand. He jerked with fierce quickness on the chain attached to the light fixture. The chain broke off as the light went out.

"No! Oh, please, no!"

Pitched into total darkness, underneath the town of Spale, Amelia couldn't see the door close. But she could hear it slam with a dirt-muffled thud, and she heard the awful sound of the long wooden bar being thrown across it.

And she could hear her own screaming.

My God, what a fool she'd been.

Tuesday, September 16

"Ghost towns of *Kansas?*"

In New York City, in the office of the managing editor of *American Times,* Amelia Blaney had slapped the palm of her left hand against the side of her head, as if to clear her ears. The spontaneous gesture was meant to indicate, humorously, that—surely—she had misunderstood her boss. It was not possible, her facial expression suggested, that she had heard him correctly.

One side of Dan Hale's thin mouth lifted in wry acknowledgment of her humor, but he didn't say, "Just kidding." Instead, he inquired, bitingly, "Is it the word *ghost, town,* or *Kansas* that gives you trouble, Amelia?"

She was merely young, not stupid. She knew that Dan himself was orginally from the state. Maybe he hated it; maybe he loved it. Already regretting her comic miming, Amelia trod carefully with her next words.

"No doubt," she said tactfully, "Kansas is beautiful in September. All that golden . . . wheat."

"It's not a wheat state."

"It's not? Corn, then."

"Corn is green in the fields."

Amelia grasped the edge of her chair to keep from throwing up her hands. *Okay!* she thought in exasperated surrender. *Whatever!* She decided to skip over Kansas altogether and cut to the truth.

"I'm afraid of the dark," she admitted.

She said it lightly, not really expecting her boss to believe her, much less to feel sympathy and to change his mind. But it was embarrassingly true. Ever since she was a small child, Amelia had been nearly pathologically afraid of the dark. As much as a claustrophobic hates closets, as much as an agoraphobic is terrified of open spaces, Amelia was scared of the dark. She felt panicky and sick on the rare occasions when she got caught without sunlight, nightlight, flashlight, or headlight. She didn't know why, hadn't even been able to tell a shrink what it was—exactly—that she was scared was going to "get" her in the dark. She only knew the fear was excruciatingly real, and only as far away as the next sunset.

Sure enough, the characteristic little curve appeared at the side of Dan Hale's mouth again. She could see that he thought she was joking. Nearly everybody did, including her last boyfriend, who had finally walked out, angrily accusing her of ignoring his needs because he couldn't sleep with a light on in the bedroom. She couldn't sleep without it. She had cried when he left, but the truth was that she was less afraid of being alone than she was of the dark.

In one scathing word, Dan summed up his reaction: "So?"

Amelia tried one last time, though she knew that no reporter with only six months of job experience between this moment and journalism school could afford to reject an assignment, no matter if it turned her knees to custard and made her feel queasy. Dan Hale could have told her to interview a serial killer, and she might not have trembled, but this—this hit her where she knew she had a gaping hole in her courage.

"So," she explained, "that's where ghosts live. In the dark."

Amelia smiled tentatively at her boss, knowing it must look more like a grimace. A skeleton's grin.

He didn't appear to notice. In fact, he next uttered what at first sounded to Amelia like a total non sequitur.

"You're an animal nut, right?"

Startled at the change of subject from ghosts to animals and taken aback at his phrasing, Amelia replied with a cautious, "Yes?" She was surprised that Dan knew of her passion for animals. She supposed it must show on her college transcript that she had had a brief flirtation with veterinary medicine, before switching to J school. The transcript would not, she hoped, betray how disastrous and tragic the outcome of that flirtation had been. Amelia had ghosts of her own that she would have hated for any reporter, such as herself, to investigate.

"I thought so," Dan said. His voice was brisk now, and she knew it was a done deal. She was going to Kansas. He said, "That's why I've made reservations for you at the Serengeti Bed and Breakfast."

Amelia nearly whacked the side of her head again. Incredulously, she said, "The *what?*"

"It's a bed-and-breakfast inn on the grounds of an exotic animal farm," he told her, which only increased her astonishment. "Camels, llamas, giraffes. Ostriches, elks, kangaroos. It's all owned by a vet."

"Now, *there's* a story," she murmured, then flushed with embarrassment because she'd said it loud enough for him to hear. But good grief! She couldn't keep herself from reacting. An exotic animal farm? In Kansas? Could such a thing be true? And if so, would she get to see these animals, maybe even touch them? As unlikely as it seemed, Amelia began to feel excited about the assignment.

"No." Her boss's tone was annoyed, sarcastic. "That's *not* the story. Ghost towns are your story, remember that."

His blunt words slapped her back to earth, and to her fears.

The dark honestly frightened Amelia, down in a deep, shadowy cave in her soul. But the man seated across from her scared her in a more immediate and direct place: her pocketbook. She had student loans to pay off. She was only a beginner. She couldn't afford to beg off just because an assignment unnerved her.

Amelia didn't have to look at the crowded walls of Dan's office to recall how pivotal this man's opinion could be, to her, to the city, to the world.

Those walls held awards and photographs, personally and admiringly autographed, of Dan Hale with so many heads of state that Amelia was hard pressed to identify all of them by name and country. He might be only thirty-six years old, but already he was managing editor of one of the four most influential weekly newsmagazines in the world. He was a man whose opinion, it was rumored, could end a war or start one.

Amelia was, in the old-fashioned parlance of her adopted trade, only a cub reporter. She doubted she would even get to compose any of the eventual story; more likely, she would type up her notes and turn it all over to a senior writer. Dan was sending her out as a researcher, that was all. But it was really something, to receive an assignment personally from the man himself.

If I'm a cub, she said to herself, as all these thoughts flashed through her mind, *then he's a bear.* It was an animal he resembled: tall, overweight, with a small-eyed, jowly face and a deceptive shambling gait that disguised a legendary ability to attack fools, in print and in the newsroom, viciously and without warning.

She felt flattered, even honored, by his interest in her.

There was nothing remotely romantic or sexual about it, Amelia felt sure. Dan Hale gave no sign that he even noticed Amelia in that way, and that was a relief to her. She liked very much meeting "brain to brain," as it were, editor to reporter. Amelia had been so saddened by her last failed love that she still tensed when a man showed any attraction to her. Compliments made her feel uncomfortable. She didn't want love, she had decided, it was work she needed, only work.

Thank God, she thought, that this interview between her and the legend was strictly professional. For some reason, this feared and respected journalist seemed to think that Amelia Blaney was worth his personal mentoring. Amelia sat up straighter and tried to swallow her doubts about the assignment. She concentrated instead on pleasing this difficult boss and reminded herself of how much she loved animals. He was doing her many favors with this assignment. She would try to appreciate it and live up to it.

Even if it meant ghost towns in Kansas.

He handed her airplane tickets and a highway map of Kansas, with certain town names circled in red ink. Then he impatiently dismissed her from his office. Only when she was standing outside his office, feeling rather breathless, did Amelia realize that he hadn't given her a single clue to *why* this assignment was made or what in the world she was supposed to be looking for.

She turned around, intending to barge back in and ask him.

But he was already on the phone, his back turned toward his window.

When she asked an older reporter about it, the woman advised her, "Don't expect explanations. Sometimes he never says why he wants you to do a story. That might prejudice your investigations. You're supposed to dig up the facts and figure out for yourself what the real story is." The older reporter grinned at Amelia. "And heaven help you if it doesn't turn out to be what he knew it was all along."

Oh, God! thought Amelia, feeling a terror that had nothing to do with the dark.

Wednesday, September 17

On the connecting flight between Kansas City, Missouri, and Wichita, Kansas, the next day, Amelia studied the map Dan had given her. She decided the order in which she would drive to the abandoned, or nearly deserted, towns of Spale, Bloomberg, Wheaten, McDermott, Flaschoen, Parlance, and Stan. She loved the name of the last one. A town named Stan. It sounded friendly and, well, small-townish. Bemused, she wondered if New York City could ever have become the center of the universe (as she considered it to be) if the founders had named it Stan. On the plane, she laughed to herself.

While she was in an organizing mood, Amelia read over the bits of research she had pulled out of the library as well as from the magazine's files (which were a veritable library themselves) and the Internet. What she found was intriguing and went a long way toward explaining why her worldly-wise editor had considered the topic newsworthy in the first place. It was going to be a story of a changing America, she predicted to herself, of rural residents leaving for the cities, and of the towns they abandoned turning back into prairie dust.

These ghosts wouldn't scare her, she felt sure.

They might be sad, but they wouldn't be frightening, at least not to her personally. And, with any luck, she could do all of her research by daylight and retire every evening to the well-lighted security of her hotel room. *B&B*, she reminded herself as the outskirts of a small city appeared below the plane. Amelia had never stayed at a bed-and-breakfast lodging before. She wondered what they would serve her to eat at an exotic animal farm. Oats? Hay? *It's all cereal to me.* She laughed to herself as they landed.

She was beginning to appreciate just how deliciously bizarre this assignment could turn out to be. Giraffes and ghosts. In Kansas. Oh, my. Why, she could dine out on this story for weeks back home. Her New York friends would laugh till they begged her to stop.

Although she put away her paperwork, Amelia left the reading light on overhead. They were flying through a cloud cover that had darkened the cabin. Amelia wasn't particularly afraid of the storm or of a bumpy landing. She just liked the way the little lamp cast a circle of security around her in the passenger cabin.

Her first clue that she was nearing her destination was a camel hanging its head over a fence. Behind the camel—dromedary, she corrected herself when she saw only one hump—there were several zebras, including an adorable colt running circles around its elders. In her rental car, Amelia drove past another pasture, where huge ostriches lifted their beautiful wings and fluttered them over their backs. She was tempted to think, like Dorothy in *The Wizard of Oz,* that she "wasn't in Kansas anymore." But a large sign spelled out, "Welcome to the Serengeti." Below that:

"Bed & Breakfast Inn." And farther down, stating the obvious in graceful script: "Exotic Animals." Visitors were advised: "No Tours without Permission."

Amelia turned onto a gravel lane.

Along a fence line, she stopped to stare back at the ostriches which ambled over to stare at her. As they batted their white eyelids at her, she shocked herself by nearly bursting into tears. Once, at a time that now seemed long ago, she had dreamed of being an animal doctor. And not just for any dogs and cats, either. A large-animal vet was what she'd wanted to be. "You," Amelia told the ostriches in a thick voice, "are certainly big enough, but I didn't quite have you in mind!"

Horses, cows, even sheep.

A practice in upper New York state, where she had spent summers with her grandparents. Farm country. Dairy land.

But it had all come to an ignominious, horrifying end. And she had slunk off to journalism school, not really caring anymore what degree she earned or what job she landed or even what her future held. She had, in fact, lost any grasp of the concept of future. Time became divided into then and now, and there was no tomorrow.

Suddenly impatient with herself (Amelia's grandmother had never tolerated what she called the "pig wallow of self-pity"), Amelia sniffed, blinked, and hurried on toward a white ranch-style house that waited at the end of the drive. She saw an ordinary-looking long, white motel structure to the right and metal pens and gates and a series of connected wooden barns. Nearly everything was painted white with red trim. It looked like a perfectly ordinary, well-maintained ranch. Except for the inn. And the zebras.

In a pasture beyond the barns, Amelia spotted a giraffe.

She wasn't quite sure she was going to approve of this place, this zoo on the prairie, because why weren't these wild creatures back in Africa, where most of them belonged? Still, she couldn't help but grin at the sight of the giraffe, and as she parked her car, she wondered if she ought to keep an eye out for wandering lions.

At first, it seemed as if the farm itself might be her first ghost town. "Nobody around but us chickens," she observed to a beautiful, glossy brown rooster that had walked up to the front door with her. "Are you the guard bird around here?"

When nobody answered the doorbell or her knock, she obeyed the sign that said, "Come in," and walked into a living room that had been transformed into an office. There were two desks with bulletin boards behind them. The walls were covered with photographs of people posing with animals, tear sheets from newspapers and magazines, and cute letters of appreciation from schoolchildren.

To pass the time until somebody showed up to sign her in, Amelia walked around the room, looking at all of the pictures and reading everything, feeling as if she were searching for the "real story" that Dan had sent her on. *Was* it about the economics of the heartland? Or was it about the traffic in exotic animals? How did these animals get here, anyway? Were they treated decently? Did they include endangered species that were illegal to own? Maybe, instead of researching ghost towns, she should have looked up references on the international wild animal trade—

Of late, Amelia had begun to get the sinking feeling that she was just not cut out to be a journalist. In truth, she didn't enjoy being suspicious of people, and she wasn't even particularly nosy. Curious, yes, in a courteous and scientific kind of way, but not nosy in the way of natural-born gossips. Or, she often thought wryly, journalists. She hated to ask rude questions. She much preferred to give people the benefit of the doubt rather than to suspect them. She'd drifted into feature writing, because investigative reporting was absolutely impossible for her; she always felt bad for the families of people whose lives were exposed. She stared, unseeing, down at one of the desks and thought, *And here I am, looking for a story, and I don't even know what it is!*

She had lost track of what she was reading and now discovered it wasn't about wild animals at all. *What?* she asked herself, confused by what she was seeing. Having worked her way around the room, she was now standing behind one of the desks, looking at the newspaper clippings tacked up there.

The word *murder* was in the headlines.

It was a set of clippings from local newspapers, dating back almost seventeen years. They were all about a long-ago murder. Of a girl named Brenda Rogers. Seventeen years old. A senior at Spale High School. Honor student. Valedictorian. Homecoming queen. Voted Most Likely to Succeed. Winner of a full scholarship to the University of Kansas in Lawrence. Oldest child of a couple who farmed outside town.

The photos showed a smiling, pretty blond girl who appeared to enjoy having her picture taken.

A terrible crime and loss revealed itself to Amelia, and she felt sadness for the girl, the families, the town where, it was reported, "nothing so heinous has ever occurred before."

The killer's name was Thomas Rogers.

"Same as hers," Amelia murmured, transfixed by what she was reading. Also seventeen. Her brother? "My God, her *husband?*" Not only that but the father of—

"Her *child?*"

To Amelia, it seemed an unlikely combination of facts for a small town in the Midwest around 1980. But what was it that was so improbable, really? An early pregnancy? Or the fact that the boy married her? No. It was the continued high achievements of the young mother, and the scholarship, the full four-year scholarship going to a seventeen-year-old with a baby. To Amelia's mind, it all suggested an extraordinary young woman, a generous-hearted high school, a forgiving town, a trusting scholarship committee, and—more than likely—a wonderful, supportive family. Her glance passed quickly over the obituary that named the survivors.

My Lord, she thought sadly, *what an awful blow to all of them.*

And the boy? The husband/killer?

Also a senior. Also a straight-A student. A football, basketball, baseball star. Almost as outstanding as she was, and honorable to boot, in marrying her. Honorable, that is, except for the appalling fact that he killed her. Amelia read how her body was found in an old tunnel under the town, that it was discovered she had been strangled and dumped there. She read of Thomas's confession, conviction as an adult, sentencing to a federal penitentiary, the town's stunned grief over the fate of these young people.

He never said why he did it, she read, only that he did.

She realized that Spale was one of the ghost towns circled in red on her map, which meant that the town had emptied in the time between the murder and now.

And then she turned over one more clipping and saw, to her regret, that this was the story she was looking for and that she was going to have to go after it. The final clipping, and the most current, reported that Thomas Rogers, having served his time for the murder of his wife, Brenda, was getting out of prison at last. This week. He was quoted as saying that he would return home to live in Spale, "because there's nobody left to hate me."

Amelia knew what to do now: call Dan Hale in New York and get his approval. He would tell her to locate the released killer, alone in his ghost town, and interview him. *So tell me, Tom, how does it feel, coming back to the scene of the crime? Did you love her? Why did you kill her? Our millions of subscribers want to know!* Amelia felt frightened and sick at the idea of what she was going to have to do. Track down the girl's remaining family, her high school friends, some teachers, get them to relive a horrible time in their lives.

I don't want to, Amelia thought, but her practical brain inquired: *Do you prefer to be unemployed?* No, she did not. She'd do it. Maybe it wouldn't be so bad, maybe she was making too much of the whole thing. Maybe Dan wouldn't even like the story idea. That thought cheered her up, and she smiled to herself.

The front door opened, admitting a breeze and a tall man.

"You always find murder amusing?"

"What? No, I—"

"That's my desk you're—"

"I was reading all of your—"

"Yeah. Are you checking in?"

She was tempted to say, "No way," and stomp out. But giving him her usual benefit of the doubt, Amelia realized that his first sight of her could have annoyed anybody. She softened her voice and said, "I'm sorry. I've been looking at all of your photographs and mementos, and it led me around back here. When you came in, I was thinking of something else. Not the murder of that poor child. And yes, my name is Amelia Blaney, and I think there's a reservation in my name."

He stared at her for a moment, giving her enough time to realize that he was an extremely attractive man. Possibly near thirty. Tanned face with wonderful dark eyes, thick dark brown hair that curled down around the top of his shirt collar. The wide shoulders of a man who had tossed a good many hay bales. He wore dirt-streaked blue jeans over cowboy boots and a red and white plaid wool jacket over a denim work shirt. He was a big presence in the room. Amelia stepped quickly around to the front of his desk and then stood off to the side of it.

"I'm the sorry one," he said, shaking his head. "No excuses. Jim Kopecki. Welcome to our zoo. I'm the head jackass."

They both grinned, and suddenly the air was cleared between them.

"Dr. Kopecki?" she inquired.

"Yeah. The locals call me Dr. Doolittle behind my back."

"I'll bet they do. How'd you end up in the Wild Kingdom?"

"I've always been here," he said easily. "Inherited the farm. And the animals, too, in a way. First, it was just a few llamas out of a local rancher's estate. Nobody else wanted them; they weren't a cash crop at the time." His tone was wry. Somewhat to her dismay, Amelia felt herself being attracted not only to the story but also to the man. "Then it was a couple of abandoned ostriches from a wild animal show, and then people took to bringing me orphaned mule deers, that sort of thing. Then I read about a mistreated giraffe, and I went and got him." The young vet grinned. "You should have seen that, driving down the interstate with a hole cut in the top of an eighteen-wheeler and a half-grown giraffe sticking out of the top."

Amelia laughed. She was delighted with the story, and she was feeling warmed by Jim Kopecki's obvious feeling for animals.

"And," he concluded, "things just pretty much got completely out of hand from that point on." He made a comically rueful face and laughed along with her. "I figured that a lot of wild species are being born now in this country, and somebody's got to take care of them. When I was a kid, I dreamed of owning my own kangaroo, so maybe this falls in the category of 'Be careful what you wish for.'"

"I envy you," Amelia blurted. "I wanted my own elephant."

He shook his head and looked sincerely regretful. "Sorry, I don't have one of those yet. You might not envy me if you could see me trying to pull a calf out of a water buffalo when it's freezing cold and the middle of the night."

Yes, I would, Amelia thought.

He cocked his handsome head at her, and she easily read the interest that showed in his beautiful dark eyes. "So what do you do?"

"I'm a reporter," she told him, feeling like a fraud as she said it. "For *American Times* magazine."

Later, she would decide she had never seen a human face shut down so fast. All of the good humor and warmth drained out of his expression. Briefly, there was a look of shock, then disappointment. And then he returned to the cold-looking man who had first opened the door and caught her smiling beside the homicide stories.

He looked down at his desk, saying in clipped tones, "Would you like the Giraffe Room, the Zebra Suite, the Kangaroo Single, the Elk Double, the—"

Astonished by the alteration in his behavior, she managed to reply, "A single will be fine," but what she wanted to say was *What did I say? What happened? What's the matter?*

In fact, she opened her mouth to ask that very question but only got as far as "What—" when he ruthlessly interrupted her.

"You get a full breakfast with your room and a tour of the animals."

He shoved a reservation card over to her, and when

she had finished filling it out, he pushed it aside without even looking at it and grabbed a key from a box on his desk. "I'll carry your bags."

"You don't have to—"

"It's my job."

Without another word, he carried her luggage into one of the motel rooms, leaving Amelia to follow along behind. But when he unlocked the door and let her in, Amelia exclaimed with surprise and pleasure. There were beautifully rendered giraffes painted right onto the walls, a thatched-roof canopy over the double bed, a lovely quilt with images of giraffes printed into it, a grass cloth carpet, and many artifacts that looked straight out of Africa. It was charmingly, whimsically designed to look like a room in a safari lodge.

"This is wonderful."

"My niece designed the rooms. Let us know if you need anything," he said formally, and then he was gone, out the door with a firm click of the lock.

Feeling offended and angry, Amelia changed into jeans, a long-sleeved shirt, socks, boots, jacket, and cap and hurried back outside, wanting to visit some animals before it got dark. As she headed toward the giraffe pasture, she saw Kopecki standing beside a beat-up, old white truck. She could have sworn that he saw her and then practically jumped into his vehicle and started it up and drove off as if a demon were chasing him.

What was it, she wondered, about the word *reporter* that scared him? Most people didn't run like that unless they had something to hide. She felt a lump of disappointment in her chest as she trudged over to the giraffe pasture.

It didn't take long for the sight of them to lift her spirits.

She propped herself against the gray metal fence to stare.

"Excuse me? Are you the new guest? Ms. Blaney?"

Amelia turned, frowning, to find a teenage girl standing close to the fence, her hands shoved down in her pants pockets. The tallest giraffe started slouching toward her, and several of the smaller giraffes pricked up their ears at the sound of her voice. When Amelia answered, "Yes," and remembered to erase her frown, the girl looked relieved. One of her hands emerged to offer itself to Amelia to shake.

"Hi, I'm Sandy Rogers. Uncle Jim said I should show you around."

Amelia heard the girl say her last name and had to work hard to keep from visibly reacting to it. *Rogers? Wasn't that the name of the girl who was killed and the boy who killed her?*

"You want to see the 'roos first, or you want to start with the giraffes?"

She looked about sixteen, Amelia thought. She had a fresh, pretty face and a sturdy little body that looked at home in the red flannel shirt, tight black jeans, and cowboy boots she wore. She had twisted her dark blond hair into a French braid, from which tendrils were escaping charmingly. Luckily, since Amelia couldn't find the right words to say, the tallest giraffe had reached them by then. He stood behind Sandy Rogers and bent his neck low, until his long-lashed, gentle face was cheek to jowl with her.

"Hey, Malcolm," she murmured affectionately. She blew gently into his nostril, and he shook his head a bit and lifted one great hoof and set it back down again. "This is one great guy, but he doesn't like to be touched, do you, Mal? The giraffes don't much, but they're sweeties, and curious as hell." She looked into the great, black, liquid eye so close to her. "Aren't you, big guy?"

Amelia stared at the two of them together—huge animal and petite girl—and felt such a painful longing that she brought her hands up and pressed them against her heart. She managed to say, "It looks as if Malcolm thinks we ought to start here. Kopecki's your uncle?"

"Yeah. Okay, Malcolm, let's tell her all about you and the ladies. Correct me if I get anything wrong, okay, big guy?" By then, two of the shorter giraffes had also loped over. Sandy bent down and picked up a clear plastic bucket from the ground. Amelia saw that it contained sliced carrots and apples. Without waiting to be invited, she reached in and picked out a slice of carrot and offered it to Malcolm. An amazingly long gray tongue curled out of his mouth and twisted itself around the vegetable, lifting it gently out of her grasp.

"Believe it or not, giraffes have only seven vertebrae in their neck, just like us, but their blood pressure is twice as high as ours—"

While the girl talked, telling facts Amelia already knew—facts she felt she had been born knowing—Amelia continued to feed the giraffes until the carrots were gone.

"Want to see the 'roos now?" asked Sandy.

"Oh, yes." As they walked together toward the big kangaroo pen, she asked the girl, "How'd your uncle get wild animal training?" She couldn't think of a single vet school that offered it.

"Oh, he just makes it up as he goes along," was the airy reply. "He calls it the school of oh-hell-what-do-we-do-now veterinary medicine." She giggled, and Amelia found herself laughing, too. It was sympathetic laughter on her part, because she well knew that while some wild animal species might resemble domestic ones in some ways, on the inside a zebra was not a horse, and a gnu was not a cow. And animals as odd as giraffes and kangaroos had special needs that no amount of training in cats and dogs could teach a young vet.

They entered the 'roo pen, with Sandy telling her, "A group of kangaroos is called a mob. Adult males are called boomers." Amelia smiled to herself, remembering the joke in vet school: If an adult male kangaroo is a boomer, does that make a young male kangaroo a baby boomer?

A young joey hopped over and stuck its dainty, fingered paws into Amelia's hands to steal the slices of apple she had hidden there. She stroked the soft back and remembered that this was what it felt like to be happy.

By the time she returned to her room, a bright half-moon was rising. Amelia heard a donkey braying in the barn, answered by the trumpeting of an elk, sounding for all the world like an elephant.

She turned on all of the lights and was, for a few more moments, content. She knew she still had to drive out for dinner, in a rural setting with no streetlights. But that's what headlights were for,

Amelia figured, to cut a reassuring path for her after dark.

As there were no telephones in the motel rooms, she went searching for a pay phone, which she found in the unlocked office. She was relieved to find Jim Kopecki gone, so that she had his office to herself again.

The first thing she did was to check the names of the survivors of Brenda Rogers. She read that Brenda had left her parents, Alfred and Betty Kopecki, a twelve-year-old brother, James, and an infant daughter, Sandra Gay. This time, the obituary was a shock. Amelia had half expected Sandy to be related to the victim and her uncle to be distantly connected. Instead, it was as close as it could be: Sandy was the daughter of the victim and the killer. Dr. Jim Kopecki was the victim's brother.

Amelia wanted to give him credit for providing a home for his niece, but what kind of home could it be for her with such a nasty uncle?

She walked over to the pay phone to do her next duty.

Amelia felt naive and nervous, calling her boss long-distance. Three times, she coughed and cleared her throat. When he picked up the receiver and barked, "Hale," into it, Amelia blurted out the whole story—of an old murder and of a killer returning to a ghost town—almost in a single breath. It was proof of Dan Hale's quick mind, she thought later, that he didn't have to ask her to slow down or to repeat herself.

"Do it," he said.

That was it, and he hung up. No advice. No caveats.

Nothing but "Do it." She only wished that she wanted to! He had hung up too fast even to hear her say, "Thanks, Dan."

But Dr. Jim Kopecki did hear her, having walked in the front door at just that moment. He nodded at her curtly, a look of distaste on his face, transforming him, in Amelia's eyes, from a handsome man to an ugly one. He crossed to his desk without a word to her.

Appalled by his behavior, Amelia lost her own natural sense of courtesy. "Don't you think it's cruel," she asked him, "to keep those articles up there? Aren't they constant reminders to your niece of what her father did to her mother?"

He looked up, his face thunderous. In a voice as cold as the winter winds that blew across her grandparents' farm, he said, "I wondered when you were going to get around to asking your first question. Here's your answer: sleep in our bed, eat our food, pet our animals, pay your bill, and leave my niece and me alone."

Stunned, she could only stare back at him.

"Got it?" he asked her.

Amelia's reply was to walk out the door with as much dignity as she could summon. In truth, she was shaking. The man was nuts, clearly. He was a crazy man, with a farm full of wild animals and one young girl, all totally dependent on him. And all those articles pinned to the wall? They looked like vengeance to Amelia. They looked like a constant reminder: *remember, remember.* And just what was this vengeful, unpredictable man planning to do, now that his sister's killer was coming home? And how would it all affect that sweet girl?

Amelia wasn't hungry anymore.

She returned to her room, locked her door, and remained there throughout a mostly sleepless night, until the light of morning.

Thursday, September 18

When she saw that it was Sandy fixing breakfast in the cookhouse and not the lunatic uncle, Amelia decided it was safe to eat there. Within a few minutes, she was delighted with her decision. The home-cooked buffet included scrambled eggs, sausage, biscuits, whipped butter, local jelly and honey, cinnamon rolls, cereal, coffee, and juice. None of the farm's other guests was present, so she ate alone while gazing at the camels and zebras lining up to eat at their troughs.

"Heaven," she said gratefully to Sandy when she carried her own dishes back into the kitchen. "Thank you so much."

"You're welcome. Sleep well?"

"Great," Amelia lied. The girl seemed so friendly that Amelia could only suppose the crazy uncle hadn't yet poisoned his niece's mind against her. "You do all this work and go to school, too?"

"Only 'cause I love it."

And your uncle forces you to, Amelia suspected. *How can I get you to tell me the truth about what goes on around here and about what these years have been like for you?* There wasn't an opportunity, because the girl was pulling off her apron and hurrying to grab a backpack from the floor.

"See ya!" she called gaily.

Too gaily, Amelia thought, for a girl facing a week

in which a father she did not know was getting out of prison and returning to the town—only a few miles away—where he had made her a veritable, if not literal, orphan.

Amelia's heart ached for her.

And suddenly, she had all the desire she needed in order to pursue her story. Maybe by publicizing this child's plight, she could liberate her from the monomaniacal control of the vicious uncle.

Overnight, the weather had changed into Indian summer.

Amelia put away her jacket and donned a short-sleeved white silk blouse and summer-weight gray wool slacks with gray silk socks and black loafers. She wished it were shorts, a T-shirt, sandals, and a baseball cap, like Sandy had been wearing when she hurried off to school.

In her rented car, with the air conditioning on, Amelia drove back into Wichita, where she spent the rest of the morning in the main library. She found out that years of a depressed economy had emptied Spale. Between the lines, she intuited that the incomprehensible murder of their brightest girl by their brightest boy had wounded Spale to its heart, perhaps dealing the final blow. What an interesting town it once had been, she thought, with its amazing system of tunnels and underground shops.

While she was at the computer, she researched the status of imported wild animal species. When she located no condemnatory information about Jim Kopecki's farm, she didn't know whether to feel disappointed or relieved. She settled on relieved, but only for the sake of the animals, she told herself.

She avoided the local newspaper, acting on a competitive instinct she didn't know she had. Maybe they'd be helpful, but maybe they'd want to keep the story for themselves.

She did, however, place a call to the federal penitentiary where Thomas Rogers was incarcerated to find out exactly when he was due to arrive back in Spale.

"Should be there by now," was the clipped reply.

She attempted to hold the prison officer on the phone by asking, "What kind of prisoner was he?"

"Model," was the answer, followed by a string of accolades that made Rogers sound more like the honor student he used to be than the murderer he was. "Perfect record. Early release. Earned three college degrees. BA, MFA, PhD. Created convict tutoring program. Taught prison classes in reading and math, plus led a creative writing class. Started a prayer/meditation group. Anything else you want to know?" Amelia said no, but she was thinking, *Yeah, where's the eagle scout badge?*

Feeling as cynical as a veteran, world-weary journalist, she got back into her rental car and drove to Spale. All the way, she felt fueled by righteous fury aimed at the man she was planning to interview.

"Don't you *dare* try to give me any of that born-again crap," she fumed aloud, as if speaking to Thomas Rogers himself. "I've met the daughter you betrayed so horribly!"

Amelia had not realized how many other journalists might also consider the return of a murderer to a ghost town to be a juicy story. When she got within sight of Spale, she saw that it was, in one of the clichés she was trained to avoid, a media circus.

As it turned out, there was only one thing missing among the television vans and the other rental cars: Tom Rogers, the ex-convict himself.

"He arrived," a writer from *Newsweek* told her, leaning against her car. "That we know, because we saw him dropped off at that building." He pointed to a falling-down storefront on the former Main Street. "But he must have sneaked out the back. Maybe he had another car waiting. I don't know. We've been in there, and there's nobody there. We're packing up and going home. He'll surface again someplace. But who the hell cares now? It's not a story now. Killers walking the streets of cities are a dime a dozen. But one of them living alone in his own private town full of ghosts? That was going to be good, damn it. You find any decent place to eat around here?"

She didn't tell him about the Serengeti Bed and Breakfast.

And she didn't tell him where Thomas Rogers probably was, either, although Amelia was pretty sure she knew: in the old forgotten tunnels, beneath the town. Where he had dumped his young wife's body. And where he now had a perfect place to hide for the rest of his life, if that's what he wanted to do.

Amelia was regretfully willing to give him what he wanted, because there was no way she was going into the darkness underneath the ground in order to search for a man who had already killed at least one woman.

No way.

"No," she said to her boss, back at the pay phone in the Serengeti office. "I'm sorry, Dan, but I won't do it. It would be stupid and dangerous for me to go down there alone."

She was surprised at how calm she felt saying that, almost as if she was relieved that she was about to be fired. Finally, she could admit to herself and to the rest of the world that she had never been meant to be a journalist. She didn't have a clue what she *was* going to be once she was out of a job and a salary, but now she knew that reporting wasn't it.

"Why the hell do you think I want you to do anything that idiotic?" Dan Hale demanded, to her surprise. "I only ask war correspondents to do stupid things that could get them killed. For God's sake, this story isn't as important as Bosnia. But I still like it, so here's what I'm going to do—" He was going to fly a more experienced reporter down to join her, he informed Amelia, and she was going to meet him at ten in the morning in the town of Spale.

Although she still wanted very much to help Thomas Rogers's daughter, Amelia found herself wishing that Dan Hale had just gone ahead and fired her. The only good thing about the exchange, from her point of view, was that Dr. Jim Kopecki hadn't walked in during the middle of it. She hadn't, in fact, seen him or his niece all that day.

She couldn't do any more that day, so she spent the remainder of it typing up her notes and observations, then wandering around the farm, communing with the animals. And composing, in her head, the right questions to ask a killer.

Friday, September 19

Amelia awoke suddenly that night and stumbled to a window, pulled by the sound of an engine running. The bedside clock displayed the time: one-thirty.

The headlights of a white truck dimly illuminated a scene: the veterinarian and his niece outside at the edge of a pasture, pulling something dark and heavy from the truck bed, dumping the object into a depression in the ground, then shoveling—dirt?—on top.

"Oh, God," Amelia whispered. "What are you doing?"

What were they burying? Should she try to call local law enforcement? But how? From Kopecki's office, where she might get caught? And if she ran to her car, he'd hear her leave . . .

Amelia had a terrible feeling that she would not find Thomas Rogers in the tunnels. If she didn't, she would advise the local police to dig up the fresh hole—grave?—in the pasture.

And then what would happen to the girl?

"Oh, God," Amelia whispered again, but this time it was a prayer.

For a second night, she hardly slept. By the time the sun rose, she was exhausted and badly frightened by her own vivid imagination. The hours alone in the bedroom, surrounded by the darkness outside, took a heavy toll on her heart.

"I can't do this," she told her image in the mirror.

It didn't try to argue the point with her.

When she walked out after breakfast, pretending to take a casual stroll, she saw dirt covering what appeared to be a fresh hole in the ground. Amelia ran back to her room, grabbed her packed bags, and got quickly into her car. Let New York take care of paying her bill, she thought, *I just want out of here.* Her brain said it never wanted her to return to the Serengeti, but her heart felt bereft at the sight of the zebras fading from view in her car mirrors.

It was still early when she arrvied in Spale.

Amelia parked at the edge of town to wait for her reinforcement to arrive. She wasn't quite so terrified anymore about going down into the tunnels, because she no longer expected to find anybody alive down there.

When the backup reporter's rental car pulled up next to hers and the driver got out, Amelia reacted with shock.

It was the man himself, Dan Hale.

His mouth wore its characteristic one-sided smile when she hurried out to greet him.

"Surprised, Amelia? You shouldn't be. Don't you remember where I'm from?"

"Kansas, but—"

"Spale, Kansas." His tone implied that she ought to have known, and Amelia felt instantly humiliated. She also felt resentful, because how was she supposed to have known something that she had never heard or seen mentioned before? In fact, she specifically re-called hearing that he was from Kansas City. She was rebelliously tempted to answer his contempt with her own sarcastic, *So?*

"I didn't know," she said instead. "But still, why—"

"Because I knew them. Brenda and Tom. We were best friends."

Her eyes widened. "Oh, Dan! Gosh, I'm—"

"Sorry? So will he be, when we're finished with him. He's going to wish he'd stayed in prison."

"But Dan, Thomas Rogers may not be here," she said, and felt a petty satisfaction that this time she had managed to shock him. "He may not even be alive." Amelia told her boss what she had witnessed from her window.

Hale looked confused, disturbed. He said, "That's impossible."

Amelia didn't see why. It seemed horribly possible, even probable, to her.

"Stay here," he commanded her. "I'm going down into the tunnels to find him."

He left Amelia standing by herself at the edge of town, sweating in the warm prairie wind that was blowing dust from one side of the abandoned town to the other and then back again. She waited for more than half an hour, coughing now and then and thinking, *Well, at least there's one good thing about Dan showing up. He knows how to get in and out of the tunnels.* But when forty-five minutes had passed, she began to worry about him and to fear that she was going to have to go down to look for him.

Still, she waited, hot, exhausted, frightened of many things.

What if something fell on him? she thought. *What if he's been injured?*

But he emerged from a decrepit storefront—different from the one he had entered—and walked toward her. For once, Dan Hale was smiling fully.

"He's down there, all right," he told her.

"He *is?*"

"Go on down and interview him, Amelia. He's waiting for you. Don't worry. He's harmless now. You don't have anything to fear from Tom Rogers."

When she hesitated, he grasped her elbow and pulled her along, saying reassuringly, "Don't worry! I'll be right behind you."

"But the dark—"

"It's not dark. He's got an old generator up and running, so there's even electric light."

Amelia thought that if Dan told her one more time, "Don't worry," she would hit him. Reluctantly, unhappily, she let herself be led into one of the old buildings, through a door in the floor, and down a wooden ladder into a cool, earthen chamber. He had told the truth; it was lighted, if dimly.

Amelia relaxed a little.

She could stand anything, she thought, if there was light.

"Dan?" she asked in a low voice. "How'd you ever get out of Spale?"

Behind her, he answered in a normal voice, as if he didn't care what Thomas Rogers heard them saying. "I got her scholarship. Brenda's. They couldn't very well give it to Tom." His chuckle was a warm breath on her neck. "I never looked back."

They reached an open door with a sign still visible beside it: "Barber Shop."

"Go on," he urged her. "Tom's in the last chair. He'll tell you the whole story." Hale thrust something warm into her hands: a trim black gun. "Here. If it helps you feel safer."

Amelia stepped inside the barber shop.

Amelia recognized the dead man in the chair from his recent photograph in the local newspaper: Thomas Rogers.

Feeling overwhelmed by the tragedy of all of their

lives, she had turned and also recognized the face of the man in the doorway: Dan Hale. He broke the light chain, slammed the bar across the door, and left her there in the utter darkness with a corpse. Before the light went out, she saw that Tom Rogers had been shot several times. As she screamed and screamed, the warm gun in Amelia's hands slid to the floor.

The darkness felt eternal.

She knew she would lose her mind before she died.

Amelia's brain played those two messages over and over, and it seemed an eternity, indeed, before another thought could fight its way past the terror: Dan had gone in one store and come out another.

Two tunnel exits. At least two, maybe more.

In the nightmare that had become her life, Amelia found the slimy walls and felt her way entirely around her burial chamber. There was no other exit, no other way out. By feel, she located one of the other old barber chairs and sank into it. She thought about the endless time that lay ahead of her. And then she remembered the gun, and she realized that she could kill herself now and foreshorten her own suffering. Frantically, she found her way to the floor and felt around until metal touched her fingers.

The end of the gun barrel was resting inside her right ear when she changed her mind.

Slowly, in the dark, Amelia brought the gun down and placed it gently, lovingly, in her lap.

In case there was even the slightest chance that she would be found, she must stay alive to clear the innocent name of Sandy's father, to give the girl the final peace of knowing that her father had not killed her mother. It seemed clear to Amelia that Dan Hale had killed them both. The one for a scholarship that was his exit to a grander world. The other for his silence. She couldn't imagine why Tom Rogers had never told the truth, if that was it.

Amelia wept and cursed her own conscience.

What good would it do to stay alive if she was out of her mind with horror when they found her—if they ever did? She started screaming again. *Please, somebody, hear me!*

A sound awakened her.

A rat? A ghost?

Amelia screamed again.

Someone yelled back at her. And soon she heard a thud, and then the door opened, and Brenda Rogers's little brother stood there in the doorway, holding a huge flashlight. The beam paused on her face, and he said, "Thank God!" Then it passed over onto the face of the dead man, and the little brother . . . the young brother-in-law . . . the grown-up veterinarian . . . came over to Amelia, collapsed to his knees, dropped his head in her lap, and began to cry.

"Dan Hale killed sis for the scholarship."

Amelia, Jim, and Sandy were huddled on hay bales in a corner of the barn, while two young black llamas sniffed around their feet and knees. Jim was explaining to Amelia, while he kept an arm wrapped around his pale, sad niece. "Then he threatened Sandy's life. He told Tom that he had to confess to the crime. Dan said that he'd kill Tom's baby girl unless Tom took the rap for him. And Tom was young and scared and didn't know what else to do."

"How'd you find out all this?"

"Tom wrote to me from prison and told me to take care of Sandy for him. And he told me the truth, and also why we couldn't reveal it, not even to my parents. They raised Sandy, and when they died, I asked her to stay on the farm with me. Dan still could have killed her, at any time, and he was very powerful by then."

"You believed him?"

"Oh, yes. I knew them both very well. I knew what they were capable of. I'd never liked or trusted Dan Hale, and I'd always loved Tom." He smiled wryly. "Little brothers know these things. What broke everybody's heart was that Brenda died, and also that we couldn't believe Tom would do that. And yet he claimed steadfastly that he did. If you knew what it did to his parents . . ." Jim Kopecki closed his mouth and shook his head. After a moment, he continued, "When he told me the truth, I knew it *was* true."

"You saved all those articles—"

"So we wouldn't forget him. I told Sandy the truth, when she was old enough to contain it. I wanted her to be able to love her father."

Amelia reached out to grasp one of the girl's hands.

Over Sandy's bowed head, the adults looked at each other.

Sandy whispered, "I was so excited to meet him. We fixed up a room here, for him to live. He was going to hide out in Spale until the publicity went away, and then we were going to try to sneak him onto the farm and make like he was just a hired hand so he could be with us."

"It might not have worked," Jim admitted.

"Because of Dan Hale?" Amelia asked, and he nodded. She didn't say so, but it sounded to her as if Tom Rogers might have had a miserable existence if

143

he had lived, although at least he would have had the comfort of the love of his daughter and his brother-in-law. What she did say, to Jim, was, "No wonder you hated me."

"Not you. Dan Hale."

"He was using me as bait."

"Yeah."

"If anybody ever found me, they'd say that Tom Rogers had trapped me in the tunnels, probably attacked me, I'd shot him in self-defense, and then killed myself when I found I couldn't get out."

Jim looked horrified at the idea of it. "Amelia, would you have—"

"I don't know. Maybe, eventually. Wouldn't you?"

He thought a moment, then sighed. "Yes."

Later, when it was just the two of them, she told Jim about how desperately she had wanted to be a vet herself. About her straight A's and about the woman-hating professor who had blamed a stable fire on her.

"Three calves died. The professor had been smoking in there, but he said it was me, and who was I against his word?"

"But now you love being a journalist."

"I hate it!"

He laughed in surprise.

She whispered, "Tell you a secret? I'm a rotten reporter. I hate to hurt people's feelings!"

Impulsively, Jim hugged her, and impulsively she returned it, and suddenly it became an embrace that turned into a kiss, which lasted and lasted and then repeated itself again and again.

Much later, Amelia sighed. "I wonder what I'm going to do for a job now."

"Stay here, of course."

She stared at him, holding her breath.

"Room and board," he said, smiling at her hopefully, "and a small salary, and all the hay you can lift. Do you want to, Amelia?"

She read between the lines, looking into his eyes, and said, "I do."

"I do, too," Dr. James Kopecki told his new stable hand and future wife.

Go Quietly into the Day

Eleanor Taylor Bland

Dawn was breaking as Katey McDivott walked up the tree-shaded, gravel path that led to her cottage. She walked without leaning on her cane, pleased that for the first time in more than a week, she did not need it for support. These predawn walks were helping her regain the strength in her right leg. When she was able to sit for long periods without moving, she would go birding again with her friends. For now, these walks and her yard—with the white picket fence, the birdhouses that hung from the tree branches, and wildflowers that attracted butterflies—would have to be enough.

Katey walked to the back, where she could look across a bluff of scrub and see the Atlantic, gray-blue and white-capped today. The perfume from the pink and yellow rosebushes that edged the porch wafted toward her. Squirrels were already trying to raid the bird feeders set up on poles, thwarted by the metal rims that blocked their path. The awakening trill of the birds would soon be joined by the low hum of the bees. She sat on the steps that led to the porch, winded from the walk through the woods to the beach and back. Her binoculars felt heavy, and she took the strap from around her neck.

Perhaps she should have retired sooner, before the series of small strokes that forced her to leave. Even then, she had been reluctant. Multilingual teachers and staff were not easily replaced. Indeed, her school had not yet replaced her. Nor had she replaced her need to be there. She would always miss the children.

There was a sudden scrabbling sound as a squirrel scurried down a nearby tree and paused, tail jerking, a few feet away. She had fed them during the winter, and would now if the weather weren't so nice and sources of food so abundant. When she didn't move toward the screen door, the squirrel gave her another two shakes of his tail and scampered away. He just missed the peanut butter, that was all.

When Katey stood to go inside, her leg was stiff and in need of the cane from just that short period of inactivity. The coffee she had brewed earlier was still hot, although she enjoyed it less after it had been sitting for more than an hour. She searched the bottom shelf of the kitchen cabinet for her medication, remembered that she had just had the prescriptions refilled the day before, and retrieved both bottles of tablets from her purse. Then she sat by the window, enjoying the flash of wing and tail feathers and the chirping and chatter as the birds began swooping in for breakfast.

Katey wasn't sure how much time had passed when she noticed the dryness in her mouth and the numbness in her left hand. Like with the stroke, she thought, only it wasn't. This was different. When she tried to stand up to go to the phone, there was no strength in her legs, and she slumped to the floor.

The sun was rising as Tori Roberts drove into Boston. Her elderly friend, Lat Nhu, was with her, a reluctant but curious companion. Lat, always a contradiction. Unwilling to venture to a place she had never been before, she sat with her shoulders tense and her hands clasped tightly in her lap. At the same time, she leaned forward, straining against the safety harness, forehead almost touching the window, eager for her first glimpses of the city. Lat's birds, a pair of canaries and a pair of finches, were in bamboo cages on the backseat. As sunshine streamed in through the windows, their predawn twitters became tentative chirps. Lat greeted the morning, speaking Vietnamese. "It is a good day," Tori agreed.

Tori had rented a small trailer for those things she did not want to keep in storage. The trailer bumped along behind them. They would just be here for the summer. After that? Tori didn't know. She had lost her job teaching Asian and African-American Studies at the small college in Connecticut where she had received her baccalaureate and master's degrees. Here she had a few friends, and she hoped Lat would feel at home in the growing Vietnamese community where they would stay with Thanh's mother. Thanh. She hadn't seen him in eight years. They had been lovers. Tori smiled, remembering.

The household was in chaos when they arrived. The order in the small apartment—rolled sleeping mats, a stack of zafu, chests filled with belongings—was disrupted by crawling infants and squabbling toddlers and giggling, arguing school-aged children. Mothers, grandmothers, and aunts, at least a dozen in all, were gathered in the kitchen, speaking in rapid Vietnamese, oblivious to the noise the children were making. There was no sign of Thanh.

Lat stayed in the second-floor hallway, one birdcage in each hand. Tori went to the women, feeling at home. Their faces were as broad as her own, their cheekbones high, their hair as black and as straight. Only their skin color was different, hers a much darker brown. Born African-American on her mother's side and Vietnamese on her father's, she had learned to speak French and Vietnamese and could understand what they were saying. A little girl was missing. How far would the child go from what was known and familiar? South Boston was a slender finger jutting into the Atlantic with water on three sides. Most likely, the girl had misplaced herself within the Vietnamese community and was not lost at all. Above the din, a baby cried, silencing women and children. One woman detached herself from the others and picked up the smallest and soothed him. The others gathered their children in their arms, too, a collective reminder of the child who was missing.

"Tori," Thanh's mother, Mrs. Diem, saw her and came over, arms wide. She was so short Tori could see the part in her hair as they hugged.

"It is Thanh's daughter who is missing," she said. "My little Ngoc Thuy."

Had Thanh named her? *Knock Twee,* Tori thought, *precious virtues.*

Again, the women all began speaking at once. As Tori sorted through what they were saying, she realized that the child had been missing since the day before, that each woman thought she was with another, that now they had no idea where the child was, and Thanh and the other men had set out to look for her. The police had not been called. That would be their last resort, based on the chorus of dismay when Tori mentioned it.

"She is so quiet, that one," one of the women said. "She has wandered off somewhere, listening to what no one else can hear and not paying attention to what is around her."

"How old is she?" Tori asked, hoping that Thanh had not lied to her eight years ago or just neglected to tell her about a child—and a wife, since he kept to the old ways.

"She was just seven in May."

"Where is her mother?" Tori was surprised by her own reluctance to meet the woman Thanh must have married. There had been nothing so serious between them that she should care.

"Gone, that one is," the mother said. "Thanh's wife is dead." The irritation in her voice and the dismissive wave of her hand made Tori wonder if that was indeed true or only wishful thinking on the part of a less than pleased mother-in-law. Perhaps the marriage—Tori assumed there had been one—had not been arranged by their parents.

"How long has the child been missing?" Tori asked.

"Almost a day."

"Since this morning?"

"Yesterday."

"Before supper or after?" If the child was nearby, she could stay away longer on a full stomach than on an empty one.

"After."

153

"Has she stayed away overnight before?"

"She often stays with one of us or another." A young woman spoke, one of three women without a child in her arms.

"Yes. Yes."

The other two vied to agree.

Perhaps the child's mother *was* dead. And perhaps, Thanh being the romantic Tori knew him to be, there was another woman, or several, who also vied for his affection, unknown to these three.

"Who watches the store?" Tori asked. Thanh was a shopkeeper by day and taught martial arts most evenings. There was a rapid search for the keys, an argument among the three single women over who should mind the store, and a noisy exodus when they could not agree. Whatever the state of Thanh's marriage, he was still considered eligible by some.

Lat stepped into the kitchen and put the birdcages on the floor. Tori motioned Lat closer and pulled a chair from the table so she could sit down.

"Lat, this is Mrs. Diem," she said. "Mrs. Diem, Lat Nhu."

The two women took each other's measure quickly and smiled.

"And what of this child who is missing?" Lat asked.

Thanh's mother explained what Tori already had picked up from the others. The little girl, Ngoc Thuy, was often in a world of her own but fussed over by women who were much more interested in the father than the child.

"School is out now for the summer. There is a teacher who will not come back in the fall. Ngoc Thuy was fond of this teacher. She is sad because she will not see her again. She does not want to go outside to play. She does not want to play with her horses and dolls. She does not ever want to go back to school. I was pleased when she was not sleeping on her mat last night. School has been out for two weeks now. That seemed like a long time for someone so young to be sad."

Thanh came in as they spoke. "Tori! You did come."

He seemed older than when Tori had last seen him, his face filled with brooding concern. "Ngoc Thuy is not yet home?"

Their silence answered him.

He stood there for a moment, muscles rippling as he folded his arms. Eyes downcast, he gnawed at one corner of his lip. "We have looked every place we could think of. She has never walked farther than the school."

He walked over to where Tori was sitting. "You have come."

"Just for the summer," she said, inhaling lime-scented aftershave that was much too familiar. Eight years no longer seemed like such a long time. "Perhaps I can help."

"Perhaps," Thanh agreed.

Tori moved her chair away as he pulled a chair over and sat beside her. Lat and Mrs. Diem nodded at each other. Lat looked eager for a conspiracy; Thanh's mother looked ready to play matchmaker.

Thanh clasped his hands together so tightly his knuckles were white, then he relaxed them. "You have searched for your family for a long time now, Tori, since before you and I met. Perhaps there are things you know about this that I do not, although Ngoc Thuy's disappearance seems much different."

"You do not want to call the police."

"I have gone to them." He brushed back unruly black hair, highlighted with strands of silver, although he was only two years older than Tori's twenty-eight and looked several years younger than that. "They know what she looks like. They will watch for her. We cannot even be certain that she did not leave early this morning. They did agree to have someone go into the school and look for her there, and I accompanied them, but they, too, think she is here somewhere, in the neighborhood."

"She is not in the attic," his mother said. "She is not in the little room under the stairs. She is not with the laughing women."

"School seems important to her," Tori said. "Did she have any friends there who don't live nearby?"

"No."

"Maybe if we look through her things."

Thanh was taken aback by the suggestion, reluctant to participate in what seemed to him a major invasion of privacy. His mother shook her head in agreement.

"There might be something there," Tori said. "Something that might tell us where she would go." She didn't add that if something special were missing, that might indicate that the child had run away.

By the time the sun was high, Ngoc Thuy had ridden on three buses. She got off the third and began walking in the direction the driver had pointed out, seeking the sign for the next bus she must catch. She had waited until morning for the third bus because a woman who was also waiting had asked her why she was outside alone after dark. Afraid that the woman would point her out to the police, Ngoc Thuy walked to a park nearby and hid there until morning. Now she must catch the bus into Sudbury. Ngoc Thuy pulled the folded piece of paper from her pocket again. Miss McDivott. She had crossed out "Sadury" and printed "Sudbury" because that was how it was written on the sign, but Sudbury didn't sound like where Miss McDivott said she would live. Sadury didn't, either, but Miss McDivott had written the word on the chalk board. Ngoc Thuy waited until it was time for recess to copy it down. She was sure it had looked like Sadury.

As she walked, Ngoc Thuy took long, deep breaths. Miss McDivott lived near the ocean. Once she could smell the salt water, she would be certain that she wasn't lost, even though Miss McDivott lived far away. She could not smell the ocean yet, but soon she would. She went into a small store and bought two Devil Dogs for breakfast. Her stomach groaned as she looked at the white cream between the chocolate cake with no icing. Although her grandmother would not allow her to have them this early, when she slept away from home at one of the laughing girls' apartments, it was always what she asked for. They would give her whatever she wanted, even money, which they thought she spent. They did not know that she saved it.

Ngoc Thuy kept away from the other people in the store and went only to the man with the tan apron, who sold groceries just as her father did. She gave him her money. When he smiled at her, she said, "You would please tell me where to catch the bus for Sudbury." When he did not understand, she showed him the word printed on the piece of paper. He took her outside and pointed directions.

It was hot waiting in the sun by the pole with the bus stop sign. She had not brought a change of clothes because she did not think it would take so long, and now her dress was stained from the grass she had sat on and the orange tonic she had spilled. Perhaps Miss McDivott would be too pleased to have a visitor to notice. Ngoc Thuy had watched as the others spoke of Miss McDivott in whispers that became silence if a child came near and had known that her teacher had gone away to die just as her mother did. She did not want someone as kind as Miss McDivott to die all by herself. She did not want Miss McDivott to think she would ever forget her. She wanted to bring Miss McDivott the hard butterscotch candy she had been saving for her mother and watch her smile as she unwrapped it. She wanted to hear her speak again, her voice soft, like the wind. She did not know that it would take so long to come to this Sudbury, though. She thought she would be there by morning, before the others missed her, and could call to let them know where she was.

The bus came. Ngoc Thuy asked again if it would go to Sudbury. Again she unfolded the piece of paper. Again she asked the fare and counted out the change. Perhaps it would not be long now. Once she got there, she had only to go to the ocean and walk along the beach until she saw the house with the pink and yellow roses. Perhaps they were wrong. Perhaps although Miss McDivott would not come back to school, she would not die. Perhaps she would walk among the flowers in her garden and watch the ocean from her back porch forever, or at least for a very long time.

* * *

GO QUIETLY INTO THE DAY

At first, Katey was able to move her left arm and leg, but as she tried to make her way across the room to the telephone, her strength failed. Now her mouth felt dry, and her tongue was swollen, and her throat felt as if it was closing. There was this buzzing and ringing in her ears. She didn't know what time it was, but she thought she must have slept. She heard noises that she thought might be the mailman, the only person likely to come to the house today, but she was unable to make even a sound. What was happening to her? This was nothing like having a stroke.

The window was open. The day must be hot, because the birds were quiet. She tried to concentrate on hearing something other than the noises inside her head. She tried to imagine that she was in some peaceful copse watching the most delicate, most colorful bird, one she had never seen before. There was nobody who would call or come to visit her. No family, and until she had retired, this was only a summer place where she spent most weekends. Perhaps, if enough mail accumulated, the postman would suspect something. Otherwise, unless this was something that would pass, she would lie here and die. Her throat felt even more constricted. It hurt to swallow. Soon her air passage would be cut off. For a moment, she panicked. No. Even though she could neither speak nor move, she would not yield to fear or despair. Perhaps, if she listened very carefully, she would hear the roar of the ocean or the song of a bird. Katey closed her eyes.

Ngoc Thuy's room was little more than a closet with a sleeping mat. Open shoe boxes held a carefully arranged collection of tiny dolls with long hair in shades of red, brunette, and blond, and horses, all plastic, some with fake hair manes and tails. Tori knelt beside a mahogany chest. The lid was a forest scene, with birds and fawns and rabbits carved into the wood. Inside were Ngoc Thuy's clothes, and at the bottom some school papers and butterscotch hard candy.

Tori took out the papers. "All of her clothes are here?"

Thanh watched from the doorway. His dark eyes flashed anger at the question. "She did not run away."

"She is a little girl. Her mother died a year and half ago. And now her teacher has gone away, too." That argument had persuaded him to allow her to look through Ngoc Thuy's belongings, but he was not pleased with her suspicions.

"She left her mother's candy," he said.

Tori touched a yellow cellophane wrapper but did not pick it up. Something special. Something she would not have left behind if she wasn't planning to come back. Thanh thought she might be able to help because she had gained some knowledge or experience from searching for her own family during the past dozen summers. Tori thought she might be able to help because as a little girl she had run away from foster homes so many times. She had never run away from her real home. She couldn't even remember having a home of her own. There were vague recollections of a mother and siblings that she couldn't even be certain were real. Her heart said they were. Logic didn't.

"Has she ever gone away for a few days?" Everything in the room said that the child who lived there intended to come back. And Tori knew this community was so close-knit that there were many who were like aunts and grandmothers to the children.

"Just to the laughing women's places."

"Laughing women?"

"That is what she calls them. You know, they come and smile and laugh and bring food and . . ."

"Flirt," Tori said.

"They are friendly."

"There are other laughing women Ngoc Thuy knows about but these women do not?"

When Thanh didn't answer, Tori sat back on her heels and looked up at him. "Well?"

"Is that a personal or professional question?"

Tori hesitated. "Both." She found it difficult to be less than straightforward.

"My wife had cancer. It took her six months to die. The last two, she was in the hospital. I was there with her as much as I could be. I have not been with a woman since."

Tori began sorting through the child's schoolwork. Letters and numbers marched halfway across lined paper, then began slanting as they reached the edge, as if the child was in a hurry to be done with it. Was she an impulsive child or easily bored? Or was she persistent and plodding? Tori didn't ask. She would form her own impressions for now. The lines and circles were perfectly formed even when they sloped. A child who was in control, Tori decided, or wanted to be, even when she was in a hurry.

When she looked at the crayon drawings, they made her eyes hurt. Variations of a very small person standing outside a door looking in at a very large person in a big bed covered with a multicolored blanket. The blanket was divided into squares, and each was filled in with a thick layer of crayon. There were twenty-eight drawings. As Tori reached the bottom of the pile, the person in the bed became smaller and at the end was even smaller than the child at the door.

"Did Ngoc Thuy visit her mother in the hospital?"

"Until she was in too much pain and sedated all of the time. Ngoc Thuy would cry to see her, but it would have upset her too much. Her mother did not look at all like herself."

Tori couldn't imagine what it must have been like for a small child to know that her mother was sick and have her taken away and then see her no more. She did know, with unwavering clarity, the void caused by that abandonment.

"And she liked this teacher."

"I went to pick her up at school one day this spring, and she came skipping toward me. She was laughing and holding Miss McDivott's hand. She looked like a little girl again, and not my sad-faced old woman."

Tori returned the papers to the chest. "I think she has gone to find her teacher." She did not attempt to explain closure to him or the need to say final goodbyes.

Ngoc Thuy tucked her sandals under her arm and walked along a narrow strip of beach that was separated from the ocean by huge rocks. The sand was warm between her toes. There was no shade, and it was hot, but when the waves crashed against the rocks, some of the water sprayed her.

As she walked, Ngoc Thuy looked up at the houses. Some were big. Most were small. When the trees got in the way, she could see only rooftops. She did not see a house with birdhouses in the trees or bird feeders on poles or lots of rosebushes. Perhaps this was not the right town. When her legs got tired, she sat and watched the sea gulls for a while. Maybe this was the wrong part of the beach. No people were here. Maybe all the houses were empty. She unwrapped a piece of butterscotch candy and sucked on it. Then she began walking again.

She saw the red bird feeder first. Then one that was yellow. She could see only the top of the house. There was a pole with an arrow and a rooster on the roof, just like Miss McDivott said. Ngoc Thuy ran across the street and pushed her way through the bushes and up to the house. There were so many bird feeders. And a little white house. When she reached a clearing near the wooden fence, she could see the roses, hundreds of pink and yellow roses.

Ngoc Thuy ran to the steps. "Miss McDivott! Miss McDivott!"

Nobody answered. The screen door was closed, but not the other one. She went up the steps and looked inside.

"Miss McDivott!" She flung open the door, then stopped and stared at Miss McDivott on the floor. When her eyes opened, Ngoc Thuy tiptoed over.

"You're not sleeping. You're still here."

Only Miss McDivott's eyes moved.

Ngoc Thuy sat beside her. "You're sick, aren't you? My mommy was sick, too, but when I went to see her, her eyes were closed. She couldn't talk, either, but she was sleeping in this little bed with a shiny white pillow and a wooden blanket. I couldn't wake her up. But you're awake." She waited for Miss McDivott to speak, but she didn't. She didn't move, either. "If I sit with you, will you stay awake? I don't want you to leave me. I'll stay right here, I promise. See, I brought you some candy."

Miss McDivott couldn't eat the candy. She needed a doctor, but sometimes, when you went to the doctor, you didn't come home anymore.

"I'm going to call nine-one-one," Ngoc Thuy said. "They'll come and put you in an ambulance and take you to the hospital, and you might never come back again. But if you do come back, I'll give you this candy and learn to write cursive and bring my ponies to see you."

Miss McDivott blinked.

"I really want you to see the ponies. I have lots of them. And this candy is real good, you'll like it when you feel better. So please come home, okay?"

Ngoc Thuy went to the phone.

It was after five when Tori and Thanh reached Sudbury. Tori drove along a narrow, winding dirt road until she reached the mailbox with the cardinal on top. A police car was parked on the shoulder. She wouldn't meet Miss McDivott today, but maybe tomorrow. Thanh took her arm as they walked up the path to the cottage. A little girl was sitting on the steps.

"Ngoc Thuy!" Thanh rushed to scoop her into his arms. The little girl clung to him, and Thanh sat hugging and rocking her and murmured something in French. Tori remained at the foot of the steps. Ngoc Thuy had Thanh's broad face and straight hair, but her features were not Asian, and her hair and her eyes were brown. Perhaps that was why Mrs. Diem did not seem to have liked the child's mother.

The last time Tori saw Thanh, eight years ago, the day was as hot and the sun was as bright, and pigeons strutted along the sidewalk at South Station. She took the train to Connecticut. Thanh went to visit relatives in France. Ngoc Thuy's mother must have been French. Precious virtue. Lat and Thanh and most Vietnamese that she knew did not seem to place much importance on what one was called, but this child seemed precious indeed.

That she should set out alone to find her teacher with only the name of a place that did not exist had not surprised Tori at all. She could remember running away to New Mexico when she was six and becoming afraid when she reached the corner and turning back. By the time she was seven, she had set out for Seattle and made it as far as the el train station. Now she understood the fear that stopped her; the fear of what she would find at the end of her journey made not knowing so much safer. She could put faith neither in herself nor in the family, the mother, she was seeking. Even now, when she had all the time she needed to search for them, she held back, coming back here again, to a community of women she felt safe with, to a man who had taught her martial arts years ago because he didn't think she was brave. It was still so much easier to come here with Lat and hide from that mother, that other culture she had been born into.

Like Tori, Ngoc Thuy must have become curious about that different culture that peered out at her from the mirror. Unlike Tori, she had her mother's courage. Enough to let go of Miss McDivott without knowing if she would return. Tori didn't know if she was that brave, if, when that time came, she would be able to let go of Lat Nhu. She didn't know if she had the courage to make more than a feeble foray into that unknown world of her mother and, perhaps, her brothers and sisters, if there were any. Thanh was wrong; she had not searched for them at all. But if this child could . . . perhaps.

Thanh tousled Ngoc Thuy's hair, and father and daughter laughed. Tori's eyes met Thanh's for a moment, then she looked at Ngoc Thuy and smiled.

Sibling Rivalry

Brendan DuBois

I n my parked and stolen car, I sat in the front seat, looking up at the lights in the third-floor apartment building, right in the middle of a run-down section of one of Boston's far-flung suburbs. It had been a long night, and my job wasn't complete yet, not by a long shot. As it stood, I was just fifty percent there, and I wasn't going to be happy until I reached a full one hundred percent. As I waited, I listened to the radio, listened to the night sounds of talk shows that went on and on about relationships, about families, about problems. I only half listened to the electronic noise, concentrating on my own problems at hand.

Well, not at hand. Under the seat, wrapped in the day's *Boston Herald,* was a 9mm Smith & Wesson, complete with attached tube silencer. That was one problem, because I wasn't sure what I'd do if a local cop came by and rousted me. While I did have a good excuse for being on this deserted street at one A.M., I'm sure it wasn't an excuse a cop would want to hear.

My other problem was the third floor of the apartment building. A living-room light was still burning brightly, along with a kitchen light, meaning that the occupant of that apartment—one Adam Crui-shank—was still awake. I had seen some movement not fifteen minutes ago, and I didn't want him to be awake much longer.

I sighed and tapped my fingers on the steering wheel. Car lights appeared from the end of the street, and I lay down in the front seat of the car, hiding myself. The interior lit up as the car went by, showing me the crumpled coffee cups, fast-food wrappers, and other trash that the previous and legitimate owner had piled up. Maybe if I had time tonight, I'd clean everything up before returning the car to its condo parking lot, next town over, to show my appreciation. If I had the time, if I had the luck.

Luck. I got up from the seat and looked out the window, and both the living-room light and the kitchen light on the third floor were off. The only illumination showing was that ghastly blue light that comes from a television set being left on. I took a couple of deep breaths, tapped on the steering wheel again, and continued listening to the radio. When the top-of-the-hour news came on, about a half hour had passed since the dimming of the lights upstairs, and that was enough time for me.

I reached under the seat, pulled out the newspaper and pistol, and stepped outside. The May night air felt good, and I walked quickly across the street and into the apartment building's lobby. Most nice apartment buildings, you need a key to get into the lobby door. This wasn't a nice building. I went in and then went upstairs, dodging trash cans, kids' toys, and a bicycle that had been torn apart, leaving nothing but a blue and rusty frame.

At the third floor, I bent down and took a lock-picking kit from my coat pocket. I knew the routine. Adam Cruishank didn't know this, but I had been in his apartment the day before, when he was out drinking with some buddies, to view the layout. In the annals of stupidity, breaking into an occupied apartment in the middle of the night, where you don't know which hallway leads to the living room and which one is home to a Doberman, ranks right up there.

The door popped open. Success. No Doberman, nothing save Adam and the sound of the television. I went in and closed the door behind me and silently put the newspaper down on the kitchen table. The layout was simple. Kitchen and a bathroom off to the right. Through the kitchen, living room on the left, bedroom on the right. I went forward, pistol in both hands now. Kitchen was clear. All right. I went to the right. Bedroom, which consisted of a box spring and mattress on the floor and a jumble of blankets and sheets. Clear and empty. Right.

Off to the living room, where a late-night black-and-white movie was on, something about a trip to the moon. Couch, two chairs, all empty. Clear. I lowered the pistol.

Damn.

And then there was the flush of the toilet, and a young and sleepy and naked Adam Cruishank came into the living room. He saw me, and he quickly became unsleepy. He started to say something in his startled state, but I didn't let him. Taking advantage of his unclothed situation, I kicked him firmly between the legs, where it counted.

He collapsed on the floor, and I got behind him, grabbing his long brown hair—tied up in a ponytail, how convenient—and I forced him up, making him kneel. I put the base of the pistol's silencer at the base of his neck.

"Shut your mouth, Adam," I said, making my voice as low and as menacing as possible. "You know what this is about, don't you?"

He was shivering on the floor. "It's about last week, man, right? Is it about last week?"

"Very good," I said.

His voice got whiny and pleading. "But it's not my fault! It was Tony's idea!"

"That's funny," I said, just before pulling the trigger. "I just saw him a couple of hours ago, and he said the same thing about you."

A week earlier, I was in the next state up north, in the city of Porter, sitting uncomfortably in that community's police station. I appreciate their work and what they do, but I've never felt at home in a police station. The cops here had tried to make the station lobby look warm and friendly, with pictures of softball teams and kid charity events up on the wall, but in front of me, behind bullet-resistant glass, was the desk officer, uniformed and staring at me. He knew why I was there, knew that it was something simple and nonthreatening, but he kept on looking at me every few minutes.

I knew why. In some base way, like a highly trained hunting dog catching the faroff scent of a dangerous quarry, he knew I was a threat, was someone that he had to be careful with. And even though I knew it myself, there was no way to hide it. It's just the way I am.

The door leading into the station proper buzzed open, and a woman police officer came out carrying a clipboard in her hands. She was a few inches shorter than my six feet, and we both shared blue eyes and light sandy hair. Mine is cut close, almost a buzz cut, while hers was pulled back in a small bun. Her name tag said "L. Sullivan," and I knew that the L stood for Lynn.

"Are you ready, Jason?" she asked.

"That I am," I said, getting up from the hard plastic chair. I joined her at the desk officer's window, and she handed over the clipboard to me. "Read it and sign it," she said, smiling slightly. "If you're not too scared."

"Too soon to be scared," I said, and I looked over the form. It was a photocopy of a standard form from the police department, basically discharging them of any responsibility if I were to be shot, injured, crippled, captured, burned, flayed, or talked rudely to while participating in the department's civilian ride-along program. I gave the form a quick scan, scrawled my signature at the bottom, and looked over at the young woman. She tore the sheet off the clipboard and passed it over to the desk officer.

"All set?" she asked me.

I winked at her. "Lead on, sis."

And so she did.

Outside, we were at the rear of the police station, and I watched with quiet fascination as my younger sister went through the motions of getting a cruiser ready for a night out on the streets. There were four cruisers, parked in a small lot that had the brick police station on one side and residential homes on the other. A black duffle bag went into the trunk, and in the trunk was a wooden case, orange raincoat, fire extinguisher, two flashlights, chains, road flares, and a light brown teddy bear. I picked up the teddy bear.

"Mascot?"

She gave me a wry smile. "No, it's something we give to a kid to distract him or her if we're pulling Mommy out of a wrecked car or arresting Daddy on a bench warrant. Keeps their minds off what's really going on."

Inside the cruiser, she started the engine and then tested the headlights and the blue strobe lights on the roof, and then flipped on the siren for a quick *whoop-whoop*.

"Guess it's better to test it here than find out it doesn't work behind a drunk driver," I said.

"You got it," she said, backing the cruiser out of the spot. "But it sure ticks the neighbors off."

"I thought they'd love to have cops next door."

"Sure," she said. "They especially love it when drunks get bailed out at three A.M. and they decide to use their front lawns as toilets."

We went out into the streets of Porter, Lynn driving the cruiser sure and true. It was early evening, and I spared her another glance. The uniform was a dark blue, and she had on a heavy utility belt with pistol, handcuffs, and other gear. There was also a portable radio at her side, with a microphone attached to her shoulder.

"Doesn't all that stuff get heavy?" I asked.

"Certainly does," she said. "All the stuff weighs

about twenty pounds, and that doesn't even include the vest."

"What are you carrying?"

As I listened to her talk, I saw that as she drove, her eyes were darting around, observing, evaluating, watching.

"Let's see, besides the pistol, there's two extra clips of ammunition, two sets of handcuffs, keys, expandable baton, pepper spray, and lipstick case."

"Really?"

A hint of a smile. "No, not really. And the radio, too. Actually, they're new. See the little red button here?"

I looked down to where she was pointing, at the radio at her hip. "Yep."

"That's the panic button. I press that twice, and dispatch gets an automated message, officer needs assistance, and within five minutes, every patrol unit on duty will be backing me up. Nice."

Seeing her in uniform and full police gear was still a bit of a shock, not only because of the fact that a family member was a cop. The last time I had seen Lynn was a few days ago, drinking a beer on a deck outside her harborside condo as she officially welcomed me back to the frigid northeast after spending many years in California. On that day, she had on a loose, light pink T-shirt and white tennis shorts, and her hair was loose and flowing around her shoulders. Nothing like the trim and proper cop sitting next to me.

And the time before that . . . well, I wasn't sure what she was wearing, but the next-to-the-last time I saw Lynn, she was a skinny and awkward twelve-year-old, seemingly all elbows and knees.

"Here we go," she said as she reached over to the console to flip on the overhead lights.

"What's that?"

"See the black Trans Am up ahead?" she said. "Just crossed the double yellow line."

We were in a section of Porter that was a mix of old residential homes, subdivided into apartments, and small corner stores. The Trans Am pulled over to the side, and Lynn picked up her radio and spoke low and quick, "Dispatch, P-five, doing a traffic stop at Congress and Ahern."

"Ten-four, P-five," the radio crackled back.

She threw the car into park, and I said, "Crossing the double yellow line?"

"There's a reason. I'll tell you later."

She clambered out of the cruiser and walked over to the Trans Am. As she neared the trunk of the car, she touched the smooth black metal and then stood by the driver's door. I now noted that when she had pulled the cruiser over, she parked a few feet out in the street, to give herself a buffer from the passing traffic. She also stood to the rear of the door, forcing the driver to crane his head back. Good work. She was pretty sharp.

The driver handed over license and registration, and after some talking back and forth, she gave him back his papers and went back to the cruiser. Lynn picked up the radio mike and said, "P-five is clear." When the Trans Am went out into traffic, Lynn pulled the cruiser out, and we were back on the prowl.

"So," I said. "Why did you pull him over?"

She tapped on the steering wheel a few times. "Because he was there, and because I needed a target."

"A target?"

"Sure," she said. "Look, complacency at any other job is fine. You can doze at your desk or play solitaire on the company computer, and you still get to go home at the end of the day. Complacency out here on the streets can get you killed. And you need to start your shift off with a bit of a start, to get the juices flowing."

I nodded. "So a traffic stop, no matter how minor, gets you in the right frame of mind for your work."

"That's right, big brother."

She took a sharp left and sped up Monroe Street, accelerating, and I was going to make a joke about speed limits working for everybody else save for cops, and decided against it.

Instead, I asked, "What was the other thing you did over there?"

"What thing?"

"When you touched the trunk of the car. It looked like you were checking something. Were you?"

"Nope," she said. "I was leaving something behind."

"And what was that?"

"My fingerprints," she said.

"Excuse me?"

Her voice suddenly became tired and patient, and sounded much older than that of my younger sister. "If I ever get gunned down at a traffic stop, and they later pull the driver over, he can't say he wasn't at the crime scene if my fingerprints are on the car. Right?"

Dear me. My little sister.

"Right," I said.

* * *

Later, we did two more traffic stops, and she wrote a ticket for someone with a burned-out taillight—"I would have let her go with just a warning, but she wanted to be a jerk about it," she had said—and then we parked behind a bridge abutment, down by the harbor. It was now fully dark, and with the cruiser's lights off, the only illumination came from the blinking red lights on the radio console. Out on the harbor, soft red and green lights marked the position of moored boats.

"Time to slow down our happy motorists," she said as she started working with the radar unit, which was set up on the dashboard. She manipulated a few buttons until two readouts glowed. The one on the left said "OO," and the one on the right said "45."

"See the two sets of numerals?" Lynn asked. "The one on the left gives you the speed of a car or truck going by. The other is the alarm set point. Anyone going faster than forty-five, a chirpy little alarm goes off."

"And what's the speed limit here?"

"Thirty-five. It's a clear night, little traffic and no rain. I'll give 'em a ten-mile margin to play around with. Anything more than that, then it's money for the state."

"Sounds reasonable," I said.

"Thanks," she said in the darkness. "So. How did California treat you, all these years?"

"Treated me fine, Lynn-Lynn," I said, using an old nickname from when we were kids. "But after a while, I got tired of the perfect weather and the people trying to be perfect, and decided to come back home."

"How was your business out there?"

I thought about the different answers I could use

and said, "It was busy. But after a while . . . well, I know *burn-out* is a popular phrase, but that's what happened to me. I put enough money away and made some good investment choices, and now I'm taking some time off."

"Which is another reason why you came back east?"

"Among others."

A car flew by, and up on the console, where the radar detector sat, the yellow numerals on the left indicating traffic speed said forty-two. "And what exactly did you do out there, big brother?"

Another popular lie. "I was a systems engineer. Something go wrong with a system, it was my job to go in and fix it."

"Was it exciting?"

God, too much so, I thought. "No, it was pretty boring. Just the same old stuff, day in and day out."

Another car flew by, and the radar unit squealed and the display said sixty-one. My sister the cop ignored it. Instead, she shifted in her seat and said, "Well, things must have gotten fairly exciting, big brother, considering what the police computers in California have about you. You've been arrested almost a dozen times, everything from attempted murder to suspicion of murder to a bunch of assaults. And yet you've spent hardly a day in jail. And why's that?"

I suppose I could have lied. I suppose I could have danced around the truth. I suppose I could have said, "Mistakes were made," and leave it at that. But this was my sister, after all.

"Good lawyers," I said.

A dark green van sped by, the radar unit squealing sixty-five. Lynn cursed and reached down and flipped on the blue dome lights, turned on the cruiser's headlights, and pulled out onto the street, the surge of the acceleration pushing me softly back into the seat.

"That's not the question I was asking, why you didn't spend a day in jail," she said, eyes straight ahead on the speeding van. "What I really wanted to know, what were you doing out in California, Jason? And what made you like that?"

For that, I had no ready answer.

The van pulled over after less than a quarter of a mile, and when Lynn called in the traffic stop, she put the microphone down, stepped out of the cruiser, and waited. And waited. And waited.

I shifted in the seat, uncomfortable about everything that was going on, from the unexpected inquisition to the mystery of why Lynn wasn't approaching the stopped van. The blue lights illuminated the rear of the cruiser's window, and I twisted my head and looked to the rear. Another Porter police cruiser pulled up, this one unmarked and with its flashing blue lights mounted in the radiator grill.

Two male cops got out of the car, and when one joined up with Lynn, she approached the van. The other male cop stood by our cruiser, and I felt a little shiver as I saw that he had his service pistol out and was holding it down by his leg. The first male cop went to the van at its passenger side, and then Lynn approached the driver's side. She and her male companion had their flashlights out and were illuminating the front of the van, and after a couple of minutes, Lynn came back to the cruiser, the van's registration and the driver's license in her hand.

She called in the information on the traffic stop and got a quick reply from dispatch, saying the driver was clean, with no traffic record, and she muttered, "Well, he's gonna have one before the night is out."

"Who are your two friends?"

"My backup?" she said, not looking up as she filled out the traffic citation form. "They're from what we call the trouble car. Every other cruiser has a sector to patrol except for that one. They go wherever backup is needed or where something might break out, like a nightclub letting out for the evening."

I looked over at the van and said, "It was the van, right?"

A small nod. "We hate vans. We call 'em cop coffins. You don't know if there's one guy in there or six. You could walk up to the back of the van, and the rear doors could pop open, and there might be a couple of bank robbers on the lam, armed with shotguns and ready to cut you in half. That's why we try to back each other up, as much as we can, whenever we stop a van."

She clicked her pen shut, then tore the citation form from its book, and went back outside. She laughed at something one of the cops said to her and handed the ticket over to the van driver—even now, I couldn't tell what the driver had looked like—and then she came back to the cruiser.

As she switched off the lights and eased us back into traffic, she said, "So. Enjoying yourself?"

"Like you wouldn't believe."

We took a brief coffee break, sipping from white Styrofoam cups as we watched the lights around

Porter Harbor. The cruiser was parked in a small lot near Gebo Park, and we watched the night strollers go by on the park pathways. Even sitting there, Lynn's eyes were quite alive, moving around, checking out the pedestrians and night bicyclists, glancing up every now and then at the rearview mirror, ensuring assassins or some such weren't sneaking up on us.

"So," she said. "What happened to you?"

"What do you mean?"

"You know what I mean," she said. "We both grow up here, go to the same schools, and somehow I end up as an officer of the law, and you end up . . . I don't even know what to call you. How did you end up that way? The rigors of being the oldest brother or something?"

The cup of coffee felt warm in my hands. "I joined the Army after high school. I found out I had a talent with weapons and how to use them. When I left the Army, certain . . . agencies and companies hired me for these skills. That's what happened."

"So, a domestic mercenary?" she said, her voice filled with scorn. "A crazed militia type, trying to save the world for Aryan Christians?"

"No," I said. "Just trying to take care of a few bad guys, that's all, the ones that fall between the cracks, the ones that never make it on law enforcement's radar screen. You could say I was doing your work, just from a different side of the street."

"Oh, that's so bogus—"

And by then, I had had enough. "Excuse me, little sister, but who elected you guardian of my morals and responsibilities?"

"What you've done was criminal!"

"Says who?"

This caused her almost to sputter in anger. "Says anybody with reason, that's who!"

"Reason? Is it reason when you know—just as well as I do—that certain criminals never get caught, never get convicted, never get put away, because they have connections? Or because they have lawyers with million-dollar legal retainers? Or because they live in estates and steal with briefcases and computers, instead of living in a trailer park and stealing with a tire iron or a cheap pistol?"

"So, it's your job to clear up problems like that? Who elected you?"

"Nobody," I said, not quite believing I was having this conversation with a police officer, even if she was my sister. "I'm hired by people I trust, and I do my job, and I don't lose any sleep over it."

"And that's all right by you?"

"Don't get all mushy on me, Lynn. I know enough about cops to know about the things you do. You turn away from a small-time crook if he can lead you to a bigger crook. If someone slightly dirty comes to you for help, he doesn't get that help unless he gives you some information you can use. And I'm sure not many cops in this city pay for a meal when they're on duty."

"What I do is different and is within acceptable levels," she said. "You have bloody hands, Jason, bloody hands."

"You'd be amazed what can be done with soap and water," I said.

She put her coffee cup down on the seat. "Well, listen to me, and listen to me well. I don't want to know what you did in California or who you've hurt or whatever. All I want you to do is leave it back west. Don't you dare try pulling any stunts like that in my town or my state."

Now it made sense. "So that's the purpose of tonight's little ride-along. No brotherly-sisterly bonding. No showing off what you do for work. Just a warning, right?"

She refused to look at me. "I'm doing well, for the first time in my life. I'm on my own, and I'm doing great on the force, and if I do well, I can make detective next year. Then my roadway is clear, and I don't need roadblocks up ahead."

"I've been called a lot of things before, but never a roadblock."

"Well, get used to it. I've got a good future ahead of me, and I don't want the black sheep of the family screwing it up for me."

Right about then, I was getting ready to get out of the cruiser and walk back to the police station and go home from there, but then the radio flared into life, a message about a cop needing assistance at a bar brawl, and we were out of that parking lot so fast, Lynn's coffee spilled all over the seat.

The bar was a roadhouse clear on the other side of the city, and I quickly found myself holding onto the door handle and stiffening my legs against the cruiser's floorboards to keep my distance as we screamed over there in response, lights on and siren blaring. I spared a quick glance at the speedometer and saw that we were doing 105 miles per hour, and then I didn't look anymore. I've been in many a scary situation before, but during those times, at least I've been in control and could do something about it. There was no control here. I was a mere passenger.

So instead of gazing in amazement at the speedometer, I looked over at Lynn, and she looked like a woman possessed, all wired and tense and seemingly one with the cruiser. With a tiny flick-flick of her wrist, we dodged around cars and pickup trucks that pulled over to the side of the road.

We zoomed down Route 1, and I could actually feel the cruiser lift off the pavement as we slid through gentle curves. I was going to say something and then kept my mouth shut. First, it wouldn't be polite. Second, she was doing her job. And third, I was scared to death that a word on my part would distract her, and the cruiser would fly off the road and wrap itself around a tree.

Strictly speaking, though, at these speeds, we wouldn't wrap around a tree. We'd probably shatter in a couple of dozen pieces, all about the size of a suitcase.

Then Lynn gently pumped the brakes a few times, as Route 1 entered a mixed commercial and residential area, with homes and shops and small strip malls. Then she braked harder and swung the cruiser right, onto a street that had a "One Way—Do Not Enter" sign, and we went up the street the wrong way, about a half block. Two other cruisers were there, and about fifty or sixty people were on the street and on the sidewalks.

She slammed the cruiser into park and practically leaped from the car, and I followed her, my hands suddenly feeling tingly, as if missing the comforting weight of a weapon, any weapon at all. The bar was in a two-story block of offices and shops and called itself the Aaron Room, and from the clothing and demeanor of the crowd, I could see that it attracted the current young generation, whatever we're calling it nowadays. Rock music boomed from the bar's open door, and lights were flashing inside. The crowd was edgy and not happy. There were hoots and some whistles from the people in the street, and everything moved fast, with a nervous edge and energy.

Two young men were facedown on the sidewalk, being handcuffed, and Lynn was talking loudly to another man with baggy pants around his hips and a loose sweatshirt. The sides of his hair were dyed orange, and he had a stud through his nose.

"I'm just tellin' ya that you're treatin' my boys rough," he complained.

Lynn gave it right back to him, saying, "And I'm telling you, pal, that if you don't move it, you're going to join them in jail tonight."

A cop on the ground near one of the two men called out, "Lynn! You got an extra pair of handcuffs?"

And as Lynn turned and started tugging at her utility belt, the young man with the orange hair reached both of his hands under his shirt. I found myself now behind him, mentally evaluating his stance, which way he was looking and what he was doing, and when I decided to take him down by a swift kick to the back of his knees and then follow up by a fist punch to his throat, both of his hands came out from his shirt, empty. I stopped myself, breathing hard, almost shivering.

The young man turned around, just for a moment, to look at me, and then he stepped away and melted into the crowd, looking at me one more time before fading from sight. The look on his face was that of a lamb, seeing a hungry wolf eye him and then let him go.

I shivered. It had been close, and somehow, deep in the back recesses of that kid's mind, he knew it had been close as well.

In a few moments, the guys on the ground had been tossed into the rear of the cruiser, and, with the urban entertainment over, the crowd began to disperse, going back into the bar or walking away. I got back into the cruiser, and Lynn joined me, wiping a napkin over her forehead and then saying a series of naughty words as she noticed the mess on the front seat made by the spilled coffee.

"Some call," I said.

"Oh, it's typical, especially considering the amount of booze that gets consumed during a weekend like this," she said. "You know, I'm no prohibitionist, but if people saw the number of lives that we see, day in and day out, that get destroyed by fun, legal alcohol, they would be amazed. I'd say about two-thirds of the people in the lockup tonight are drunk. And that doesn't count the car accidents, the accidental drownings, and the domestic disputes that happen, all fueled by alcohol."

"I thought that guy with the orange hair was pretty fueled," I said.

"The usual," she said. "His mouth was writing checks his butt couldn't cover."

"Well, I don't know if you noticed, Lynn-Lynn, but I was ready to kick his butt," I said. "When your back was turned, he put his hands under his shirt, and I thought he was reaching for a knife or something. He came about three seconds away from having some serious problems."

By now we were traveling back on Route 1, at about seventy miles per hour slower than before, and I could see Lynn tense up. We traveled in silence for long seconds, and she said, "Don't ever do that again."

"Lynn, it was pure reaction. I thought he was going to—"

"Not that, you idiot," she said, interrupting me. "Don't you ever call me Lynn-Lynn again. You long ago lost the right to say that, a long time ago."

I couldn't think of what to say at first, and then I said, "Lynn, it's just a nickname. You used to call me Jay-Jay, and I used to—"

Her lips were tight and drawn. "Right, I know. Jay-Jay and Lynn-Lynn. Big brother and little sister. Very cute, very nice, except you forgot the rules of brothers and sisters."

"What rules?"

She glanced at me, eyes flaring. "Damn you, the rules that say brothers and sisters look out for each other. The rules that say big brothers take care of their little sisters, and little sisters look up to their big brothers. The rules that say you never lose touch, ever, because a little sister, her heart is quite easy to break and never, ever repairs."

I couldn't bear to look at her. I stared out at the passing landscape of Porter and cleared my throat, but she beat me to it.

"You care to remember how many birthday or Christmas cards I got from my big brother after he joined the Army and moved to California?"

Me, a person who has been to one end of this

hemisphere and back in service of dark companies in service of this country, was now slouched down in the seat, warm with embarrassment and humiliation. "I don't remember."

"Why shouldn't you?" she shot back. "The number was pretty small. There were exactly three. That's it. All the years growing up, going through adolescence and finding out what it's like out there by myself without anyone to protect me—my big brother, my Jason, was too busy to write or call or check up on me. So don't think you can come bouncing back here with a smile and a happy attitude at being back home. It's gone beyond that."

"Lynn, look, I know I wasn't the best of brothers, but I—"

The radio crackled again. "Forget about it," she said as she turned the cruiser around and we headed toward downtown Porter.

It was just past two A.M., long after the bars had closed and the drunks had stumbled home. A light mist was falling, and the streets were empty, and we pulled up along a block of stores and little restaurants. Lynn didn't bother with the strobe lights, just parked the cruiser with its engine running.

"Silent alarm at a toy store," she explained, grabbing a flashlight and putting her hat on. "As bogus a call as you'd ever get. Who'd want to rob a toy store?"

"What are you going to do?"

"Make sure the doors are locked and report back," she said. "Some of these old alarms, when we get wet weather, they short and send back a false report. Or maybe a truck went by and the vibration set it off. Won't take more than a sec."

She stepped out into the mist, flashlight in hand, and headed over to the store, about ten feet away. Just a sec, she said. Just a sec to fix this little problem. *And how long to fix the little problem we face tonight, of a younger sister who's about ready to club you just for spite?*

I was thinking about that when I looked out the windshield of the cruiser again, just in time to see my younger sister get shot.

There were two of them, and they sprang out of a door adjacent to the toy store, a door belonging to a goldsmith, running to a parked car up the street, their hands carrying something, their hands carrying something shiny, damn it, their hands carrying weapons!

I got my hand on the car door handle just as Lynn shouted at them to stop, her free hand reaching to her side for her pistol.

I got the door open as the two men spun and looked back at her, and I froze their faces in my mind.

I got one foot out as they raised their pistols and fired, the noise obscene and loud, the muzzle flashes bright and blinding.

I got both feet out and was standing up as Lynn was thrown to the ground by the force of the shots, her flashlight and hat falling to the ground, her body hitting the asphalt, making a hollow noise that sounded like an ax handle striking a ripe pumpkin.

And I was running toward her and forcing myself not to look down. *Don't look down at her, don't look down at your sister.* And I saw the late-model Chevrolet with the Massachusetts license plate parked under a streetlight, and I froze that in my mind as well, as the two men clambered in, and the car sped away with both doors hanging open.

And then I reached my sister.

Her face was pale, except for where the blood was dribbling out of her mouth. "Lynn?" I whispered, looking her over, running my shaking hands over her body. The center of her uniform shirt was a torn mess, and there was stickiness on the ground from her flowing blood. Her eyes remained closed.

And I remembered something and reached to the radio at her side and pressed the red button twice, paused, and then pressed it again. And again.

Sirens in the distance began whooping and wailing, getting louder as they got closer. I stayed on my hands and knees with my sister. The noise of the approaching units got closer and closer, and each few moments I asked the same question, over and over again, raising my voice so that it could be heard over the sounds of the sirens.

"Lynn? Lynn?"

And her eyes remained closed.

Soon the little street was jam packed with ambulances, police cruisers, fire engines, state police cars, and even a car from the local fish and game warden, all because of that little red button.

Lynn was bundled up and taken away, and I wanted to go with her, but her fellow cops were insistent.

I was asked questions by the first arriving officers.

I was asked questions by the shift supervisor.

I was asked questions by the police chief, called out of bed and hastily dressed.

I was asked questions by the state police.

And to all of them, I said the same thing.

It was dark. There were two men. Maybe three. A dark-colored car. Maybe blue, maybe black. No license plate that I knew of.

And that was it.

Hours later, when they finally let me go, I took a deep breath and focused, then cut short my retirement and went back to work.

There's a saying that a little knowledge is a dangerous thing. Which was proved during the subsequent week when I went out hunting. I had a little knowledge, of two men's faces and the car they drove and the license plate it bore, and after several days of phone calls, meetings in bars and restaurants, of money being paid off in plain brown envelopes and favors being arranged, I ended up with two names and two addresses.

So the little knowledge did indeed prove dangerous.

But not to me.

When my work was finally done, I slept nearly a day and then took a short drive into Porter, finally to see my sister.

She was in a hospital bed on the third floor, looking as cheerful as one would expect under the circumstances. One leg—the left one, which had received a flesh wound—was bandaged and hanging from one of those torture devices that pretend to be medical equipment. She smiled when I came into the room and winced as she shifted in the bed. She had on one of those ugly hospital johnnies, and the day's *Boston Globe* was scattered over the bedding.

"How are you doing?" I asked, taking a chair near the bed.

"Better," she said. "My leg's doing fine, and my ribs are healing up. The vest is a wonderful thing, except afterwards it feels like someone took a baseball bat to me."

"You're right, but think of the alternatives."

She stuck her tongue out at me. "I'd rather not."

I looked around the room. She had a private room, which I had arranged for, and the windowsill was jammed full of flowers and cards. The television set was on without any sound, and the sun was shining through the tall windows. Even wired up to the bed and with bandages and hospital clothes, she looked great.

She looked down at her hands and then looked up at me and said, "Jason . . ."

"Yes?"

"Thanks."

"For what?"

She wadded up a piece of tissue and tossed it at me. "You know what for. Thanks for not losing your head and for using my radio. The docs told me that I had lost a lot of blood. A few more minutes . . . well, a few more minutes might have made things more interesting. Thanks for not letting things get interesting."

"You're welcome."

"And one more thing."

"Yes?"

Lynn took a breath, winced again. "I said some things last week. Things that weren't fair to you, things that were hurtful."

"Look, you had a right—"

"No, just let me finish. I said some hurtful things,

and I just want to say, please, forget it ever happened. All right? Let's . . . let's just go from here, brother and sister, and enjoy each other's company. I'm glad you're back from California. It's going to be good to have you around."

"No longer a roadblock?"

"Hardly."

I smiled at her. Suddenly, my shoulders felt light indeed. "Then you've got a deal."

"Then why don't you give your sister a hug? And don't break any more ribs in the process."

Which is what I did. I gave her a gentle squeeze and kissed her on the cheek, and as I stepped back, I glanced down at the *Globe*. At the Metro page, a story about two men with long criminal records who had been mysteriously murdered, the same night and only a few hours apart. Two men who had been friends, who were suspects in several crimes, and whose deaths were a puzzle.

Then Lynn noticed that I had seen the story, and she looked up at me and smiled and winked and said, "Thanks, Jay-Jay."

I nodded back. "You're welcome, Lynn-Lynn."

The
Haggard Society

Edward D. Hoch

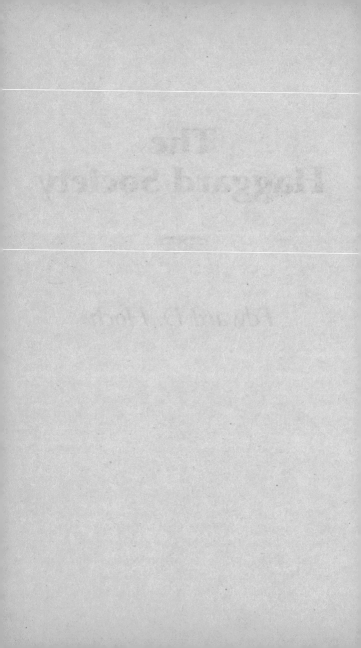

The first time Jean Forsyth heard of the Haggard Society, she was at her desk at the radio station, checking the advertising log for the previous night, trying to establish whether they needed to schedule make-goods on any of the thirty-second spots that were supposed to run during the baseball game. As always, a loudspeaker carried the station's current programming to every office in the building, and though it could be turned off if necessary, none of the people in the billing department was ever brave enough to do it.

So Jean heard the brief public service announcement along with everyone else: "Tonight's monthly meeting of the Haggard Society has been rescheduled for tomorrow evening at eight o'clock at Fenley Hall. The guest speaker will be Eugene Forsyth."

Jean turned to the young woman in the next cubicle. "Marge, what's the Haggard Society?"

"Beats me. I never heard of them before. Maybe

one of those self-help programs. Why the sudden interest?"

"Their guest speaker is my brother. I haven't seen him in two years. I didn't even know he was back in town."

"Maybe it's just someone else with the same name."

"Maybe," Jean agreed. But there couldn't be that many Eugene Forsyths around these days. Her brother was three years older than she, and all through their growing-up years he'd resisted using "Gene" as a nickname because it would be confused with her name, something that had never occurred to their parents when they were christened. Eugene had gone off to college in Ohio when he was eighteen, then dropped out after a couple of years. He told them if he worked a year and established residence there, he could attend Ohio State at a lower tuition. But he never went back, and his letters home became less frequent.

Two years ago, Jean had gone out to Cleveland where he was living. Their parents had moved to Florida, and it was a summer when she was feeling especially lonesome. She wanted to see Eugene, to establish the old ties that had withered since he left home. He had an apartment in an older part of the city, an area that had once been middle-class but was now on the fringes of poverty. From his window, Jean could see drugs being sold openly on the street corner.

Eugene professed to have a job as a camp counselor, but it was the middle of July, and he didn't seem to be working at all. She didn't ask him too much about it. After three days, she cut short her visit and returned home. She hadn't seen him since, and her trip to Cleveland didn't even prompt a Christmas card.

Now, if this was really him, he was speaking to something called the Haggard Society. Jean thought about that, wondering if it might be an organization of sickly folk. Might her brother have AIDS? She considered phoning their mother in Florida but decided that would accomplish nothing. First, she should go to the meeting and see for herself if it was really him.

Fenley Hall had been known originally as the Labor Lyceum, a meeting place for union members during the 1930s and the postwar years. The neighborhood had changed during the '60s, and it became less expensive for unions to rent a party house when they needed to hold a rally or take a vote. The Labor Lyceum became simply Fenley Hall, named after some forgotten politician. It was rented now for wedding receptions, political rallies, and various lecture series.

When Jean Forsyth arrived shortly before eight o'clock, the first thing she saw was her brother's picture out front on a sign advertising the event: "The Haggard Society presents a talk by Eugene Forsyth followed by an open discussion. Admission free!" He looked older with glasses and a mustache, but it was clearly Eugene. The hall itself was about half full, with more than a hundred people seated on the folding chairs provided for the occasion. One or two appeared to be street people merely looking for a place to sleep, but most were young or middle-aged and middle-class. Some walked to the front of the hall, where a slender black-haired woman was accepting books that they returned. Jean almost asked a man seated ahead of her what the purpose of the society was but decided she might appear either flirtatious or stupid. Besides, she would know soon enough.

Promptly at eight o'clock, the black-haired woman walked onto the stage and lit a single candle by the rostrum. She was quite slim, and her makeup seemed too severe for the occasion, whatever that might be. "Good evening, ladies and gentlemen, and welcome to the July meeting of the Haggard Society. I am Antonia Grist. As most of you know, we gather here monthly to discuss our mutual interests. We were hoping tonight to hear from one of the newer members of our group, Eugene Forsyth, but he is indisposed. We plan to reschedule his talk very shortly. Instead, may I present my husband and president of the Haggard Society, Martin Grist."

The audience applauded politely, and Jean half rose from her seat, ready to leave. Then she abruptly changed her mind. Since she'd come this far, she might as well learn the nature of the group and possibly something of her brother's involvement.

Grist was slender, like his wife, with a lined middle-aged face and thinning hairline. He crossed to the microphone with a purposeful stride. "Thank you, Antonia," he said in a surprisingly deep voice. "I am hardly a replacement for Mr. Forsyth, whom we hope to have with us at a future meeting, but I'll do the best I can. I apologize in advance to those of you who have already heard my views on this subject."

He paused for a drink of water and then continued. "She Who Must Be Obeyed is H. Rider Haggard's greatest creation, a woman at once beautiful, erotic, headstrong, and selfish, cruel to her enemies yet tender to her lovers. Ever since her first appearance in Haggard's 1886 novel *She,* readers have found her as irresistible as she is deadly. I first came upon Haggard's writings when I stumbled onto a well-thumbed copy of *King Solomon's Mines* in my high school library . . ."

Jean could hardly believe her ears. It was a literary society devoted to the writings of a British author from the last century! And her brother, who'd hardly finished a book in his life, had been scheduled to speak there. She began to think there was some mistake. Surely, this was a different Eugene Forsyth, despite the picture out front.

Martin Grist droned on for some thirty-five minutes, covering H. Rider Haggard's life and works in the most general way. Jean, who'd read a couple of the books during her teens, remembered them as being more exciting than the talk, which Grist finished by recalling the novel's most vivid image. "It is fire," he told his audience, "the Flame of Life that is supposed to bring immortality but instead brings only a withering, terrible death."

There was polite applause as Grist concluded his talk and asked for questions. One man inquired about the possible value of a first edition of *She.* "There was a misprint in the first issue of the first British edition," Grist explained. "Line thirty-eight, page 269, has 'Godness me' instead of 'Goodness me.' That version is valued at around six hundred dollars. The corrected version is worth only half as much."

A woman asked about Haggard's early adult years

in Africa and the long-rumored affairs with native women. Grist seemed a bit taken aback by the question. "We don't go into those matters here," he replied. "This is strictly a literary society."

It was the answer rather than the question that caused Jean to turn in her seat and look at the woman, seated three rows behind her. She was in her twenties, brown-haired and wearing pink-rimmed eyeglasses. She'd stood up to ask her question. Unsatisfied with Grist's response, she continued standing and said, "I have one more question."

Martin Grist seemed momentarily taken aback, and his wife suddenly appeared onstage. But before she could reach the microphone, the young woman asked, "Why wasn't Eugene Forsyth allowed to speak tonight?"

"Mr. Forsyth was taken ill," Grist answered.

His wife grabbed the microphone and said quickly, "That concludes our program for this evening. Because of the shortened nature of tonight's meeting, we will try to schedule another program shortly. If you wish to be notified of it, please leave your name and address on the pad by the door. As usual, we also have some hardcover editions of Haggard's novels for those who would like to borrow them till the next meeting."

There was an immediate hum of conversation from the crowd, and Jean sensed that the abrupt ending was most unusual. A dozen or so people came forward to accept the proffered books, doled out by Mrs. Grist from two piles, while the rest of the audience filed out. Jean hurried to the front of the hall and requested a copy of *She*. "Excuse me," she said to Grist's wife.

"I'm Eugene Forsyth's sister. I came to hear his talk. Where is he?"

That stopped her momentarily. "I know nothing of your brother," she said. "He was taken ill minutes before his talk and left the hall."

"You must have his address."

Her husband had gone on ahead, but now he returned to grip her arm. "Come, Antonia."

She looked into Jean's eyes and said simply, "I can't help you." Then they were gone.

Jean looked around with a feeling of helplessness. Most of the audience was gone, but the young woman in the pink-rimmed glasses was still there, watching her. Perhaps she had overheard part of the conversation. Jean strode across the hall to join her. "You're the one who asked the question about Eugene," she said. "I think he's my brother."

The woman put a hand to her mouth. "I'm worried about him."

"What's the matter? Where is he? What's happened to him?"

She glanced around nervously. "Look, I can't talk here. Meet me at the coffee bar on the corner in ten minutes. Turn left, and cross the street."

"All right," Jean said. The young woman hurried away without giving her name.

Jean left a moment later, lingering along the dark street to gaze casually into lighted shop windows. She was almost to the corner when she heard a woman's scream and the thump of metal against flesh. Someone yelled, and two or three people nearby turned and ran. Jean reached the corner and saw them standing by a fallen figure on the pavement.

"What happened?" she asked a man.

"Car hit her. I just caught a glimpse of it. He didn't even stop."

"Did anyone get his license number?" somebody else asked, but no one answered.

Jean saw the pink-framed glasses on the street by the body. "Is she—?"

"Someone call nine-one-one, but I don't think it'll do much good."

She didn't wait for the ambulance and police to arrive but hurried away from there. Whatever was happening, whatever it meant, was a threat to her. More especially, it seemed to be a threat to her brother Eugene. Something had happened to him, but she couldn't bring herself to think about that. The young woman in the pink-framed glasses had suspected as much, or she wouldn't have asked that question at the close of the meeting.

Jean hurried home to her apartment, parking the car in its usual place and ducking in the side door. The accident she'd almost witnessed had unnerved her, possibly because it might not have been an accident. A car had hit the woman and then sped off in the night. Did such things happen as a rule? Wasn't it far more likely that an innocent motorist would have stopped and tried to help the victim?

On the eleven o'clock television news, a report of the fatal accident was in the second spot, right after a fire in a pizza parlor across town. Police were seeking the driver of the vehicle, and the victim's name was being withheld pending notification of next of kin. She read the following morning's paper at work over coffee, as was her custom. The dead woman was now identified as Amanda Burke, an unmarried librarian employed at the main library downtown. That might explain her interest in H. Rider Haggard, but it didn't explain her connection with Jean's brother, if there was one.

On her lunch hour, she walked the few blocks across town from the radio station to the main library, dodging fire engines on the way. It was a new four-story building with a glass-topped atrium that flooded the place with subdued sunlight. Amanda Burke had worked in the literature division, and Jean headed there at once. She identified herself to the librarian at the desk and said, "I met Amanda Burke last evening shortly before her terrible accident. I wonder if you could tell me something about her."

The woman stared at Jean as if she were from another planet. "You're a radio reporter, did you say?"

"No, no, I just work at the station. I—it's very important for me to learn what I can about Amanda. I believe she was a friend of my missing brother."

The woman hesitated and then said, "Mark Jessup knew her. He might be able to tell you something."

She rang him on the phone, and after a few moments, a tall, angular young man joined them at the desk. "Hi, I'm Mark Jessup. Can I help you?"

"I wanted to ask you about Amanda Burke."

He led her over to some chairs near the window. "Amanda was a wonderful young woman. We're all still in shock over the accident."

"I almost saw it happen," Jean explained. "I'd just met her, and she wanted to talk further about my brother."

"What's his name?"

"Eugene Forsyth."

He nodded. "She's mentioned someone named Eugene. I kidded her about having a boyfriend, and she didn't deny it."

"I'm afraid something bad has happened to my brother, but I don't know what." She gave a little laugh. "I know it's crazy to be concerned, when I don't even know where he's been for the past two years."

"Have you seen him lately?"

She shook her head. "Just his picture at a meeting of the Haggard Society."

"That's where you met Amanda?" Jessup asked.

Jean nodded. "My brother was supposed to speak there, and I went to hear him. They said he'd been taken ill, but Amanda questioned that from the floor. The people running the meeting, Martin Grist and his wife, abruptly ended it."

"Strange."

"What do you know about the Haggard Society?"

"Not a great deal. Grist's wife brings flyers around to leave at our information desk downstairs whenever they're having a meeting."

"Did Amanda have a family?"

"In New York, I think. They've been notified."

She looked into his face and decided he was a man she could trust. "Could you let me know if anything turns up among her possessions here at the library? Especially anything about my brother? Here, I'll write down my home phone number."

He took it from her with a smile. "I'm sure he'll turn up, but if I hear anything, I'll let you know."

In the days that followed, it was as if the events involving the Haggard Society had never taken place.

Jean thought about it constantly, her mind dwelling on the picture of her brother every time she picked up the borrowed copy of *She* and read a few pages. There was no listing for the society in the phone book, and when she dialed a number for the only Martin Grist listed, there was never an answer.

One day she found herself back at the library, and Mark Jessup helped her search through the computer database for some mention of the Haggard group. "Not a thing except the dates of their meetings," Jessup told her, swinging the computer screen around so she could view the listings for herself.

"What about Fenley Hall?" she suggested. "Somebody must own it. They must rent it for their meetings."

"Good idea," he said, smiling at her. "I'll check on it."

But the following day, when she came again on her lunch hour, the news was gloomy. "The owner of Fenley Hall is in New York," Mark told her. "They know nothing about the society except that it's a literary group. They rent the hall for the third Wednesday of every month and pay in advance. Occasionally, someone calls to arrange an additional meeting."

She was discouraged by the news, another dead end, and perhaps that was why he invited her out to dinner that night. The idea cheered her, and it was not until they were starting dessert at a small Italian restaurant near the library that she suddenly blurted out, "This is like a date!"

Mark grinned at her across the table. "Sure. What's wrong with that?"

For the first time, she really looked at him. He wore

his sandy hair a bit long, and when he smiled, he had tiny dimples in his cheeks. She guessed him to be in his late twenties, about her own age. He was of medium build, tall but hardly athletic. "How did you happen to become a librarian?" she asked, trying to steer the conversation away from dating.

"I was recruited by Longyear Corporation just out of college. They had quite a corporate library and wanted me to run it. I always liked books, so I let them pay for my librarian's degree. Right after I got it, the company downsized, and I was out on the street. I was a librarian without a library, so I went to work for the city."

"That's where you met Amanda?"

He nodded. "A swell girl. If she was deliberately killed—"

"What about my brother? You said she mentioned his name, but you never met him."

"I think he brought in flyers for patrons to pick up, the way Mrs. Grist does. That's how Amanda met him."

After dinner, Mark walked her the few blocks to her apartment but declined an invitation to come up. Later, when she was alone, she thought about the evening and decided she liked him. When he phoned her at the radio station the following day, she was almost pleased. "How's business at the library today?" she asked.

"Fine. I have some news for you. I thought you'd want to know Mrs. Grist stopped by with another stack of announcements. The Haggard Society is holding a special meeting on Thursday, and your brother is listed as the speaker."

"My God! I have to go!"

"That's not all. I was on the information desk when she came in, and I told her we had new regulations. Anyone leaving material for distribution at the library had to give us the address of the organization. She grumbled a bit, but she gave it to me. They're out on Willow Terrace."

"That's a residential street."

"It must be where she and her husband are living now."

"I'm going there after work," Jean decided.

"Not alone! Remember what happened to Amanda."

"I'll be all right."

"Let me drive you out. They won't try anything with me along."

She had to agree it might be safer. "All right. I get finished here at five."

Promptly at five o'clock, Mark was waiting in the parking lot. "I managed to get out a bit early," he said, passing her the Haggard Society announcement on pink paper.

"You have the Grists' address?" she asked grimly.

"Right here." He showed her the slip of paper.

"Let's go talk to them."

The house was a modern colonial with a wide driveway and two-car garage. Mark Jessup parked in front of it just as Grist himself emerged to check the mailbox. He seemed none too happy to see them, but Mark had already called out his name before he could retreat inside the house. "What is it?" he asked. "I'm a busy man."

"I know Mrs. Grist from the library," Mark quickly explained. "My friend here, Jean Forsyth, wants to ask you about her brother."

Martin Grist peered at her, squinting as if the sun bothered his eyes. "You're Eugene's sister? Weren't you at our last meeting?"

"That's right. I haven't seen him in some time, and I'm anxious about him."

"He'll be speaking again on Thursday night. You can see him then." He turned back toward the door.

"But—"

"I'm sorry. I have no time now."

Jean was not to be put off so easily. She followed him up to the door and might have continued inside, but suddenly the entry was blocked by Mrs. Grist. "Go away!" she commanded. "We don't want you here. My husband and I are very busy."

Mark hurried up to Jean's side. "Come on. We can't learn anything here."

Reluctantly, she allowed herself to be led back to the car. Both the Grists had disappeared into the house and closed the door. "That was a waste of time," she grumbled.

They drove back to the station parking lot where she'd left her car. She felt somehow she should repay him for the time he'd spent going out there with her. "I've got some pasta at home if you'd like to join me for a light supper. It's not much, but—"

"I love all sorts of pasta," he insisted.

"Then come along. Follow me in your car. You know where I live."

It proved to be the most pleasant evening Jean had spent in some time, enough to make her forget the growing concern for her brother. More than that, Mark was a perfect gentleman, ending the evening with a chaste good-night kiss as he left the apartment. She watched at the window as he drove away, against a night sky lit by a distant fire, perhaps in a warehouse across town.

Rather than face the dirty dishes in the morning, Jean tackled them right away, bundling up the rest of the rubbish to drop down the incinerator chute in the hallway. By the time she'd finished and was walking back along the darkened hall to her apartment, she decided she was ready for bed. Glancing at her watch, she saw it was already a few minutes after midnight.

That was when a hand darted out from the shadows and closed over her mouth as another pinned her arms. "Don't scream," a voice whispered in her ear.

She felt a rush of terror and then a soothing recognition.

It was her brother Eugene.

"You've changed," she said when they were back in her apartment with the door safely shut. She'd poured them each a glass of wine. "You're looking a bit like our father these days."

The young man seated opposite her, barely past thirty, wore dark-framed eyeglasses and a neat mustache that combined to make him seem older. "I hope not," he said with a smile. For just an instant, he was the brother she remembered and loved from her youth, and then the vision faded, and he was this stranger who had entered her life.

"Where have you been, Eugene? I haven't heard from you in two years."

"I've been working here and there," he answered with a shrug. "Sometimes it was difficult to keep in touch."

"I never would have found you if I hadn't heard about your lecture. Are you living in town?"

"I'm here for a while," he said, keeping it vague.

"That woman Amanda, the one who was killed by the car—"

"What about her?"

"She seemed worried about you. At the end of Martin Grist's talk, she asked why you hadn't been allowed to speak."

"That was a misunderstanding. I was taken ill at the last minute."

Suddenly, Jean doubted his words. "Did you cancel because you saw me in the audience?"

"No, no. I never looked at the audience. I just felt I couldn't go on."

"When did you develop this sudden interest in Haggard's books? I can't remember you being much of a reader."

"Dad didn't exactly encourage it, did he?"

She realized that his attitude hadn't really changed with the years. "He was a fireman, for God's sake! He was out earning the bread for our table. And it killed him in the end. Do you resent that, too?"

Eugene shrugged. "They gave him a nice funeral."

"Do you ever talk to Mom in Florida?"

"I don't have her address or phone number."

"I can give you both of them."

He sighed. "What am I supposed to say to her after all these years?"

"More than you're saying to me, I hope. Eugene, you come back into my life after two years, and you don't ring my bell or knock on my door. You grab me in the hallway and scare me half to death!"

"I'm sorry about that, sis."

"What about Amanda Burke?" she asked. "You knew her, didn't you?"

"Yes," he admitted. "We'd been dating a bit."

"Living together?"

"Not formally."

"Was she murdered?"

He turned his eyes away. "I don't know what happened out there. Anything's possible."

"Is that why you sneaked into my building, so you wouldn't be seen?"

He took a sip of wine and said, "Look, sis, you've been asking too many questions. You were out to the Grists' house today, and I saw you come up here with that fellow who worked with Amanda."

"You know Mark?"

"I saw him a couple of times at the library." For a moment, his face took on an anxious expression. "This isn't about him, it's about you. I don't want anything to happen to you."

"Like what happened to Amanda Burke?"

"This is serious business. Stay away from the meeting on Thursday."

"Do you really expect that of me? You're my brother, for God's sake! If you're in trouble, I want to help you."

"There's nothing you can do." He finished his wine and stood up.

"Eugene—"

"Good night, sis. Be careful crossing streets."

As he was at the door, she said, "I'll be there Thursday night. There's no keeping me away."

"I suppose not."

"Tell me one thing. What is the Haggard Society?"

He hesitated and then said, "Ask me that question at the meeting on Thursday."

Jean didn't mention her brother's visit when she met Mark Jessup for lunch the following day. She especially didn't want to tell him about Eugene's grabbing her in the hallway of her building. It made him sound a bit weird, and maybe he was. Maybe that's why he'd stayed away from her so long. Mark had the evening shift at the library that day, so she wouldn't be seeing him after work. Following a bit of casual banter, he asked, "Are you going to that meeting tomorrow night?"

"Of course. I have to see Eugene."

"I'm worried about you, Jean, after what happened to Amanda."

"I'll be careful crossing the street," she said with a smile, remembering her brother's warning.

"It's no joking matter. From what you've told me, I think her death is connected with your brother in some manner. You said she asked a question about him before she died, and now you've been asking questions about him. I'd feel better if I came with you tomorrow."

"All right," she agreed readily. She trusted Mark, and she was beginning to wonder about her brother.

"We can get something to eat after I finish work and then walk over to Fenley Hall together."

That night, when she arrived home from the station, Jean was careful to glance up and down her street, paying particular attention to parked cars. But they all seemed to be empty, and no one was lurking in doorways. She went upstairs to put a frozen dinner in the microwave.

Thursday was drizzly with rain, the sort of day Jean would rather have stayed in bed. Her clock radio was always tuned to the station for which she worked, and the first sounds she usually heard in the morning were the jovial banter of their weatherman and the news anchor at seven o'clock. This day was no different. The weather always came first in the morning, because they figured that was what people most wanted to know about at the beginning of the new day. Then there was the traffic report and finally the morning's top story, an overnight fire in a suburban strip mall. Jean slipped out from between the sheets and padded into the bathroom.

While she was brushing her teeth, she suddenly remembered Eugene and the meeting of the Haggard Society that evening. Because she was meeting Mark for dinner first, she wore one of her better dresses, prompting Heather at the desk next to her to speculate, "Heavy date tonight?"

"I'm going to hear my brother speak at a literary society."

Heather groaned. "Sounds dull. What is it, the Jane Austen Society?"

"H. Rider Haggard."

"Does anyone still read the old boy?" she asked.

"Apparently. They loan out copies of his novels at each meeting."

Heather grunted. "What was that one where the woman burned to death at the end?"

"You probably mean *She,* but the flames simply withered her, destroying her immortality. I know because I just read it again."

She gave Jean a pitying look. "Well, enjoy yourself."

When she and Mark arrived at Fenley Hall around a quarter to eight, the place was already half full. Mrs. Grist was up front wearing a long black dress with wide, full sleeves. She was doing some early book collecting, and Jean returned her copy without comment. Some readers were continuing with the story, she noticed, borrowing copies of *Ayesha,* the first sequel to *She.* There was no sign of Eugene anywhere, and she settled down to wait.

This time, it was Martin Grist who strode to the podium promptly at eight o'clock. "Ladies and gentlemen, welcome to this special meeting of the Haggard Society. Those of you who still have books to return or exchange can bring them up to my wife after our program. We're very pleased this evening to offer the delayed talk by Haggard expert Eugene Forsyth. Mr. Forsyth established the first Haggard site on the Internet. He'll tell us about that experience, as well as the joys and sorrows of reading and collecting the works of H. Rider Haggard. Please give a warm greeting to Eugene Forsyth."

For the occasion, Eugene had dressed in an open khaki jacket such as Haggard's hero Alan Quatermain might have worn while searching for King Solomon's mines. "Is that your brother?" Mark whispered beside her.

"That's him." Until this moment, she hadn't really expected him to appear. Now he seemed like a different person as he stood behind the lectern speaking of those century-old books.

". . . Those of you who know Alan Quatermain only from *King Solomon's Mines* and its sequels may be surprised to learn that Haggard brought his two most famous creations together in the 1920 novel entitled *She and Alan.* This book is set shortly before the events recounted in *She*. . . ." As he spoke, her mind flew back to childhood days, to the shock of their father's death. Perhaps he'd changed after that, but how? One of the great mysteries of recent years had been her inability to come to grips with the truth about Eugene. That, she supposed, was why he'd remained so distant from her. ". . . If Haggard was never truly a great novelist, he was certainly a great storyteller, making up for weak characterizations and an occasionally irritating style with authentic backgrounds and an exciting imagination. . . ."

He told about his Haggard site on the Internet, which had brought him in contact with Martin and Antonia Grist. Then he concluded by saying, "I can take questions for fifteen or twenty minutes, if you care to ask any."

A man on the other side of the hall raised his hand and asked, "Is it true that Haggard was knighted in England for his adventure novels?"

Eugene smiled. "If only it were so! He received his knighthood for his studies of British agriculture and land utilization."

Jean raised her hand, but he called on someone else first. "What are you going to ask?" Mark whispered.

"You'll see."

This time, Eugene pointed to her. "The young lady there."

She stood up, making eye contact with him for the first time since he began his talk. "What is the Haggard Society?" she asked in a clear voice.

Eugene leaned both hands on the podium and smiled. It was as if he'd been waiting a long time for this moment. "The Haggard Society is a criminal conspiracy to provide arson for hire, using anonymous agents to carry out contracts arranged by Martin Grist and his wife."

Antonia Grist's hand appeared from the wide sleeve of her dress, holding a small automatic pistol. She raised it toward Eugene, but suddenly two men from the front row were upon her. Someone blew a police whistle, and all at once the Haggard Society was in the hands of its enemies.

It was a long night after that. When Eugene finally joined Jean and Mark at police headquarters, she almost sobbed with relief. "I thought—"

"I'm sorry to have made it all so mysterious, sis," he said as he hugged her. "It was important to get those people, especially after they killed Amanda. She thought they'd done something to me when I didn't speak at the last meeting. When she asked that question, it made Grist's wife nervous. As they were leaving in their car, they saw Amanda crossing the nearly deserted street, and Antonia ran her down. They claim it wasn't premeditated, but everything else they did was."

"You're with the police?" she asked.

Her brother nodded. "More or less. I'm an undercover arson investigator. It all started in Ohio when I took that year off from college. The Haggard Society was operating there at the time, and the police needed someone young to infiltrate them. I established the Haggard Internet site and tried to make myself visible enough so they'd contact me. It didn't work at first, because they were frightened off and moved here. Pretty soon, this city had a marked increase in arson fires, and the police asked me to keep up the Haggard business on the Internet. I finally managed to get a rise out of Grist. I came to see him, and the Ohio police loaned me out to the department here. At first, I still couldn't figure out exactly what was happening, except that a large number of fires were being triggered by identical incendiary devices."

"So the interest in Haggard was all a cover?" Mark asked.

"On their part and mine, too. I met Amanda one day while I was doing Haggard research at the library. I never thought I'd be putting her in any sort of danger. They must have started to suspect me, or they never would have killed her like that."

"But how was the society linked with the arsons?" Jean asked.

"They recruited a number of people willing to take part in the conspiracy. Most of them were arrested tonight. They attended the meetings, and if they were willing to earn money for starting a fire, they came up before or after the program and accepted a book from Mrs. Grist. Strangers got real books, conspirators received hollowed-out volumes containing an incendiary device, the address of the target, the best time for the job, and the necessary payment."

"They were paid before they did the job?"

"Oh, they went through with it, if they ever wanted another job. It was a perfect setup, really. The property owners, or whoever was paying for the arson, arranged for an alibi. They never knew who did it, and the actual arsonist didn't know who'd ordered the job. You know it was successful when you think about the number of fires this city's been having lately."

Jean remembered the television reports and the red skies in the nighttime. She even remembered Mrs. Grist lighting a candle before each meeting. It was all about fire, like the flame that destroyed She Who Must Be Obeyed. "Why did you cancel your talk two weeks ago?"

"I was going to use the talk to spring a trap on the conspirators, as I did tonight, catching as many as possible with the hollowed-out books. At the last minute, some lab work wasn't ready, and we weren't ready to make an arrest. Rather than give the speech, I postponed it a couple of weeks so we could follow through with the original plan. We had a dozen men scattered through the audience, with uniformed officers outside."

He walked outside with them and lingered for a moment with Jean. "Mark seems like a nice guy."

"He is." There was something else she had to ask Eugene. "This undercover work—it was all because of what happened to our father, wasn't it?"

"I suppose so. I didn't much like him, growing up, but he died in a fire. To me, fire has always been the enemy."

"It was the Grists who were the enemy." She gave him a hug. "It's good to have you back."

Something Borrowed, Something Black

Loren D. Estleman

Lʼm back."

And almost before he had the door shut behind him, she was kissing him. He let the copy of the *Los Angeles Times* he'd been holding drop to the floor to free his hands.

Afterward, he slept while she ordered room service and sent the polite young Hispanic waiter off with a generous tip on top of the guaranteed fifteen-percent gratuity, then set out the breakfast things. Splurging thrilled her. Before Peter, she'd always had to budget carefully. There was much to be said for marrying a man who'd made enough from his own retail camera business to retire comfortably in his forties; there would be no arguments over money, and he wouldn't be working late when she wanted to prepare a candle-lit dinner for two.

Or so she guessed, for she actually knew very little about her husband of twenty-four—no, twenty-*five* hours. She wasn't even sure if he ate breakfast or what he liked. But he was sleeping so peacefully, making cute little noises when he inhaled, and she hadn't wanted to disturb him.

He was a very good-looking man, in a quiet, ordinary sort of way. Even the thinning of his dark hair at the temples became him. He kept in good condition—no bulging biceps or six-pack abs, but no spare tire, either, and he seldom winded. He dressed unobtrusively but in good taste, although she would do something about those plain white shirts and uninspired solid ties. Her girlfriends politely found him dull. It was true he didn't turn female heads when he entered a crowded room, but her father had, and his unwillingness to discourage what came after had led to her parents' divorce. Laurie had had her fill of flamboyant men at an early age. Life with Peter promised little adventure. That added to its appeal.

She woke him by stretching out full-length on top of him and kissing his eyes open. He smiled, then saw the breakfast cart and declared he was starving. As she sat opposite him in her new powder-blue satin robe, sipping coffee and watching him wolf down his steak and eggs, she thought about later, when there would be time to find out how he really felt about breakfast. She was a child of divorce and knew it was the little inconsequential things that mattered. They built and built and eventually exploded if left unaddressed.

She knew so little about Peter, yet he knew so much about her. Laurie was a chatterer, mercilessly mining her background for incidents with which to fill awkward silences. He knew she was twenty-three, that she'd grown up in a suburb of Dayton, spending her summers and then her life after age thirteen on the farm following her parents' breakup, and that she'd left home at eighteen to attend nursing classes at Ohio State, interning as a receptionist in a family practice center in Toledo. There she'd met Peter, who came in to have a suspicious mole removed, returned twice more for examinations, and came back a third time to ask the pretty blond receptionist to dinner. She'd liked his looks, his quiet manner, and—professional prejudice—the way he paid attention to his health and acted upon the messages his body sent him. She could not care about a man who did not care about himself. They were married six weeks later.

Her mother, still embittered, had not approved. She had been especially hostile toward her daughter's decision not to keep her maiden name. But Laurie believed in total commitment, and anyway, she had never liked having to spell the German surname for people and correct their pronunciation. It pleased her independent spirit, in these slavishly postfeminist times, to have personal stationery printed reading "Mrs. Peter Macklin."

She waited until he polished his plate with a triangle of toast, popped the morsel into his mouth, and pushed away the plate, then asked, "What are we going to do today?"

He smiled. He was not a dour man, but he smiled only when he was amused or pleased and never to be polite—another thing she adored about him, for it presented the challenge of earning that smile. "Well, I'd ask you what you want to do, but you'd follow up on it, and I'd end up dead."

"Stop pretending you're an old man. Can we rent a car? I want to drive up the coast. The closest I've ever been to an ocean is Lake Huron."

"I'll put the concierge on it as soon as I finish my coffee. We can have lunch in Santa Barbara. Five years ago, there was a great little seafood place built on a pier. Maybe it's still operating."

"What were you doing here five years ago?"

"Business. California goes through cameras like Detroit goes through tires." He opened the *Times*.

While he was reading, she showered and brushed her teeth. When she came out of the bathroom, he was on the telephone, the newspaper crumpled on the carpet beside his chair. He made a noise with his tongue against his teeth and banged down the receiver. "I've been on hold five minutes. I'll go down and talk to the concierge face-to-face." He rose and went out.

She worried a cuticle. Had she offended him earlier? No, Peter was no prude, she was certain of that. More likely, he was preoccupied. He was that way sometimes: here with her one moment, sweet, attentive, and then a hundred miles away the next, lost in his head. Yes, there were many things to learn.

She stooped to pick up the newspaper and place it on the table, pausing to read the headline on the front page of the second section when she spotted the word *Detroit*. She wondered if that had triggered Peter's preoccupation. Detroit was his home, the headquarters for the chain of camera stores he'd owned. Coming upon it out of context, he might have been reminded of old concerns. The headline itself—

"Detroit Crime Boss Faces Grand Jury Here"—was so remote as to be harmless.

When he returned, he was as he had been before, tender and playful. He showered and forty-five minutes later, they were in the bucket seats of an apple-green Camaro convertible, fighting their way out of the valley traffic and beyond the smog, where they could put the top down and be like Cary Grant and Deborah Kerr. (Laurie was addicted to AMC.)

The morning was overcast, but after they had eaten a rather disappointing lunch in Santa Barbara, where the restaurant Peter remembered had changed hands and slipped downhill, the sun came out. By the time they turned back toward L.A., the rays were canting between orange and purple clouds in one of those heart-wrenching sunsets peculiar to the poisonous atmosphere of Southern California. Laurie, a former recording secretary of her high school environmental group, was too drunk on the violet beauty of the Pacific to care. She was on her honeymoon in a fairy-tale place with a man who, she was amused and delighted to learn, would cross two lanes to avoid hitting a soporific sea gull dozing on the asphalt.

"Oh, Mr. Macklin."

The desk clerk, a Hispanic not much older than their waiter of the morning but considerably more polished, handed Peter a message scribbled on hotel stationery. Peter read it, glanced toward the pink light of the bar, then kissed Laurie.

"Someone's waiting for me. I'll be up in a little while."

"Is she pretty?" She made it sound teasing. A small, cold fist had closed in her stomach.

"It's a he, and he isn't even handsome. We used to do business. I'm afraid I have to be polite."

He kissed her again and left, wearing the same expression he'd had on that morning when she came out of the bathroom.

Upstairs, she put on one of the nightgowns she'd bought for the honeymoon, dusty pink and weighing no more than an ounce, and slipped into bed. She intended to sit up, but the long drive and the sea air had had its effect, and she fell asleep.

She woke at dawn, alone in the room. His side of the bed was still made. The message light on the telephone was flashing.

"One message, Mrs. Macklin, from Mr. Macklin." It sounded like the same young man at the desk. "Shall I send it up?"

"No, open it and read it." Her knuckles were white on the cord wound around her hand.

"'Darling,'" read the clerk, "'A legal matter has come up over the sale of my business. I'll meet you in the dining room at eleven. Love, Peter.'"

She hung up without thanking the young man. What kind of legal matter kept a retired man out all night? She wondered if the *he* really was a he. She cried for a while. Then she decided to stop behaving like a child bride and called room service.

After breakfast, she put on slacks, a light top, and flats and walked up Sunset. In a china shop, she bought a soup tureen with a Mexican sunrise enameled on the lid—a present for her mother—and arranged to ship it east. By then, her mood was improving. On the way back to the hotel, she gave a street vendor a dollar for a map to the stars' homes.

A few minutes before eleven, a bald, brown-faced waiter seated her in the casual dining room. She explained that she was waiting for someone, ordered iced tea, and unfolded the map. She'd bought it as a joke, but she was seriously considering pestering Peter to accompany her on a bus tour as punishment for his neglecting her when she noted a newcomer entering.

He was absurdly tall, with most of his height in his long legs, encased in stiff new blue jeans that crinkled behind the knees when he walked. The heels on his cowboy boots—some kind of lizard skin, dyed bright red, with glossy black wing tips—added three inches he didn't need, and the crown of his cream-colored Stetson nearly brushed the hanging ferns as he crossed the room. He wore a calico shirt with pearl snaps, and his tan throat looked naked without a kerchief tied around it. Laurie was so absorbed in the ludicrous ensemble, she didn't realize the man was heading her way until he stopped in front of her table and swept his hat off.

"Miz Macklin?"

She hesitated. He had straw-colored hair, pale blue eyes, and a long, rectangular jaw that slid sideways when he smiled, like a cow chewing. "Yes?"

"Pleased to make your acquaintance, ma'am. I'm Roy Landis—*Le*roy, actually—but you don't have to bother with that. Folks generally call me Abilene." He unsnapped the flap on a shirt pocket, took out a square of folded paper, and thrust it at her. "This should do the trick."

She unfolded the paper. She recognized her husband's handwriting, neat, without flourishes.

> Darling,
>   The legal thing is more involved than I thought. This will introduce Abilene, an old friend, who will keep you company until I can get away. You can rely on him for anything you need.
>
> Love,
Peter

Her eyes stung, but she took her time refolding the note and opening her handbag and slipping it inside, and when she looked back up, there were no tears. She smiled politely. "Thank you, Mr. Abilene—"

"Just Abilene."

"I'm comfortable alone. I'll just wait for Peter, and you can go on about your business."

"Excuse me, ma'am, but you're my business. L.A.'s a tricky place till you get used to it. I been out here ten years, and I got a good car. Take you anyplace you want to go, and you won't even have to talk to me if you don't want to."

"You're a professional escort?"

His smile became a grin. There was no leer in it. "Call me what you want, but call me Abilene if you expect me to answer."

"How long have you known my husband?"

"Three, four years. I get things done around here for Mr. Major. Every time Peter's in town, I take him around."

"Is Mr. Major an associate of Peter's?"

"Yes, ma'am. They go clear back to Detroit, before Mr. Major came out here."

"Does Mr. Major sell cameras?"

"Mr. Major sells everything."

"Sit down, please, Abilene."

He pulled out a chair, sat, and leaned down to stand his hat on its crown on the floor.

"Texas or Kansas? I can't place your accent, and I've seen every western ever made."

"Arkansas. Little nothing town called Blytheville. You never heard of it. I ain't been back in twenty-five years."

He was older than she'd thought. There were hairline creases around his eyes, which were nearly as pale as the whites. "And where were you in between Blytheville and Los Angeles?"

"You call it. Chicago, Vegas, Miami, Atlantic City. Wherever there was doing to be done."

A waitress brought Laurie's iced tea. She ordered the breast of chicken and offered the menu to Abilene, who glanced at it and surrendered it. "Steak sandwich for me, ma'am, rare as it comes, with a shot of rye. And bring me the bill."

"That isn't necessary," Laurie said.

"Mr. Major's orders."

When the waitress left, Laurie asked, "What business can Peter have with Mr. Major now? He says it's something legal."

"He said that?" The grin broadened. "Well, I wouldn't know. I'm just one of the injuns."

Over lunch, Abilene confessed he'd worked as an extra in a Clint Eastwood film: "Mr. Majors had an investment." Laurie's glance fell to the map folded on the table. "Do you know the way to Harrison Ford's house?" she asked.

"I don't keep up since they stopped making westerns. I can show you where Joel McCrea used to live, and Randolph Scott."

"You like old movies?"

"If there's horses and guns."

She didn't know if it was anger at Peter or delight at the absurdity of the man, but she touched his wrist. "Abilene, I think this is the beginning of a beautiful friendship."

It was a good day, although it would have been better with Peter. Abilene, who really did know his way around, took her to the Chinese Theater (where she stood in Jean Harlow's footprints while her escort measured his boots against John Wayne's), pointed out Tom Mix's old house, and drove her to a canyon in Malibu where silent westerns were shot. Abilene drove a black Jeep Grand Cherokee with a chromed custom exhaust system that gleamed like his boots. They had dinner at a place where the stars no longer came and returned to the hotel, where there was no word from Peter. At the elevators, she turned to thank Abilene.

"Juarez tomorrow," he said. "Show you where Will Rogers went to get laid. It's a fudge factory now."

"Thank you, but I'm sure Peter will be back by morning." She was suddenly very tired. She had had enough of her escort's good ole boy chatter for one day.

SOMETHING BORROWED, SOMETHING BLACK

"I'll call you at eight. Just in case he isn't."

He was still standing there wearing his lopsided grin when the doors closed.

On her floor, she rummaged through her handbag and realized she'd left the key in the room. Wearily, she rode the elevator down to the lobby, where a different clerk gave her another. She turned away— and stopped when she saw Abilene's lanky frame stretched out in a club chair. He lifted his Stetson off his nose to look at her, then resettled it.

She hovered, undecided whether to approach him. In the end, the hat was too much of a barrier. She went back up.

She double-locked the door and put on the chain. Quickly, she undressed and got into her simple cotton shift, the one she'd wondered if she'd have use for on the trip. In bed, she thought. Did he imagine he was protecting her? Maybe he lived too far away to bother going home if he were planning to look in on her in the morning. Either way, he'd passed beyond what even a brand new husband would expect of the friend he'd asked to entertain his wife in his absence. Was she being stalked? More than ever, she wished Peter were there.

The telephone woke her. She hadn't realized she'd slept. Light was coming in around the heavy curtains on the window. The digital clock on the nightstand read 7:59.

"Miz Macklin?"

"Abilene." She'd hoped it was Peter.

"What do you say we strap on the nosebag downstairs and get an early start on Juarez?"

"I have a headache. If you don't mind, I'd like to

233

stay in the room today. Anyway, Peter might come back or call."

"I can fetch you some aspirin. These hotel folks'll sock you ten bucks for a teeny bottle."

"No, I just need rest."

The pause on the other end was just long enough to notice. "I'll call you later."

An hour later, dressed and made up, she couldn't stand to spend another minute in the room. If she could get away for part of the day, visit a mall or something, she felt she could shake this sensation of being trapped. She considered, then decided against calling down for a cab; if Abilene were within earshot of the desk, he might overhear the call. Once outside the hotel, she would take a chance on flagging down a taxi.

On the ground floor, she stepped carefully out of the elevator, looking around. The chairs in the lobby were empty, the clerk behind the desk busy checking in a heavyset man in a suit wrinkled from travel. She started for the door—and withdrew behind a potted palm just as Abilene looked up from a display of neckties behind the glass wall of the gift shop. From there, he had a clear view of the main entrance on Sunset.

For a long moment she stood frozen, uncertain whether he'd seen her or where she should go from there. She and Peter had always used the main entrance. She hadn't got her bearings.

A carpeted hallway next to the elevators led to sunlight, perpendicular to the main lobby. She turned that way and followed it to a side door opening onto a one-way street. Just before she pushed through the door, she glanced back. No one was following.

She walked toward Sunset. It was a busy street; there were bound to be cabs. Twice she tried to hail one, but both times the cars cruised past, and she saw they had passengers. She kept looking back toward the building but saw only the bored-looking doorman in conversation with the bell captain.

At length, a canary-yellow Capri with a light on top swung into the curb, and the doorman opened the rear door to let out a woman in her fifties. While the driver was grappling a matched set of luggage out of the trunk, Laurie stepped toward the open door. A long arm reached past her and swung it shut.

"You can waste a lot of money on cabs in this town," Abilene said. "How's your head?"

He towered over her in a red and white yoke shirt, crisp black jeans, and glossy black boots with silver caps on the toes. Only the Stetson was the same. His crooked grin was bright against his clean-shaven jaw. He must have had a change of clothes in the Jeep and done his toilet in the men's room.

"Oh—much better." She tried to keep her face from turning red and knew by the heat in her cheeks how badly she'd failed. Her heart was hammering. "I thought I'd go shopping."

"My crate's out back. Where you want to go?"

"Please don't be offended. I'd rather be alone."

"No good. Something was to happen to you, I'd never hear the end of it from Mr. Major."

"You mean from Peter." When he didn't respond, she said, "I'm a nurse in training, Abilene. I've visited neighborhoods alone at night that make the worst in Los Angeles seem like Disneyland. I just want a day to myself."

"I'll keep my trap shut. You won't even know I'm around." His hand closed on her arm.

Laurie looked around. The doorman was holding the lobby door for the woman in her fifties. The cab driver, a husky black man with a gold earring, hesitated, then, when Abilene turned her away from the cab, got in and drove off. She thought, *I'm being kidnapped.* But she said nothing. She went with Abilene.

As they pulled away from the hotel, Laurie made a plan. It was probably unnecessary and would make her feel silly later, but she had begun to realize there was no talking to Abilene. She wondered how he and Peter had ever become friends. It was probably a business thing: win over the boss by becoming chummy with the help.

When Abilene stopped for the light at Western, she hit the door handle and pushed.

A hand shot out and grasped her wrist. It wasn't the polite hold of before; his fingers were strung with wire. When she resisted, pain shot up the bone. The light changed. They shot forward with a chirp of rubber. Still holding her with one hand, Abilene swung right around the corner from the inside lane, earning a chorus of horn blasts from other drivers, gunned the Jeep halfway up the block, and made a hard right into the parking lot of a 7-Eleven. He circled behind the building and braked just short of the cinderblock wall. A Dumpster on the right prevented Laurie's door from opening.

SOMETHING BORROWED, SOMETHING BLACK

She turned just in time to see the blur of his fist. A blue light burst. She fell back against the door; her head struck the window. Her mouth stung. She tasted salt and iron. When her vision cleared, Abilene's face was two inches from hers.

"This ain't the farm, Heidi. Mr. Major wants you kicking, but he didn't say you had to keep your teeth."

It took all her strength to force back a wave of hysteria. Her lip was puffing. She spoke slowly. "Who is Mr. Major?"

He slid a folded newspaper from its perch atop the sun visor and spread it on her lap. The only photo on the page showed a short, middle-aged man standing slightly hunched between two younger men carrying briefcases. "Carlo Maggiore, reputed former Detroit mobster, arrives at Superior Court," read the caption.

"You work for a gangster?"

"Don't look down on me. So does your husband."

"My husband is retired from the retail camera business."

The grin slid farther sideways. "He sold cameras, but just to police photographers. You might say he helped create the demand. Pete's a wet worker, little nursie. He kills to live."

"Why are you lying?" she said after a moment.

He pushed back his Stetson with a knuckle. "If I show you, you promise not to try and jump the fence? I'd hate to bust that cute little nose, smear it all over your face like a bad pepper."

"You can't show me what isn't true." She could see her reflection in the dead pale blue eyes. "I won't try anything."

He shifted into reverse. "There's Kleenexes in the glove compartment. We don't want you bleeding all over the police station."

The building looked familiar, but it wasn't until they'd parked around the corner and climbed the steps to the entrance that she placed it. It was Los Angeles City Hall, and she had seen it in every episode of *Dragnet* on Nick at Nite. The central tower, row upon unimaginative row of office windows, rose for eighteen stories above a neoclassical ground floor with marble arches in front. It even appeared on Joe Friday's badge.

Abilene gave his full name to the short-haired female officer at the front desk, who used the telephone, then told him to go on up. On the sixth floor, they entered a large room paved with desks, each equipped with a computer console. Abilene shook hands with a young man who rose from behind one of them and put on his suit coat before wishing Laurie good morning. His eyes noted her split lip, but he said nothing about it.

"Jake, I need the FBI file on Peter Macklin." Abilene spelled the last name and added Peter's date of birth, which Laurie hadn't known.

The young detective sat down and rattled the keys on his computer. After five minutes, he grunted and swung the console around on its lazy Susan.

The first thing Laurie saw was Peter's photograph in front and profile. He looked years younger, but she didn't need the raw data printed out beneath to assure her the likeness was her husband's. Then the screen began to scroll.

* * *

SOMETHING BORROWED, SOMETHING BLACK

She thought later that she could have summoned help from any number of officers on the way out, but even if she'd found the voice, there was no room in her head for thoughts of escape. She had become faint while reading the bright screen, the endless list of arrests, court appearances, and surveillance reports in which Peter's name appeared, and had had to sit down. Afterward, she did not feel weak so much as weightless; she could hear her heels clicking on the marble floor, but it might have been someone else's legs bearing the burden for all she felt of it.

Abilene had not spoken to her since before they entered City Hall. He had thanked Jake, then escorted her to the elevator and out to the parking area, where he'd helped her into the Jeep. Now, slumped in the seat with her head tilted back against the rest, she asked him if he was a police officer.

Seated behind the wheel, flicking lint off his hat in his lap, he laughed. "That's a corker. I'll tell Jake you said it. Mr. Major—that's what he calls himself out here, and it's legal, but try and sell that to the papers—he's got friends all over."

"You mean he owns people. Even the police."

"Nobody's that rich. But in L.A., everything's reasonable."

"Does he own Peter?"

"There was a difference of opinion about that. When Mr. Major left Detroit, Macklin came, too, and made a space for him, then went back. He thought he had his pink slip, and maybe he did. But he shouldn't have picked here for his honeymoon.

He was seen, and Mr. Major ain't one to let a handy tool lay."

"What's he doing for Maggiore?" She used the name pointedly.

"He's making up for a mistake Mr. Major made. Mr. Major trusted somebody and paid him five times what he was worth to go on trusting him. Then that somebody got a better offer. Your new hubby's job is to see he don't earn it."

She glanced down at the newspaper. "Maggiore wants Peter to kill a grand jury witness."

"Who says you're a dumb farm girl?" The absurd grin was in place.

"Your job is to stay with me just to make sure Peter comes through. If he doesn't, you'll kill me."

"I'm no killer, nursie. If I was, he wouldn't have to use Macklin. But if hubby screws up, or runs, or forgets the play, I can fix you so he won't want you back." He tugged his hat on by the brim, fore and aft. Then his right hand jerked out from behind his head. The point of a narrow steel blade stung the flesh below her right eye. "The name's Mr. Major. If you don't want to read thermometers in Braille, it pays to show respect."

She asked him to take her back to the hotel. On Wilshire, they were forced to stop and wait for the street to clear in front of a cocktail lounge, where a line of cabs waited behind customers dropping off and picking up their cars from parking attendants in uniform. She asked Abilene what it was all about.

"Cigar bar," he said. "Tourists come in from all

over to see Demi Moore sucking on a Corona Corona."

"I need a drink," she said.

"We'll never get in. Anyway, the hotel bar's cheaper."

"I need a drink," she said.

Abilene sighed heavily and swung into the curb. An attendant in his twenties gave him a claim check and slid in behind the wheel.

Tiny, crowded tables took up most of the space not occupied by the rosily lit bar. Ventilator fans worked hard to diminish the unmistakable odor of expensive cigars. Laurie didn't see any celebrities, but then most of her favorite stars were doing their twinkling in heaven. She asked Abilene to order her a Kahlua and cream and took the short corridor to the rest rooms.

There was no line, a lucky break. There was no window, either, which was not so lucky. She passed a pair of women freshening their makeup at the mirror and entered a vacant stall, where she sat on the toilet and thought.

Five minutes seemed to be the limit of Abilene's patience. She heard an outraged gasp as the door opened from the corridor, then a general shuffling of feet toward the exit, followed by the clomping of cowboy heels on tile. Abilene grunted, and she knew he was crouching to look under the first of the line of stalls. She was in the third, standing hunched on the toilet seat, holding shut the unlatched door.

She saw a glint off a silver-capped toe, heard again the grunt as he lowered himself to the floor outside her stall. She pounced, throwing all her weight against the door, pushing through the resistance when the door struck him, tipping him off his hands and the balls of his feet. She kept on going without looking back, on through the door of the room and down the corridor and across the lounge. She collided with a gaggle of customers in the entrance, caromed off through the front door, stumbled and fell to one knee on the front step, skinning it and running her hose. She was on her feet before the nearby parking attendant could help her, down the two steps to the sidewalk and waving a hand at the first cab in line. Scrambling into the backseat, she shouted something at the driver, who took off obediently without questions. Later, she wondered how many agitated females he had been called upon to sweep away from popular fun spots. Only when they were under way did she turn and look out the window, just in time to see the crown of a cream-colored Stetson ducking into the back of the next cab in line. The attendant would be too slow fetching the Jeep.

"Please go faster," she told the driver.

The car lunged. A pair of sad eyes checked the rearview mirror, then met her gaze. "I can tie this guy in knots."

"Please," she said.

Laurie had a good sense of direction but lost her bearings quickly in the tangle of one-way streets, commercial drives, and broad alleys through which they sped. The other cab kept up through the first few turns, then vanished from the back window. When they slowed down, she leaned forward. "My husband—" She stopped. Nothing beyond those two words was safe to say.

"I'm an old fart, I give advice," the driver said. 'Any husband worth running from is worth dumping." He drove six blocks in silence, then: "So where to? Courthouse or airport?"

She looked down. She was twisting her wedding ring around and around her finger. She looked up. "Airport."

The clerk at the American counter took Laurie's check and handed her a ticket for the 4:46 to Dayton with stopovers in Denver and Chicago. Laurie went to the gate for the ninety-minute wait. At 4:15 Abilene walked in and slouched into the chair beside her.

She gripped the arms of her chair, but he made no move to hold her down. "That's the thing about airports, no place to run," he said in his lazy drawl. "Can't catch your plane from the ladies' room."

She forced her heart rate to slow down. They were in a secure area; he couldn't have gotten his knife past the metal detectors. "How did you find me?"

"You didn't go back to the hotel, and you don't know anyone in L.A. I never did shoot a pheasant on the fly when I knew where it was fixing to roost."

"Mr. Major has friends all over." Her voice was hollow.

"Ohio's cold this time of year. I bet you ain't even been to the beach here."

"I'm not going with you."

He yawned, stretched, and put his hands behind his head. The knife came out of its sheath and across his body to prick her ribs. The family of Asians seated facing them across the aisle continued to stare into space.

"How—?" Laurie couldn't catch her breath.

"Stuck it down in my boot. The lady with the wand stopped looking when she got to the silver cap. Let's go." He prodded her with the point.

She looked around at the passengers waiting to board, the other passengers, well-wishers, and flight crews walking briskly up and down the concourse. "You won't try anything here."

"Tell that to Jack Ruby."

"What about security?"

"Airports are designed to keep folks out, not in."

He prodded her again, harder. The point slid straight through the fabric of her blouse. They stood up together. The Asians looked at them. She was pretty sure they were curious only because she and Abilene were the only people there without luggage.

The walk to the exit seemed twice as long as the walk to the gate. Twice, passing guards in uniform with revolvers on their belts, she took in her breath to cry out, only to expel it when the knife pricked her. Sharp objects frightened her more than guns; how could he know she'd spent a childhood hour in an emergency room with a puncture wound from a pitchfork? But then, he knew everything else.

A senior citizens' tour group in flowered shirts and Mother Hubbards clogged the corridor near the security checkpoint, wrestling bags off the conveyor and setting off the metal detector with their pacemakers and the steel pins in their hips. A skinny, big-haired woman wearing dark cataract glasses stood to one side with her arms spread while a short woman in uniform went over her from head to toe with a hand-held wand. When Abilene pushed against Laurie to step around them, Laurie pushed back hard. He stumbled into the pair. With the path past the metal detector blocked, Laurie ran through the arch from the wrong side, veering to avoid a white-haired man preparing to come through opposite.

She picked up her pace, ignoring Abilene's curse, the bonging of the detector when her pursuer set it off behind her. Someone shouted, "Halt! Security!" but she didn't know if the cry was directed at her or at Abilene. Then she heard the hollow plopping of a revolver going off.

"I'm back."

She was in the bathroom when the door opened from the hall, using powder and lipstick to hide the swelling. Her heart gave a hop when she came out and saw Peter. He was wearing the clothes he'd had on when they'd come back from their drive up the coast. He'd said the words he'd said the morning of their first married day. He even had a copy of the *L.A. Times* in his hand, as he'd had then. Everything in her wanted to throw herself at him, extinguish all the fear and betrayal of the past forty-eight hours in the frenzy of what they had been. She didn't move.

"Did you do what he wanted?" she asked.

His face had been hard to read in the past. Tired, older, as rumpled-looking as his clothes, it had not lost that quality, but she recognized something collapsing behind it. He knew she knew.

"No," he said. "Security was too tight."

She nodded. It was the answer she'd prayed for, but it brought her no gladness.

He gestured with the newspaper. She knew what

was on the front page, although she hadn't seen it. There would be a photograph of the absurd lanky cowboy sprawled on the floor near the airport checkpoint, the big black headline. The reporters would find a way to work Maggiore's name into it. There would be no pictures of her. The police had been courteous about that, sneaking her out of City Hall through a service entrance as a reward for her cooperation during questioning. Abilene had told the truth: Mr. Major didn't own all of them.

"You shouldn't have come back here," she said. "The police are looking for you."

"You told them?"

She thought of saying they would have found out anyway, would make the connection between Laurie Macklin and Carlo Maggiore's hired man in Detroit.

"Yes," she said.

He looked away. Then he looked back. "They can't hold me. I'm not wanted for anything, and their witness is alive."

"I'm glad."

He searched her face. She knew it was as unreadable as his. "I never wanted to lie."

"I wish that meant something."

"I'd put it all behind me. I only went back because of you. I don't know how much Abilene said."

"He told me. I understand."

After a silence, he said, "Where do we go from here?"

She'd thought about that constantly since she'd left the police. She'd gone back and forth with equal conviction. She told the truth. "I don't know."

"We could see a counselor."

"We might have trouble finding one with the right experience," she said.

"I'm willing to try."

She looked down. She was twisting her wedding ring. She hadn't realized she hadn't taken it off. She looked up.

He could read her then; she wanted him to. He smiled. Her heart hopped again. She made her face grave.

"No more secrets," she said.

The Witch and Uncle Harry

Angela Zeman

W hat do you think?" Rachel demanded
brightly, but her scowl alerted Mrs. Risk that Rachel
would put up with no conflicting opinions.

Tactfully hiding her amusement, Mrs. Risk scanned
the shop-lined street around them, her eyes brimming
with proprietary pleasure. The May sun, busy with its
morning chore of gilding rooftops, toasted their
chilled noses and hands. It was one of her favorite
early morning occupations, walking the boardwalk
that edged the bayfront village of Wyndham-by-the-
Sea. The boards under their feet plonked in a cheerful
rhythm, Rachel's boots producing a deeper half-beat
behind the clack of Mrs. Risk's slippers. Both were
fairly tall and their strides matched well.

Rachel was not only much younger, but also more
buxom than the leaner-framed older woman. As usual, Rachel wore jeans and a cotton shirt, her mass of
curls dangling darkly down her back in a ponytail.
Mrs. Risk's straight hair lifted and snapped like an

unkempt black banner in the breezes coming off Wyndham Bay.

Finally she said, "If gold is what you want, I suggest you buy the metal itself. You'd have something you can physically hold or even wear, and it appreciates. But gold futures? Pure speculation, dear. Possible high yields, true, but the risk is even higher. In the commodities market, one can lose even more than one invests."

Rachel snorted impatiently. "I can't afford to invest in something to wear!"

Mrs. Risk tried to interrupt, but Rachel overrode her.

"Remember how St. Boniface Hospital hired me to supply the flowers for their Gala Fund-raiser next week? Well, when I get that check, for the first time since I opened my shop, my rent and bills will be paid up to date, with a chunk left over. This is my chance to earn a little extra, using that chunk. Mel Arvin, the broker, he says—"

"Tchah! If that man told me fish lived in water I wouldn't believe it."

"Yes," Rachel crowed in triumph. "But would you trust Harry Fitch?"

"Absolutely. But what does Harry know about gold futures, or any commodity, for that matter?" Mrs. Risk lifted her face to the sun and sniffed. The yuppie coffee craze had arrived at Wyndham-by-the-Sea and roasted bean aromas wafted seductively through the salty air.

"He sells gold all the time!"

"He sells antique gold coins. Entirely different. Let's skip our herbal tea and get coffee this morning, do you mind?"

"Not now. He said if I came over early, we could talk. And FYI, *some* of his gold thingabobs are *new*. He said he could explain about the world markets. A noble metal, he called gold. One of the three in the world."

"Gold, platinum, and silver, but gold has the most ancient history."

"How'd you know—oh, never mind. You know everything, I forgot." Rachel giggled—being in those tender twenties when she could still do it attractively—and because of the giggle missed the sounds erupting from the Dallour Coin and Stamp Collector's Shop. Mrs. Risk whirled Rachel backward and around, choking her giggle into a squawk.

She mashed Rachel against the realtor's window next to the open door of the coin shop. She pointed a finger at sun-faded photos of Hamptons summer rentals (probably already snatched up for the coming season) and commanded, "Hush!"

Rachel, ignoring the order, growled, "If you want me to invest in real estate, you're going to have to be nicer about it."

"Listen!"

Puzzled, Rachel huddled with her against the plate glass and listened. The she straightened up. "Oh, that's Aunt Marguerite."

Mrs. Risk snorted. "And they call *me* a witch!"

Because of Mrs. Risk's eccentric spirit (which Rachel shared) and eerie ability to see what others often missed, the residents of Wyndham-by-the-Sea believed Mrs. Risk to be a "witch." Most were intimidated by her—an impression she shamelessly took advantage of—but some were intrigued, and some accepting. It was from this last very small group that she selected her friends. After Mrs. Risk had rescued Rachel from nearly committing a fatal act of desperation, Rachel too had been "selected" by Mrs. Risk—typically, without being consulted.

Two years into the sometimes prickly friendship, Rachel had begun calling herself Mrs. Risk's apprentice witch—and wasn't always sure she was kidding.

From inside the coin shop came a high-pitched, derisive warble, rising in volume and pitch with each breath: "Don't you dare say it's unnecessary, you undersized slug. After all I've done for you, you owe me a little sweat. I *gave* you your so-called career. Bought this shop for you, didn't I? Without me you would've ended up—if I hadn't—*Harry!* Where are you going? Don't turn your back on me! You'd still be sleeping in doorways, that's where! So! Like I said before, for every goddamn stamp and coin in this shop I want a detailed description, with value, commentary, and provenance notes. And forget fudging with your usual good-for-nothing quick scribbles. I can't understand those. Just remember. Nobody else'd hire a lifeless lump like you. Just me. With my soft heart.

"Hmmph. I'll be checking on you, too. If you've been playing fancy with the books, I'll soon know it. At any rate, like I said, start keeping the shop open nights. We need more business to make you worth the expense of keeping you. *Great* expense, with that apartment I let you use upstairs! I could be collecting rent on that."

"Yeah," whispered Rachel to Mrs. Risk. "At great expense, she lets him live in a that rattrap efficiency, making him a built-in watchdog twenty-four hours a day, seven days a week. No expense spared to keep him from drawing a real salary somewhere better. The guy can't afford three solid meals a day! And no health insurance. Remember last year's flu? If Dr. Giammo hadn't taken care of him for free, he'd be dead now!"

The voice droned on: "And keep those neighborhood brats out of here, I'm warning you, Harry! And while you're at it, scrub this place down. It's getting frayed around the edges. Like you!" She hooted with amusement. "Reminds me. Get that tux cleaned that I bought you last fall. You're going to escort me to— *now* where're you going! Stay put! St. Boniface's Gala's coming up. *Everybody* will be there. That old bat, Velma, I heard she's bringing her *sister,* isn't that priceless? Big comedy star, can't get a date." She tittered.

Then her tone changed to a coaxing croon. "Now don't be difficult. Mommie will make sure you won't be sorry. Mommie loves you. Would I leave you everything I own in my will if I didn't? Nowwww, give a kiss." A juicy sound followed.

Mrs. Risk plunged through the coin shop doorway, banging the door back against the wall hard enough to rattle the entire building's windows. Inside, a corpulent woman in a violently-flowered jersey dress sprang back from the slight figure with graying brown hair who she seemed to have been swallowing.

"Gah! *What the*—oh!" Marguerite Dallour's scowling bulldog features rearranged themselves into a simper when she identified the intruders. Lifting an arm, she patted her tightly pin-curled coiffure, exposing a dark sweat-stained circle on her dress. Crusts of face powder drifted to her gelatinous billow of bosom. "Mrs. Risk! How lovely, but *startling,* to see you *so* early in the day." Having swiftly assessed the social insignificance of Rachel, Ms. Dallour ignored her. "I'm surprised you don't sleep in mornings, instead of running about like us poor working girls. Naps are so *preserving* for women your age." She dug deep into her handbag, then lit a cigarette. "And how *do* you manage to make black look so, uh, airy on a hot day?" She fanned at her damp, numerous chins. (Mrs. Risk, who was not quite two decades younger than Ms. Dallour, habitually wore long black gauze dresses in hot weather, wool in winter.)

Behind her, Harry, with sickened eyes, turned away and pretended to straighten pennies in a dish on the glass countertop. Rachel winked at him, which brought a healthier color to his cheeks.

Mrs. Risk considered the woman. "Regarding your comment about the Gala. Velma Schrafft is a dear friend of mine and a worthy human being. She is not so insecure as to *need* an escort to go anywhere she wishes to go."

Purple mottled Ms. Dallour's cheeks. She warbled, exhaling smoke, "Oooh, getting late. Must rush. We should lunch sometime. I'll call you." She billowed away like a soiled battleship, the odor of unwashed flesh lingering in her wake. Rachel shuddered.

The rest of the hour passed in a discussion between Rachel and a subdued Harry Fitch about gold and its relative stability in world markets.

As they left, Rachel announced, "Somebody should boil Aunt Marguerite in all that oil on her unwashed face."

"Why in heaven's name do people call that woman 'Aunt'? Even though this is our first meeting, I'd heard of her before, but never understood the appellation."

THE WITCH AND UNCLE HARRY

"Because everybody calls *him* Uncle Harry. I think calling her 'aunt' is a sarcastic thing, because of how opposite they are, but still connected. Nobody can stand her, but everyone adores Uncle Harry. He draws kids to him like a magnet. They're in the shop every afternoon, listening to his stories about the coins and stamps. That's where his nickname came from—the kids."

"Yes, I've heard that quite a few teachers and parents are grateful for his influence."

They walked on in silence. Then Rachel said, "Harry joined my pottery class a few weeks ago, at Randy Blume's. That's how I got to know him."

"Why does he put up with that—that person?"

"Well. Only what I've heard, mind you. Every time he wants to leave, she dangles that inheritance in his face. She's over twenty years older than he, so he has a good chance of collecting. It's true, though, about him living in the street. He told me. He was a Viet Nam veteran, and never readjusted to normal life until she put him in that shop. Stamps and coins were his hobby before the war. He said the quiet life in Wyndham and his love for those stamps and coins slowly turned him around. He says he can't forget what she did for him."

"That explains a lot," said Mrs. Risk thoughtfully.

"Well, I think he's earned his inheritance by now. He should murder the old gargoyle," spat Rachel.

Mrs. Risk gazed at Rachel with narrowed eyes. "Is that your past repeating itself? Be careful what brand of tragedy you wish on your fellow man."

"*Hmmph.* The real tragedy is, there's the greatest woman in our class. Named Christa. He and she—"

Mrs. Risk held up a hand. "Please. Enough."

Rachel heaved a deep sigh. "Gotta open my own shop now, anyway. See you later. Mel Arvin promised to give me more information about gold futures today. You'll see, I'm doing a smart thing."

"I'm sure you're right, dear," said Mrs. Risk, looking distracted. "Isn't your pottery class tonight?"

"At seven. Why?"

Without answering, Mrs. Risk drifted away down the boardwalk like a dark shadow in the sunlight.

That night at seven, Mrs. Risk entered Randy's pottery studio to delighted greetings of "Take some clay!" Mrs. Risk declined the honor, but perched on a stool to observe. The wide room was full of busy men and women straddling whirling wheels, digging hands into wet clay, spattering each other with muddy water, poring over glaze samples, and most of all . . . laughing. Randy, a tall talented woman overflowing with her own infectious laughter, sprang from student to student. Soft classical jazz filled the background, and the odor of glazes, clay, and fresh coffee perfumed the air.

Mrs. Risk marveled at Harry. This charming man she watched talk with animation to everyone in the room was far from the pale, despairing figure she'd seen this morning.

She soon picked out Christa. Harry was a small man of frail build, but Christa was even smaller. She had ivory skin, masses of fine ash blond curls, and hazel-green eyes. Her figure was softly rounded and appealing, like a puppy transformed into womanhood. When she spoke to Harry, he seemed to sprout confidence in that instant. And like Geiger counters nearing uranium, each one's flesh betrayed the approach of the other by flushing rosier and rosier, the color receding as the other moved away.

When all had left except Randy, Rachel, and Mrs. Risk, Randy laughed. "Isn't it cute? And everybody loves them so much they don't even tease, which is amazing. This is a pretty frank bunch."

"What do you know about Christa?" Mrs. Risk asked.

Randy said, "Oh, she works in a doctor's office in the next village. She has two little girls, ages four and six. Her husband ran off while she was in labor with the second one. Bob helped with her divorce. She once told me she was young and foolish when she married. But now she's old and smart, she says. Too tough to fall for anyone else." Randy laughed delightedly. "As tough as a butterfly wing."

"And as beautiful," added Mrs. Risk, smiling. "By the way, what is Harry making? He seems skillful for a beginner."

"He's good," agreed Randy.

"Harry's making flower pots," said Rachel. "Harry has a whopping green thumb. He's filled that ugly apartment with plants you wouldn't believe. He's really creative."

"Isn't that what you're making, too, dear? Flower pots?" Mrs. Risk asked, glancing from the misshapen lump on Rachel's wheel to the delicate symmetry of Harry's piece.

"Yes. I thought I'd sell them in my shop—if I get good enough at this. It's harder than it looks."

"I can see that."

Rachel sniffed. "Want to try it?"

Mrs. Risk arched an eyebrow. "Thank you, dear, but then I might want lessons, and Randy's waiting list is long enough already."

"Ummhmm. Right."

Mrs. Risk drifted to the door. "Is Bob at home now, Randy? If you don't mind, I'll drop in on him. I have a rather odd legal problem. See *you* in the morning as usual, dear," she said to Rachel.

"Lucky me," said Rachel.

The next morning after tea, a curious Rachel trailed Mrs. Risk to the coin shop. They found Harry laboring over stacks of paper, as pale and depressed as yesterday morning. He'd begun the intricate inventory demanded by Aunt Marguerite, Mrs. Risk guessed.

"Um, about the commodities market," Rachel began, but was cut off by Mrs. Risk.

"Harry," she gushed, "I found the oddest coin. Of course, for all I know it could be a subway token!" Mrs. Risk laughed merrily.

Rachel snorted.

"But it *could* be very old. The markings are—" She broke off, glancing annoyed at Rachel, from whom again had erupted a muffled snort.

"But you're so busy now. I have it!" she exclaimed. "Do you ever visit Harrington's Dock to watch the sunset? It's so lovely, overlooking the water. Even *you* will need a break by then. I'll bring us a lovely wine, and you can look at my find!"

"Is six-thirty too late?" asked Harry, suddenly cheerier.

"Just what I was about to suggest myself. See you then." And abruptly, Mrs. Risk grabbed Rachel's arm and hurried her outside.

Mrs. Risk said crossly, "In future, refrain from crude noises, dear. I worried that you were about to blurt out something embarrassing."

"Like how expert you really are about coins? Gee, why would I say that?"

"Tchah! Compared to Harry I know very little!"

"Oh, I see. You told a *relative* truth, then. Not a flat lie."

Mrs. Risk gazed fondly at the young woman, then sniffed the air. "I have the oddest craving for a mocha latte. Join me?"

Rachel laughed. "Watch out. You might lose your taste for herbal tea! Can I come too, tonight?"

Mrs. Risk looked suddenly disturbed. "I don't think so, dear. Your friend Harry would probably rather not have any friends nearby."

Rachel paused, surprised. After a moment, she nodded gravely. "Okay. See you tomorrow."

At 6:30 that evening, Harry arrived at Harrington's Dock. Over the clustered tables, umbrellas fluttered gaily in the breeze. The last rays of the blushing sun stained the water red as it drooped toward Wyndham Bay and sea gulls swooped low, scouting for possible treats. Nearly the whole village had collected there to salute the day's end.

Mrs. Risk detached herself from a table occupied by two men in conservative suits and beckoned to Harry to join her at the next table over. A bottle of wine and glasses stood waiting.

"What a gorgeous time of day to share with friends," she exclaimed, and insisted he relax before looking at her coin. They discussed her wine—a Simi Private Reserve Alexander Valley Cabernet that he declared outstanding—ordered a snack, and pondered the weather. Soon he was laughing, and as she watched, the lively man from Randy's class reappeared. They'd begun their second glass, when a voice from the table behind them became loud and easily overheard. She paused, and so did Harry.

"I've drawn up the wills of most of the villagers around, but I'm glad I had nothing to do with that one." The voice was Bob Blume's, Mrs. Risk's friend and attorney. Mrs. Risk wondered if Harry had ever met Bob, who was as popular in the village as his wife, Randy, but Harry gave no sign of recognition. He seemed content to wait until the speakers quieted again so that he and Mrs. Risk could continue their own conversation.

The second man, who was elderly, answered, wheezing loudly, "I just do my job."

"If you handle her affairs, though," pressed Bob, "you must know how she underpays this guy, dangling that damned will over his head to keep him in line. It's abuse, no less. He's like her slave." He refilled the older man's glass.

"If I could tell him, I would. You know that. But it's not done. Where are the ethics?"

Bob leaned forward and exclaimed, "It's not ethical to reveal what's *in* a will, but what's wrong with saying what's *not* in it, Leon!"

At the word, "Leon," Harry's eyes suddenly widened. He listened openly now, his expression uncertain. Mrs. Risk stayed quiet.

"Whattaya mean, what's *not* in it?"

"What's *not* in it. You could, out of decency and respect for a really fine guy, go to this employee and say, fella, you're not in the will. I mean, I could say the same thing to every single person for miles around without revealing that the dishonest bitch left every dime she owns to that foul, shriveled up nephew of hers. Right?"

Harry's wineglass snapped off at the stem in his hand. Without seeming to notice the bright liquid that splashed like spilled blood across the white table, he pulled himself to his feet. His plastic chair tumbled over behind him. A few people glanced up, startled.

The older man considered Bob thoughtfully. "You know, I'm gonna think it over. I am. Might be worth it, givin' the poor guy a break. I'll consider it."

Harry rushed, stiff-legged, from the pier. He didn't say good-bye to Mrs. Risk, and in his reeling flight seemed to see nothing around him. His eyes burned with a painful light turned inward.

Mrs. Risk sighed. Bob turned to her, his eyes worried. Mrs. Risk patted the back of his hand. "Thank you, darling. I know it was difficult."

Bob glanced at his colleague, whose nose was buried in his fifth glass of wine and shrugged. "Leon won't remember a thing tomorrow." He tossed his napkin on the table. "I'd better drive him home."

Mrs. Risk nodded. She stayed to see the sun safely tucked away for the night before she walked to her own home.

Throughout the next few weeks, Mrs. Risk kept track of Harry. To her amazement, he didn't quit his job.

Nothing seemed to have changed except that he suddenly began showing up twice a week at Randy's instead of just once.

One morning, Rachel called Mrs. Risk. "You won't believe this! Uncle Harry proposed to Christa at

Randy's last night! You should've seen Christa's face! What's happened to him in the last month? When Aunt Marguerite finds out, she'll pop!"

"Which would break your heart, obviously," said Mrs. Risk dryly. But when she hung up, her expression was grim.

Then came the fire.

Mrs. Risk watched with the others as the Volunteer Fire Brigade tramped through the soggy, still sizzling, blackened site. Uncle Harry had been helped to safety across the street, where he was breathing from an oxygen tank, surrounded with worried friends.

Marguerite, after a bellow of rage at the damage to her property, had theatrically clutched a mammoth breast with both hands. She weaved about drunkenly, stumbling into the paths of the feverishly working firemen. The medics politely took her pulse, then moved her out of the way. Rachel said, frowning, "There hasn't been a fire here since Uncle Harry came. That has to be . . . ten years ago?"

Marguerite, miffed that her distress had been unappreciated, began uttering threats against the "simp who let this happen," meaning Harry. That brought the attention she sought, but not quite the sympathy she desired. Her audience, most of which were Harry's friends, glowered menacingly.

The fire chief asked Harry how he thought the fire had started.

"Could be somebody dropped a smoldering cigarette into a wastebasket without me noticing, I guess. After all, stamps are dry pieces of paper, and in an old building, it wouldn't take long—"

"In that gloomy dump, the fire probably caught before you could see the smoke," consoled Jesús, who ran the nearby shoe- and leather-repair shop. He was avidly conscientious about flammable materials.

"And if that same person had been smoking in your shop, at first you might think it was leftover smoke you were smelling," added Rachel.

The fire chief asked, "But who'd smoke in there? You got "No Smoking" signs all over."

A sheepish expression came over Harry's face. He didn't answer.

The thought occurred to Mrs. Risk a half beat before the others. Following her lead, everyone turned to stare at Aunt Marguerite. She paused in the act of lighting a cigarette. "What!" She turned her back on them.

The fire chief left to consult with his men. In passing Aunt Marguerite, he snarled a few words about criminal disrepair, fire hazard, reckless endangerment, and an inspection. Aunt Marguerite's face paled beneath her scabs of face powder.

In the next few weeks, the shop received the attention it should have gotten decades ago and soon it and Harry were both restored to a brighter, fitter ability to conduct business. The damage had been mostly smoke. Insurance covered the inventory loss—a series of rare stamps—and Harry lost his cough.

Mrs. Risk, on hearing that only one group of stamps had perished out of the entire inventory, spent the rest of the afternoon in the coffee shop, musing over an iced cappuccino. At about six P.M., she decided to visit Randy's studio. Students wouldn't be arriving for another hour and Randy would be free to talk.

Once there, she asked Randy to show her Harry's latest group of pots. She examined them closely, then questioned Randy. "Oh, dear," she muttered as she

listened to Randy's information with dawning aware-
ness.

Immediately Mrs. Risk hurried to Uncle Harry's
apartment. At his door, she answered his surprised
look, "Harry, the time has arrived for us to get to
know each other better. May I come in?"

Harry gazed at her thoughtfully, then invited her to
enter. "Will you join me for coffee? I'm sorry I forgot
all about your coin. Did you bring it?"

"Thank you, I've had enough coffee for a while. No,
I didn't bring my coin. Frankly, I forgot about the
silly thing. I actually came to congratulate you on
your recent engagement, rather belatedly, I know."
She entered, then paused, taken aback by the riot of
color in Harry's apartment. "Rachel told me about
your green thumb, but I expected nothing like this!
You've made your home a garden!"

He nodded morosely. "In pots, though."

"Mostly made by yourself, too, I see. I recognize
your style. Beautiful work, dear. Do you have any
empty ones I may examine closer?"

"Sure. Here." He handed three to her, one by one.

"You've been productive in these last few weeks."

He shrugged, then turned to tend the bubbling
coffeepot on his hot plate.

She watched while he stirred cream into his cup.
His shoulders sagged, and his expression seemed
duller than she'd ever seen before. A man engaged to a
woman like Christa ought to look happier, she mused.

She put down the three pots he'd handed her,
selected one from a nearby table, held it up and said,
with a playful note in her voice, "I would very much
like to own one of your pots, Harry. This one is
exquisite. Could I buy it from you?"

Without looking up he replied, "Don't be silly. Take it as a gift. You—" he looked up, spotted which pot she held, and paled. "No, not *that* one. It's poorly done. I couldn't let you—"

"Oh, but I insist that I want this one. Although," she lifted up another from the floor, "this larger one is also lovely. Oh, look. You've inserted small decorative plugs where the bottom drainage holes should be. How clever. I suppose I just pop it out if I need the hole to be open?"

"That's right." He leaned to seize the pots from her hands, but she withdrew them just out of his reach. Then, with a sigh, she put them down.

He stared at her, his arms hanging limply at his sides.

"You're right," she said. "How inappropriate for me to choose my own gift. I've forgotten my manners. Which pot would you pick for me?" But before he could answer, she continued, "Are you free tomorrow evening? Rachel and I want you to come to my house for dinner, a small celebration of your coming marriage. I've already mentioned it to your delightful Christa, and she's coming. Bring along whichever pot you choose for me, a memento of our growing friendship, Harry. You see, I think so very much of you, dear. Our village has been richer in all the qualities that matter since you came to live among us."

Harry sat down suddenly, looking depressed.

She moved toward the door. "And six-thirty would be perfect. Such a lovely time of day in May."

When Harry pulled his car into the witch's glade the next evening, he was dismayed to discover that despite his early arrival, Christa, her two small daughters, Rachel, and an older man were there already, seated in old aluminum lawn chairs in the velvety grass fronting the witch's cottage. The little girls rushed to seize his legs and propel him to a chair. Christa nestled contentedly in the grass close beside him. Although it was clear how much they loved him, he sunk into a deep gloom.

"You already know most of these present," said Mrs. Risk with a smile, ignoring his misery. She handed him a glass of red wine and in return received from his trembling hands her gift—the pot she'd first selected yesterday evening, although missing the decorative bottom plug. The smaller girl climbed into his lap and nestled there.

"Thank you, Harry. How forgiving of you to give me the exact pot I selected. I shall treasure it."

Tears welled in Harry's eyes. "I took away the plug, the . . . the hole's empty, but I want to explain—"

Mrs. Risk turned her back on him. "Who's ready for more wine?" She busily passed around the bottle. "Harry, dear, I'd like you to meet an old friend of mine, a retired industrialist, Aisa Garrett. He owns, among other things, the North Shore Industries Corporation that occupies part of the bayfront in the village. I'm sure you're familiar with it."

Harry nodded, but politely, not really interested.

Mrs. Risk patted the back of his hand and continued, "I hope you don't mind, I don't normally interfere in people's lives—"

At this statement, Rachel and Aisa hooted in wild laughter. Christa smiled, but looked puzzled. Harry gazed about in bewilderment.

When they'd subsided, Aisa, still chortling, said, "What she means is, Harry, without interfering in the slightest in either my life or yours, she's decided my corporation should go into a small sideline business, with a partner who knows what's what—meaning you."

Harry frowned. "I don't follow—"

Christa said firmly, "Just listen to Aisa, Harry."

Harry blinked at her in astonishment.

"Here's the deal," began Aisa, and then he outlined a partnership proposal in a coin and stamp store, with generous terms to Harry, resulting in Harry's ultimate sole ownership of the store.

After a stunned pause, Harry gasped, "Why?"

"Blamed if I know," admitted Aisa.

"Are you interested in coins and stamps? Are you a collector?"

"Absolutely not. I fish, as it so happens."

Rachel beamed. "Which means you'll be in complete control, Harry." She picked up a platter of appetizers and began passing them around. "Dinner will be ready in a while. More lemonade, girls?"

Chatter picked up in the small glade. The oak trees towering over them, newly filled out in their spring leaves, rustled and shimmered in the breeze from the nearby Long Island Sound. The setting sun lit the cottage behind them in soft gold. Harry leaned back in his chair, cradled the child with one arm, and sipped his wine. He looked more tense and unhappy than any man had a right to look, surrounded by love and good fortune.

Finally, he put his glass on the polished stump being used as a table. Reaching behind the little girl into his pocket, he pulled out a soft bag that made muted jingling noises. The little girl laughed in delight at the sound.

Everyone looked up and stopped talking.

Harry began, anxiety choking his words, "I can't go into business with anybody. I've made a huge—I've done something terrible. Later tonight I'm going to confess to Marguerite. Christa, you can't marry—"

Mrs. Risk calmly interrupted and pointed over her shoulder at her cottage. "Girls, see the nice black cat sitting in the window? She's waiting for you to play with her." The adults paused while the two children rushed to see the cat.

Then Mrs. Risk turned briskly to Harry. "A man of your intelligence—certainly you could find some way to adjust Marguerite's . . . inventory in a less self-destructive manner. By the way, how did you accomplish the theft? She's totally oblivious to their disappearance."

Harry reddened. "About a month ago—"

Mrs. Risk interrupted again. "After our drink on Harrington's Dock?"

Harry nodded. "The next day. A young man came into the shop. His uncle had died and left him a coin collection." He jiggled the bag again. "This is that collection. It's extremely valuable, but he was more interested in stamps, so we traded." He shrugged sheepishly. "I didn't record the transaction."

"Ah. And after a space of time for safety, the fire," put in Mrs. Risk.

Harry nodded. "The fire. I burned some blank bits of paper. I told everybody they were the stamps which I'd given the young man, to account for their disappearance. Then I kept—stole—the coins. When I made my flower pots, I made drainage holes in the bottoms slightly larger than the size of each coin. Then I bought some of that clay that air dries without firing. I pressed it on and around the coins in pretty designs, and fitted them into the holes. They just looked like decorative plugs." He nodded, shame-faced, at Mrs. Risk. "To everybody except her." He sneaked a look at Christa, who sat listening unperturbed. "I was desperate," he finished miserably.

Rachel said firmly, "She'd been treating you like a slave all those years, and you were in love."

"Yes. I—I didn't think things through. Well, maybe I didn't want to think. I guess I wanted a little revenge."

Mrs. Risk examined the shattered man before her and smiled. "Your revenge certainly contained no sting for Marguerite. The insurance company reimbursed her for the stamps."

He sunk even lower in his chair. "Yes. I didn't think that through either. I cheated them most of all, and they didn't even do anything to me."

Christa rose, kissed him on top of the head, and sat down again. "If anyone can understand about anger and desperation, it's me."

Rachel shrugged. "Me, too."

Aisa grinned. "It's a common condition, young man. We've all been there. So how long will you need to straighten this out?"

Harry gaped. "What?"

Mrs. Risk prodded. "How long will you need to manipulate things so that the stamps can reappear? The coins, too, of course. Will you need help with a plan?"

Christa leaned forward. "How about if he discovers a misplaced transaction invoice, or something like that? He could say that in the trauma of the fire, he forgot about making the deal. So he'll 'realize' the stamps weren't burned after all. He can reveal the young man's name, who can confirm the trade. He can sneak the coins back into the shop easy, right? Then the insurance company can get their money back from Marguerite and she'll have her coins back in inventory. That would work, wouldn't it?"

"Christa!" Harry gasped. She laughed.

Mrs. Risk lifted her face to the breeze and sniffed. "Ah. I think our roast chicken beckons. Time to eat."

When Harry and his new family finally left, Rachel studied Mrs. Risk and Aisa sitting half asleep in their chairs. The glade was lit by a three-quarter moon and all the greens and golds had turned to silver and gray.

"Look at you two sitting there," she said crossly. "Like grandma and grandpa God."

Aisa said, "He's a good investment. Look how well he's done for that woman over the years."

"I don't mean your money. I mean his crime."

Mrs. Risk smiled, her eyes still shut. "Justice is fickle, seldom does it go where it ought. A little nudge here and there doesn't hurt. Harry's a good-hearted man. He needed a little straightening out, that's all. His conscience would've torn him apart, ruining the rest of his life." She opened her eyes and looked at Rachel. "Admit it. You're as happy about this whole thing as we are."

"*Humph.* Maybe. Well, seems to me *real* justice would be if Aunt Marguerite got *some* kind of payback for the way she treated him for so long."

"Don't be greedy, dear. Don't forget the help she gave him when he needed it most." Mrs. Risk again closed her eyes, but not before Rachel caught a certain gleam.

While Rachel washed dishes, she could be heard

whistling. The next day, she asked Aisa what he meant by saying Harry was a good investment.

Soon after Harry and Christa's June wedding in Mrs. Risk's glade, Rachel called Mrs. Risk on the phone: "Remember what you said about justice being fickle? I just heard that Aunt Marguerite never told the insurance company about the stamps' reappearance and the coin trade, can you beat that?"

"Oh, my," said Mrs. Risk. "Cheating is such a bad habit."

"And she would've gotten away with it, too, if somebody hadn't anonymously tipped off the insurance adjuster. Rumor is, she's up on charges of fraud!" Rachel crowed with laughter. "Do you think it's true?"

"Count on me, dear. It's true."

Delta
Double-Deal

Noreen Ayres

M innie Chaundelle was a beautiful big woman with waved hair swept close to her head like raked copper. The color was by way of her stylist boyfriend, and a front tooth rimmed with gold came courtesy the neighborhood dentist. The dentist never charged Minnie and Minnie never charged him, so it was a nice arrangement that kept Minnie in a wholesome smile.

How I met Minnie Chaundelle Bazile was a phone call. She wanted her brother found.

I always ask to see my clients first time face-to-face. She said she wasn't about to truck all over town no matter how nice a man I was.

"What makes you think I'm a nice man?" I asked.

"The word get around," she said.

Gross Street, offa Dallas. There's a Corrections for boys on one side of Dallas and a school for the retarded. On the other side's a cemetery. No one comes there anymore, she said, not even to die. If I took the right road past the cemetery I'd see her on her porch. If I took the wrong road I wouldn't.

It was the first day after a hard rain and the sun was boomin' hot already. When I turned my key to lock up, the mosquitoes were spraddle-legged up against the siding of my house, stunned by the heat themselves.

I stay in Neartown, about a mile from the heart of Houston. Gangstas and old-time politicians call it Fourth Ward. Despite a few bad apples, I like it here. From my office on the second floor I can see trees green as broccoli, and skyscrapers the color of turquoise, rust, chalk, and shined silver against a clean blue sky. At night I watch the moon play games between the towers, and when it's wet, their edges go soft in the rain-smoke.

And from my perch I watch old men black as roof paper cross the road to talk to each other, hands in their pockets like they're countin' change. Or a kid on a bicycle hoppin' holes. I could afford better but I'd have to work harder, and then I'd own more things and things lock up your freedom.

I came in off Clay near a condo complex walled off like a fortress for folks who make more money than God. An old black dog with his tail drooped under ambled across the road, fixin' his eyes the color of pennies on me.

Down the way were four wood-frame houses with plants spillin' off the porches. One porch had a line strung between its pillars holding cinnamon-colored work jackets pinned upside down, the arms danglin' like dead men hung up for show.

I drove my old brown complainin' Plymouth easy over chuckholes worse than on my street. At the end was a lot filled with patches of water and weeds. Opposite were six tiny houses sunk down in the tall grass and so far gone of paint you could see right through to air. A baby carrier leaned against a tree stump in one yard, and in the next were so many rusted gadgets it made you want to come up and browse. There, at the next house, sat a woman on a porch swing, just as she said she'd be. I parked and got out and crossed a drainage ditch laid over with crunchy dirt.

When I got a good look at Minnie Chaundelle, without hardly realizing it I sucked my stomach in before she got a good look at me. She was talkin' into a blue cell phone and wore a purple dress lit with orange embroidery, the skirt spread from one end of the bench to the other. On her feet were gold wove slippers Japanese ladies wear.

"Miz Bazile?"

"Catch ya latuh, Asyllene," she said, and punched off, then slipped the phone between her thigh and the side of the swing. From her heft and manner you could take her for thirty-five, but I knew from a source she'd just made thirty.

I put my hand out. "Cisroe Perkins."

"Minnie Chaundelle," she said and took it. Her skin was moist from the heat and had a glow like dark honey. She motioned me to sit on a barrel with a red cushion on top, and we talked there among her fern and trailing begonias. The air was thick with a sweet familiar scent. It mixed with that of a jasmine bush so happy by the side of the house it long ago turned itself into a tree.

"My brother's name is Verlyn Venable," she said. "He's twenty-four years ol' and still don' know enough to hold his diapers offa his knees."

I took out a notepad and made my face like I knew all things.

"He had hisself a good job," she said. *"Good* job. I got it for him, fr'en o' mine. He was doin' perfect. Then he ups and ghostifies. They owe him a pay check, but they cain't trace him down. I call ovah his place, call and call. What kinda man don' know enough to catch gold nickels fallin' out the sky?"

She was sayin' all these worryin' words, but her voice could calm a bobcat in a pepper field.

"His boss been out to his place, been out there and back to Egypt. They *took* to him, like I say. But you cain't count on patience to live overlong."

I asked when was the last time she saw her brother.

Her thumb rubbed a finger like she was about to start a fire. "He drop ovah here las' week and tol' me hold sumpin' for him. I say, 'How long,' and he go, 'Oh a day or two.' Six days now I don't hear nothin'. Three days he ain' showed at work."

Minnie flicked a dark thing off the armrest. It hit hard against the wall and landed in a white plastic U.S. Post Office bin people take home full after they've been on vacation a long time. Inside was what I made out as pecan shells. Then it come to me what comprised the strip of red dirt I walked on out front and what I smelled in the air: shells, and nutmeats maybe in a pie.

I asked did she file a Missing Persons. She cocked her head and grinned like to say, What planet you from, boy?

The button in the center of the cushion was biting

into my bony behind. I shifted away from it and asked, "What was it your brother lef' off?"

"Hode on. I need to know how long you think it take to find him befoh I know I can afford you."

"I charge twenty-five a hour," I said, resting my arms on my knees. "If there's long-distance, faxes, fees for records, well, that's additional."

"I be cookin' up a *buncha* nuts for that kine money. How many hours, you think?"

"Sometimes I find people in a hour. Sometimes never. I'll give you a runnin' report of my time weekly or bi-weekly as you choose. You tell me to cease and desist anytime you want. Bi-weekly—that's twice a week."

"I may be beautiful, Mr. Perkins, but I ain' dumb."

We smiled at each other as if there was more to the words than what hung in the air. My mind was wanderin' where it shouldn't. "I just like to clarify," I said.

"Clarify all you want, Mr. Perkins. You a educated man, I c'n see that."

"Cisroe."

"Mr. Cisroe," she said, with that cat smile.

"I had a couple years after the army, but I wouldn't say I'm educated, Miz Bazile." But I don't think she heard me.

She put her elbow on the armrest and framed the side of her face with a thumb and a finger. The swing was carrying her toward me, then away.

"Come to think on it, it's not gon' take all that long to fin' that boy. He either pokin' his nose where he oughtn'ta, hangin' in Slick Willie's Billiards down Sugahland, or . . ."

I waited, one hand clasped on the other, notebook

danglin'. That woman made the hairs on my chest snap and crackle. I was listenin', listenin' hard, but I was seein' her inside her house, invitin' me in for tea.

"Or swimmin' with the mocs in the bayou," she said, and squeezed and unsqueezed the rope fixed to the porch swing. "He just a dumb baby, Mr. Cisroe. He think he Eddie Murphy. What I'm worried about: his hard head."

Minnie Chaundelle went inside to get what her brother gave her. She turned back and asked me did I want some tea. Just like that, did I want some tea. But it wasn't the time for me to offer a different tone, and I said yes with a right and decent attitude.

I sat on there on the porch and ruminated on what I already knew about Minnie Chaundelle. I had placed a call to Stinger Gazway. Stinger drifts all over Fourth and Fifth Wards. If anyone knows anything about anybody, he does. He told me Minnie married a man named Sparrel Bazile six years ago, then laid him in the grave a year later. Sparrel was comin' home from work on the Katy at two A.M., same time a drunk was comin' home from a party.

While I waited on Minnie's porch, the clouds were forming a dark blanket from the south. The air was thick enough to punch. I pulled the collar of my shirt away from my neck. Two white women with mismatched clothes walked by holdin' hands, their glasses half-down their noses and their hair cut straight across, and I could see they were short a few cards, maybe come from the school for the retarded down the way.

Minnie returned bringin' two iced teas on a tray with a high lip on it and sugar, lemon, spoons, and napkins from Whataburger. She nodded at a book with a marbleized cardboard cover like you buy for notes at school and said, "Here," and I took it off the edge of the tray.

The label on front said *Brickner Deposit* at top, and on the bottom was the company name and an address on West Loop. I turned the pages and saw typing and charts and plot diagrams. Soon I figured out it had somethin' to do with a drilling operation off the Gulf's Terrebonne Bay.

Minnie Chaundelle set the tray across the top of the postal bin and commenced asking me my tea preferences, then mixed and stirred. "That mus' mean sumpin' to some freak a nature," she said, glancing at the book. "But not t' me."

"Uh-huh," I said, making myself out to be a thoughtful man. I took the glass of tea and swallowed deep but didn't drain it, not wantin' to inconvenience her. I asked if she showed the notebook to anyone, say, that friend of hers who gave her brother the job in the first place.

"Verlyn tol' me don' show it to nobody, so I dint. Till you."

"Sounds like maybe you don't trust your friend hired your brother."

She glanced down like she was sorry for a sick puppy hid behind a chair. "It shunt be that way in this world, but I guess sometimes it is." Then she met my eyes and said, "Oh, well now, don't take me wrong. I just be steppin' on my own toes sometimes. Then again, you never know. Verlyn say, 'Anything happen t' me, you turn this ovah the *po*-lice.' I say, 'What you talkin' about?', but he don' ansah dat. Jes get in his car and go." She flapped the edge of her dress as if it got out of position, then moved inside it till she got comfortable. "He don' see me with no stickum sticker say 'Back the Blues.' Oh, cops ain' all bad. But enough o' them is." The swing went into motion lazy as a boat on a sea but Minnie's brow was scrunched up tight.

"You don't go out to where he stays?"

"One, I don' drive. Two, my fr'ens could take me, but time marches by and here it is, and you come highly recommended."

She slid down me with her eyes. I slid up her the same way.

I'd already decided Verlyn Venable was goin' to be found for about a hundred dollars.

The cemetery behind Minnie's house was dense and shadowed thick with pin oaks and two pecan trees Minnie said she took a rake to, then paid a little Mexican boy down the street a quarter a bucket to pick up the nuts. She candied pecans for people to sell in beauty parlors and gun shows at $7.50 per two paper-cones' worth. That, plus what she gets from the state for a bad back, is what she'd be payin' me from, she said. Bad back from bein' too much on it maybe—Stinger's the one told me this. But I don't judge what a woman with looks does to get by.

I didn't much want to hit the freeway down to Sugarland to check out Verlyn Venable at four-thirty when traffic's all hinky. Instead, I swung over east a couple blocks to Kroger's grocery down on Montrose, thinking I might run into Stinger.

He was sittin' in a booth by the side of the bakery, smearing mustard on a soft pretzel with a coffee stirrer. I asked if Minnie's brother was the type to mess with trouble. "Not that boy," Stinger said. "It don't fit, 'less he got mixed up with drugs down the way. He play Little League when my own boy was livin' here with his mama. Used ta, I'd see him drivin' Minnie Chaundelle the doctah when she had breathin' difficulties. They parents die young but dem two kep' they nose clean, I say dat. 'Course there's Minnie with her fellas. But hell, she give it away for free you real down and out. Used ta, anyways."

Across the room in a Formica booth a man the color of summer grizzly was sittin' silent with his knees out into the walkway, his blond girlfriend opposite. She had a cut under one eye and on her cheek, surrounded in green and yellow. "Ain't that a damn shame," I said, nodding in that direction.

Stinger looked over while he bit into the pretzel, leavin' mustard in his goatee. "Some women go outta they way to find somebody ta whack 'em," he said with his mouth full. He swallowed and said, "Ever'body got a choice wever to walk in dry socks or piss in they boots and whine about it."

Stinger wasn't a low man but he was one to take serious.

"Verlyn got a lady by Buffalo Speedway," he said. "I cain't tell you the *add*-ress, but I c'n show you."

Stinger went to his pickup truck and unlocked the door, glancing right and left, then reached behind the seat where there's space enough for his paste bucket. He hunched his shoulders then, and I knew he'd slipped his .38 into his waistband under his loose shirt. He glanced around again, shut the pickup door, and headed my way. His top half was a sandy-colored shirt and a Rockets cap. His bottom half was brown pants and red sandals, and he moved like all his tendons had been stretched too long on the rack.

How he came by the gun was one time he was drivin' home after a wallpaper job when a man was yellin' and wavin' a gun in the street with his own children lookin' on. Stinger pulls over, walks up to the goon and says, "I know you want to get rid of that piece, man." A woman who saw it said he held out his palm "like he ain't got no normal skin a bullet go through."

While we drove to the street Stinger pointed out, the air was heavy and worthless from a storm comin' in off the Gulf. Lightning flickered like dyin' neon and low thunder rumbled, making promise the sky would rip open and relieve itself so we could breathe again.

Halfway down the street we saw a girl in gray shorts and a black halter-top come runnin' barefoot toward us, wavin' her hands. "Uh-oh," I said, and slowed the car.

"Tha's her," Stinger said. "Tha's Verlyn's stuff."

Her hair was dark and curly and she had a light, fleshy look to her limbs when she came jammin' up to my window. A blue-rose tattoo showed on the rise of her left breast when she leaned in. "There's a guy with a knife! He's attacking someone!" she said.

I told Stinger to get in the back so she could get in the front, and she hung onto the dash, pointing backwards as I smoked tires up to the outside pay phone at Popeye's Chicken. She hopped out and dialed, rocking foot to foot. Stinger said, "She get done, le's go take us a look." She came back, fear still in her face, and I told her to wait in Popeye's, where there's light.

We found the apartments no sweat, and saw through a wire fence trailed in vine two lean men with no shirts standing by the pool smokin' cigarettes. The Cauc was wearin' black trousers. The other one had long beige shorts on and somethin' white wrapped around his shoulder and under his armpit with the pattern like a big red rose coming through. Stinger said, "Well, he's alahve but he's nicked."

All the while we talked, Verlyn smoked his cigarette and kept an eye on the breezeway. He could've been a golden panther, what with his hard jaw and yellow eyes.

I told him I was a friend of his sister's. She was worried about him. He nodded but kept his counsel.

There was a quiet but alert resolve about him, like he was just goin' to catch his breath before he took care of business. I'm like that myself sometimes. I once in a while get criticized over it, like by the woman who left me a few months ago. She took a bunch of things I called mine, but I didn't go after her when she very well knew I could hunt a whisper in a big wind. By the time I got through mulling it all over, she was askin' to come back, but my head was in a different place. It takes this cement a while to set, but when it does it's what it's going to be for a long, long time.

The Anglo did all the talkin'. His hair was buzzed close so you could see the metal studs embedded in his scalp down to an arrow's point. I'm not squeamish but that did catch my attention.

He said, "Me and Verlyn and Bitsy was kickin' it, watchin' the game, like that, this hype comes outta my room. Lucky he ain't stone dead, man." He laid off a bunch of rowdy names on the culprit while Verlyn stood there offering no contradiction, his eyes held steady on somethin' the rest of us couldn't see. I thought then that the only thing missin' in that young man's face was a young man's youth. Stinger and I bend the polar ends of forty, but the kid seemed worn ragged at the cuffs.

I gave out my card and said if they have any more problems to give me a call. Then I told Verlyn he might ring up his sister, too. A change came into his eyes at his sister's name. Softer. Younger.

He said, "Keep this under your hat, okay?"

"I got no problem with that," I said.

Stinger and I left out the opposite side of the courtyard when we saw the baby-blue cars of Houston's finest because we'd as soon not waste everybody's time.

When we pulled back into the lot at Kroger's the clouds opened at last. I could feel the difference in the air already.

"Thanks, man," I told Stinger.

"No problem, baby," he said, and pinched a wad of Bandits into his cheek before he opened the door. As he hurried to his truck, big drops pelted the back of his shirt like loads off a fully choked shotgun. He ducked like he thought if he was shorter the rain wouldn't hit so hard.

I drove away, thinking Minnie Chaundelle would sure be grateful to know her baby kin was still healthy. Maybe she'd give me some pecans in a paper cone, or bake me a pie.

It was comin' on to six o'clock and the rain was drummin' so hard I thought the ark would have to be broke out. Lookin' through my windshield was like lookin' through seven sheets of waxed paper. But when I got to Gross Street and parked, like magic, the rain sucked back in a heavenly tide.

I was about to get out when I saw a tall man in a light suit emerge from a car and cross the culvert to Minnie's. Up on the porch he closed his umbrella and tugged at his jacket before he knocked. The front door opened and the screen door right after, and Minnie beckoned him in with a big sweet smile. She was framed in the golden light and I imagined I smelled candied pecans cooking on the stove.

I drove on by.

Seven the next morning my phone rang. I reached for a glass of water on my lowboy and slugged some before I answered.

The voice said, "This is Verlyn. Could I talk to you?"

I met him at Starbuck's off West Gray. He was wearin' olive-green pants and a pale green polo, butterscotch loafers with no socks. In one ear was a gold earring and on his hand a class ring from U.T. We got our orders and sat outside in the pleasant morning. He drank juice and took a bite out of a dry croissant I knew was dry because I had one too. I asked him did he call his sister. He said he woke her up and apologized for bein' absent without leave, told her this before she had it together to yell at him too much. Once in a while he'd flex his shoulder a little and wince. Each car pulling in he gave a long stare.

I said, "You ready to tell me who's the snook got a grudge against you?"

"Somebody don't like what I know, okay? Somebody thinkin' to scare me." He pressed his middle finger to the fallen powdered sugar on the paper and put it to his tongue.

"And did he do a proper job on that?"

Verlyn leveled his eyes at me. "A bee don't flee."

"Say again?"

"You swat him, he bite," he said in an old man's mimic.

"Thataway you can get a buncha trouble comin' at you, brother."

"Not if you go after the head nacho, right?" He blew on his coffee, took a sip, then said, "I need to go pick up a computer I left at the office. I could use some company."

Am I workin' for you now?, is what I wanted to say, not a complete damn fool, the man's got money to spend. But what I did ask was, "Cain't your friend there, Toolhead, what's his name, come with you?"

"William? Not the right one."

"I charge twenty-five an hour," I said.

"I'm down with that," he said, causing me to ponder just how much he made on his job. He said, "It may already be takin' up window space at E-Z Pawn," he said. "Cheapskates. Making me bring in my own computer."

"So far, not a capital offense, far as I can see."

"Well, there's stuff going on . . . ," he said, leaning closer to the table so his chest hit the edge. "Some of these wildcat drillin' outfits will do any damn thing to get money for the next hole. They take on more investors than they can handle. And they get away with it because they tell people they're drillin' in a 'prohibitive frontier,' kinda like drillin' on the moon, so nobody should be all that fried when it comes up dry."

"Makes some kind of sense," I said.

"But the thing is, good people invest in these things, people like my rich aunties, if I had any. And too many times they get the hot yanked right out of their fire."

"I don't quite get the scam here."

He took a bite of his pastry and chewed awhile and got a look of a man still plannin' what his next step would be. I let off the pressure a bit and asked him a side-question. "So why didn't you show up for work three days?"

Verlyn sat back and crossed his legs. "Disgusted," he said, and turned in his chair and crossed his legs the other way. "There's this one temp agency I been with for more than five years. They had a rush job, so I filled in. Hey, I know it's not stand-up to do Mitchell Corporation that way. But what they pull is worse. I'm serious. I got names. I could hurt 'em."

"Most people would just shut their eyes and go to lunch."

"Most would, I give you that. You met my sister? She raised me right. Tomorrow I go to the D.A."

"That's one you might want to think over."

"A bright man don't chew on something that's eating him."

"I'd just hate to answer to Minnie Chaundelle over you."

"That's something I'd hate myself," he said, managing a grin.

We went to a high-rise off the West Loop and rode a glass elevator lookin' down on Buffalo Bayou, where a dozen gray shapes cut the green water—turtles with their long necks out, or baby 'gators.

Verlyn's lip was beaded with sweat.

"Nobody gonna shoot you here, boy," I said.

He rolled that shoulder but smiled and said, "Can't be a hundred percent on that, now, can we?"

Verlyn went to an office along one wall of a roomful of cubicles. He said to stand by, and I did, leanin' against a wall and cleanin' my fingernails with my pocket knife. Before long I heard a raised voice say, "You leave me high and dry like this? Thank you very much." Someone down a lane poked a head out a cubicle, then pulled back in. I moved so I could see into the office where Verlyn was and got a look at a short man with a lot of scalp edged with white hair, over a fall of red face. When the man saw me he stared, then flipped his hand at Verlyn, like Go on, get out of here.

In the car Verlyn unzipped his laptop case and fired up to look at his files. What files? The machine was wiped clean. He cursed and hit the door with the side of his fist, but then seemed to resign himself.

"How about we go get the book you left with Minnie Chaundelle?"

He said maybe later, he had to grab some sleep. I caught him in a smile again. He said, "My girl likes a wounded man."

Back home, I phoned Minnie and told her her brother might be along, maybe with me, except I had a job to do early in the evening so I didn't know.

"Oh honey, that is a great relief," she said. "Anytime you want to drop on by, I sure be happy to pay you what I owe." I wondered if she was sittin' on her porch swing talkin' to me.

When I hung up, I checked my closet to see what shirts I had clean, fried up some okra and sausage with red bell peppers and leftover noodles, then took a nap and dreamed of a bayou I lived on as a child, and how a yellow butterfly used to land on a bush outside, and the smell of jasmine and apples and pine.

That afternoon I did a records check on the drilling company. Mitchell Corporation had racked up litigation against them draggin' on for years. On a hunch I ran a criminal history on the president, the V.P., and the operations manager, Guy Grundfest. The president had a domestic on him two years ago. The V.P. was clean. Grundfest had two assault convictions, one in El Paso, one in Houston, and a theft-by-check out of Huntsville. What rang a bell, though, was the name of the company CEO, Ray Wayne Wooley. I'd seen that name before but didn't know where. It gave me a funny feeling. The more I wanted to shake it off, the more it hung on.

In an hour I'd have to get ready for my evening job, the one I mentioned to Minnie Chaundelle.

I called Stinger. "Who you know named Wooley? Ray Wayne Wooley."

"Not a single sinnin' soul."

"Don't sound familiar, nothin'?"

"Nope."

"Okay, what do you know about drilling outfits? That Bazile boy's workin' for a company might be doin' some fishy stuff, but it seems like he's not quite ready to lay it all out."

"Sonny's maybe got to boil in his own oil a while," Stinger said.

"I'd like to see what I can do to avoid that."

"You'd like to see what Minnie Chaundelle's sugah tase like."

"That too. But in the meantime I don't want to see no jacko playin' slice-'n'-dice with that boy again neither."

"Lemme ask around. You up the car lot this evenin'?"

"That's right. I'll have my cell phone with me, you need to call."

"I don't know, maybe I need a new car. Maybe I'll see ya around."

I rang up a reporter I met at a legal investigator's conference one time, nerdy guy named Jobar Wilson, liked to go by Buck. Once you saw him you knew how bad he needed to, but it was hard for me to remember to say that name. He was rackin' on a story about the blues bands playin' for the Juneteenth festival. That's the three-day annual celebration marking the about-date when word reached Texas the slaves were freed. Buck supported what Verlyn told me about wildcatters sometimes overselling a well. "An investor might put up the million it takes to drill a hole, okay?, but then the wildcatters get greedy. Say they meet a guy at the Petroleum Club's got another million to toss around. They take him on, don't happen to mention they already got their million to start the drill. That way they're sure to have enough money in case they run into problems. Or, they're lookin' ahead to the next hole. Say, then, their kid's buddy has a daddy with money to invest. Okay, they take him on too. Problem: Now the well comes in productive. Oops.

They got too many people to pay, 'cause it's not going to be *that* productive. Ass-is-grass time."

"So they go bankrupt," I said. "Happens every day."

"Wrong deal." He waited like an actor thinking he invented timing. "Nuh-uh. What they do, *they plug the hole.* Plug the hole and *say* it's dry."

I said, "And they go unplug it later."

"No. What do they care if the poor schmucks don't get a return? They're not in the production/refining business, they're in the drilling business."

"Hey now," I said. "Grifters everywhere."

I was letting him go when I got him back and asked, "Jobar, does the name Ray Wayne Wooley mean anything to you?"

There was a pause and I wondered if he was playin' me, till he said, "Might be, Cisroe. But I'd sure rather you call me Buck."

"Sorry, man. Buck." I could hear him clacking on a keyboard.

"Ray Wayne Wooley," he said. "He's the brother of Brant Wooley. D.A. down the courts building. Saw that name in the Society page the other day."

I rang up Verlyn several times. He either didn't have a machine or it was turned off. If Verlyn knew the connection between Mitchell Corp.'s CEO and the chief district attorney for the city, that boy owned more sap than I'd given him credit for. Maybe more stupid, too. Maybe that's what his sister meant.

At six I had to give it up and get to my evening job. It was for a rich brother bought a fancy pre-owned car and suspected the dealer fooled with the odometer. Asked me would I pose as a salesman to see if I could sniff out their practice—didn't matter what-all it would cost him, it was the principle. I said I'd do it for a week but how'd I know I could even get hired? He laughed. His voice sounded like a nail coming out of hard wood. "You Sneaky Petes just another kind of con man. Tell me different and I'll show you a hog can dance."

This business, you do a lot of things for a dollar.

So I was up on the auto corridor on North Shepherd, standing outside in a shirt with too much starch in it and listening to a blues station over headphones hooked up to a radio clipped to my belt. Now and then I'd roll down the sound and take out my cell phone and try Verlyn's number again.

Two couples came in, took my time, walked away. I was going for a bathroom break when I saw Stinger's faded tan truck. He got out and put on his shades against the lot lights. When he reached me, he said, "You might want ta come with me, Cisroe. They got your boy."

Verlyn Vincent Venable, twenty-four years old. Ideals, character, history, brains, beauty. All that, ready . . . for what? To be put in the ground for worm feed. Officials said he didn't make one of the curves up on Allen Parkway, the tree-lined drive that streams along in sync with the bayou.

Stinger guessed better, and so did I.

But it wasn't till the next morning at four A.M. that I knew for sure. Buck Wilson reported the findings to me after I gave him a call and he reached a contact at the morgue down on Old Spanish Trail. A single .40-caliber round sent parts of Verlyn's skull zinging over the black bayou waters that carried a full moon on its back. Rage and sorrow filled my soul. I shattered a pane in my bedroom window when my loose shoe went through.

My heart cinched down for Minnie, that big lovely woman struck with grief, and I was going to go over her place, when Stinger said he already called and a friend of hers answered, and he could hear some awful wailing in the background, and what women need at a time like this was other women.

By the book, I had no more to do for Minnie Chaundelle. I'd found her brother briefly, and that's all I was paid for. But it made me sick thinkin' I could've maybe done somethin' to prevent him being given over to evil.

I stayed away from Minnie's but I thought of her and that poor boy in and out all that day. After a while, I played back what Stinger said about pissin' in your boots and whinin' about it, and about Verlyn himself saying spit or swallow. I decided I wanted to have a second look at that book he left at Minnie's.

Around five I was leavin' my house to get dinner when Stinger came by. I stood talkin' to him outside his pickup.

Across the street, men were handling pieces of tin for a new roof. The sun was a gray, sharp light through the clouds, and the brilliance it gave off struck Stinger's face in a way that made him look hard and mean.

"We gon' get him," he said.

"Which one? We got no idea—"

"The hail we don't."

I said, "It could be Grundfest, sure. He's got assaults. It could be a high muckety like Wooley. Or it could be a low-ass snake-clambake like the one cut the boy in the shoulder. How you gon' pick which one?"

"Young brother down, Cisroe. Could've done good in this world."

"I know that. But there are ways to handle it."

"Sure there *are*."

"Legal ways."

"Bullshit," he said, and yanked the far window handle in circles till the glass got down low enough he could spit. Then he pulled out a white sock he carried in his pocket and wiped his mouth with it. "Who gon' tell Minnie Chaundelle that? You?"

After dinner we drove to Minnie's. A woman named Ardath Mae was there. She had silver in her hair and a church look about her that I guessed made Stinger all of a sudden shy. Ardath Mae said Minnie went with another friend to make Verlyn's funeral arrangements. "That child *all* broken up," Ardath Mae said. "Don't know how she gon' come out thothah side."

I asked if it would be all right if I checked Minnie's bedroom for something Verlyn might've left there.

Ardath looked at Stinger before giving me a nod. As I was leaving to the back, I heard her say, "Whatchu been up to, Mistah G.? Been a long time, ain't it, now?"

Minnie's room was full of picture frames and vases glued with beads and nutshells, and more hanging in strands in front of the closet like something out of the hippie days. It took me all of a minute to find Verlyn's book under a shoebox on the closet shelf. When I came out, Stinger and Ardath Mae were standing kind of close together. I showed her what I was going to make off with and told her to tell Minnie. She frowned but said okay, and then I saw her hand slip out of Stinger's, which was hiding behind a fold of her skirt.

Back at my place, I set a bottle of JW Black on the table, got glasses, the ice tray, hot peppers and pretzels, and commenced to read Stinger the list of investors in Mitchell Mining and Drilling Corp. He'd nod at each one, sip his whiskey, and let the sounds roll by while his lids were half-closed. There were eleven names, with sums from a quarter million to a cool eight zeroes posted. When I got to name number nine, Stinger's eyes came open. He said read that one to me again.

Houston is rich in gentlemen's clubs—Centerfolds and Baby Dolls, La Nude and Peter's Wildlife; Rick's and a dozen others. The one we were headed for you had to know was there to know was there. It was a sandstone stucco box with soft-lit arches guarded by two palm trees and had no sign out front, but I knew the place from when it did, remembered it when Stinger said to read that name to him again—Barsekian's Lounge.

We found a place to park at the back of the lot. In the shadows off to the side a security cop in a black uniform sat still as cardboard in his golf cart. The white wafers of his eyeglasses drew him into a cartoon.

Inside, I asked of a man with bleached hair and a face like a chunk of chipped concrete for Mr. Barsekian. He gave us the twice-over, asked our names, then left off through the crowd.

Armen Barsekian used to be one of the biggest bookmakers on the Third Coast, but he retired at the behest of the *federales*. Maybe he was trying to go legit now, run with the bulls down the slick streets of Oil and Gas. If he was the same A. Barsekian listed as an investor in Verlyn's notebook, maybe he'd just like to stimulate an accounting of the Brickner Deposit operation. Only thing was, if this was the hood I thought he was, he also used to be the kind you don't mess with unless you have a fondness for medical personnel of the emergency kind.

Glamour-boy came back and said Stinger could see Mr. B. I'd have to wait at the bar. I started to object but thought maybe Stinger, with his lighter skin, thinner build, and grayer hair, wouldn't be so terrifying as Cisroe Perkins to an old, beat white man.

I went up to the bar and ordered a stout from a woman whose outfit left little to the imagination. She looked about ready to blow and shower us all with beer fuzz. She wore a skirt that could make a man holler and not even know he did.

The crowd was mixed, but not very. I thought I recognized a cop smiling pretty at a dancer and figured you take your pleasure where you can. The music wasn't over-loud, but it was that kind of music anyway, and before long I felt a pulling need for someone with heat and perfume and a great, kind heart.

When Stinger came back I was on my second. He swiped at his goatee, then tipped his head back toward the office door, and said, "It's done, man. It's in the right hands."

Armen Barsekian was an influential man. I didn't much like what I might have guessed about the various businesses he was in nor how he conducted them, but sometimes, I thought, you have to let water cut the channels it is born to cut.

Minnie's baby brother Verlyn Vincent Venable had died on a Wednesday night. The Friday following, way out the Katy, a hunting dog learning to retrieve on a swamp-lake by a shooting range found Guy Grundfest, operations manager at Mitchell Corp., in a dive to its muddy depths. And Ray Wayne Wooley suffered an unfortunate mishap that broke both his legs at the knees, jet-skiing, he said, on Lake Houston on Saturday midnight when he knew he'd had too much too drink.

Monday I took a trip to Chicago, work-related. I was gone four days. When I came back I had other things to attend to, so I didn't make it by Minnie Chaundelle's till the Saturday following.

When I drove down Gross Street, the sun was bright enough to score diamonds. The radio reported ninety-five degrees and about the same dewpoint and I thought it would be all right on this sticky day if it turned out Minnie Chaundelle wasn't there. She didn't answer the door. But then I walked around back and looked through the thick stand of glowering green oak in the cemetery and saw that lovely full-figured woman who from here seemed tiny as a child as she stood by a gravestone.

I walked through the high weeds, watchful for

snakes. Walked by headstones broken and stacked in piles and others whole but overturned as though a tractor had plowed them down. I took my time, glancing at the stones, wanting Minnie Chaundelle to see me and get used to the intrusion. Some of the graves had sunken so the names barely showed above the soft earth, and I thought what a shame it was: Gone, then double-gone.

As I got closer I saw the clean mounded earth Minnie stood by. At its head was a shiny black stone with Verlyn's name and dates on it. Minnie turned eyes on me deep as the River Sorrow. No words could cover a time like this, so I didn't try. I just poked out a finger in the direction of her slack hand, and she took it and held it hard as if she were slipping in quicksand.

She said, "This here ain' the real stone. They'll be more on it latuh."

"I know it will be nice," I said. "The best it can be."

She nodded and clamped her lips and leaned into me, wiping her left eye with the ball of her palm. "It's gon' say, 'A ray of sun would be enough. But there was you.'"

"That's real nice, Minnie Chaundelle."

"Ain' it evah?"

The wind took a path alongside us and blew Minnie's skirt forward and tunneled through the brush and leaves ahead as if showing a new way. We stood there, Minnie Chaundelle and me, head touching head, arms about each other, like old lovers locked in memories too hard to name. After a while, I walked back with her to her house, where I comforted her some more.

* * *

Later that night, I left my desk to go to the window where the moonlight painted the sill blue and powdered the tops of trees and houses in the same cool shade. I felt sorry for those men caught in the wash of greed, and for the weak ones who open the gates, and for those women held blameless who somewhere wait for both.

And as I unbuttoned my shirt to prepare for bed and smelled the sweet scent of Minnie Chaundelle still upon me, a single tear fell beside my foot on the hardwood floor. I wondered what was becoming of me, letting other men take care of my work so that I could not in honesty lie next to a grieving woman and tell her Cisroe Perkins looked after justice the way he best knows how.

I resolved to do better next time.

About the Contributors

The rugged beauty of the Massachusetts coastline is where Sally Gunning both lives and sets her mystery novels. Her series character is Peter Bartholomew, a small-business owner who has become entangled in murders through six books so far. Her latest novel is *Deep Water.*

Joseph Hansen makes a welcome return to fiction with his short story detective, Bohannon, in "Widower's Walk." Hansen is known primarily for his excellent novels featuring David Brandstetter, a homosexual detective. The Brandstetter books illustrate the world-within-a-world of Southern California, with finely detailed settings, inventive characters and plots, and an engaging, complex protagonist. Hansen has ten novels under his belt in the Brandstetter series, and one can only hope more are on the way. His latest novel is *Jack of Hearts.*

Sarah Shankman started writing mystery fiction under the pen name Alice Storey, to distinguish those books from her more mainstream work. The mystery novels proved so successful, however, that she now writes all of her fiction under her own name. Her series character is Samantha Adams, an investigative reporter in Atlanta and the subject of six novels so far. She has started another series, this one based in Nashville. Her latest book is *I Still Miss My Man, But My Aim Is Getting Better.*

ABOUT THE CONTRIBUTORS

Nancy Pickard is the creator of the Jenny Cain series of mysteries, thoughtful explorations of life and crime in a small New England town. Her novels have won the Anthony, Agatha and Macavity awards, and been nominated for the Edgar. Her short fiction is just as impressive, appearing in such anthologies as *Vengeance Is Hers* and *A Woman's Eye*. She has also edited anthologies, most notably *Women on the Edge*.

A cost accountant who lives in Waukegan, Illinois, Eleanor Taylor Bland created mystery fiction's first African-American female detective in Marti MacAlister. Her work recently appeared in *Women on the Case*, edited by fellow Illinois writer Sara Paretsky. Novels include *Keep Still* and *Done Wrong*.

Brendan DuBois makes the stark New England countryside come alive in his novels and short stories. Appearing in several year's best anthologies, one of his latest pieces, "The Dark Snow," was nominated for the Edgar Award for best short story of 1996. His series protagonist is Lewis Cole, who finds murder and corruption on the New England coast where he lives. Recent novels include *Dead Sand* and *Black Tide*.

Another Edgar Award–winning author, Edward D. Hoch quietly produces some of the finest crime fiction around. He is a master of the short story, and his work has appeared in every issue of *Ellery Queen's Mystery Magazine* since 1973. When he's not writing, he edits anthologies, having put together over twenty volumes of *The Year's Best Mystery and Suspense Stories*.

Few writers can set mysteries in a city and make it completely their own the way Loren D. Estleman can. His Detroit is the Motor City of the past, present, and future all rolled up into one, where the rich and poor alike fight for survival. His urban jungle has some very mean streets, and private detective Amos Walker is just the man to walk them. Estleman uses degrees in English and journalism and his experience as a reporter and staff writer for several newspapers to create evocative novels in both the mystery and the western genres. His latest is *Never Street*.

Angela Zeman is known for her stories about Mrs. Risk, the older, eccentric detective, and her sidekick, Rachel. Together the two have solved several crimes around Long Island, all of which have appeared in *Alfred Hitchcock's Mystery Magazine*. Other fiction by her appears in *Mom, Apple Pie, and Murder*. She serves on the Board of Directors for the Mystery Writers of America, and has written about the history of the organization in *The Fine Art of Murder*.

Noreen Ayres is the author of three novels featuring forensic expert Samantha "Smokey" Brandon, the most recent one being *The Long Slow Whistle of the Moon*. She holds a master's degree in English, and several awards for her short fiction and poetry. Before turning to writing fiction full-time, she worked as a bookbinder, science teacher, fish cleaner, and trademark docket clerk among various other occupations. Other fiction by her appears in *Fathers & Daughters*.

Visit

MARY
HIGGINS
CLARK

At the Simon & Schuster Web site:

www.SimonSays.com/mhclark

Read excerpts from her books,
find a listing of future titles, and
learn more about the author!